syd Parker

Love's Abiding Spirit

For Sarah, who knows me better than I know myself.

Prologue

"I can't believe you could be so hateful." Soren said angrily. "Why would you take Olivia from me? She's my child too. I'll fight you for custody"

Victoria's eyes narrowed. "Fight all you want, no judge is going to grant you even visitation rights. Olivia is my daughter. You're my ex—lover. No court will recognize you as a parent or legal guardian."

Soren's eyes filled with tears, the anger mingling with desperate heartbreak. "Please Victoria, don't take my...our little girl away from me. I understand you're not happy and you've made the decision that you feel is best for you, but don't hurt us all in the process. I need Olivia."

Victoria smirked evilly, not softening even the slightest bit at the sound of Soren's pleas. "At this particular point I am not concerned with what you need. My concern is for my daughter. I know that you think it is mean and spiteful. I believe it's looking out for her best interest. Being a lesbian and raising her with another woman is not what I want for her."

"And getting married to a man and pretending to be straight sets such a great example for her." Soren retorted acerbically. "What about virtues like being true to yourself? Not lying? Keeping commitments? I suppose those don't matter."

"We had a made up ceremony Soren. Our marriage was never real."

Soren winced at the harsh words, suddenly realizing that she did not know Victoria Holmes at all. During the nine years they had been together, including four raising Olivia together, she would have sworn to anyone that she knew Victoria better than herself. What a load of crap! "If you respect me at all, please don't do this. I may not have given birth to Olivia, but I was there for everything. The birth, the two o'clock feedings, all the dirty diapers, we watched her first steps together for god's sake Victoria. How can you take her away from me?"

Victoria stiffened slightly and folded her arms across her chest, a sign that she was closing herself off to this conversation. "I don't want her to know anything about this...this lifestyle Soren. She's young, she will bounce back from this and in a few years, not even remember you. I don't want you to try and contact me or her. If you do, I'll let the police handle it." She stood up quickly, smoothing the wrinkles out of her skirt. "Don't worry Soren. I'm sure in time you will realize this really is the best choice...for everyone involved."

Soren stared dumbfounded as Victoria walked out of the house they'd shared for six years and the life they'd shared for even longer.

Chapter 1

Soren Lockhart tucked a strand of her chocolate brown hair behind her ear, sighing when it wouldn't stay. She liked this shorter cut, but there were times when she wished for her old ponytail. Foregoing the errant strand momentarily, she looked at the woman staring back at her from the oval mirror. Her blue eyes were still as dark and piercing as always, but now they were framed by deepening crow's feet. Someone had once described them as sexy, although she felt as far from that as possible today. She felt every one of her thirty—six years and then some.

She straightened her shirt, trying to tuck it back into the waistband of her slacks, but it stubbornly refused to stay. She tried to tighten her belt to keep it tucked in and frowned when she realized she'd already tightened it to the last hole. She had always been slender for five eight, but the weight she'd lost since her break up with Victoria had left her unnaturally thin. Nothing in her closet fit anymore, but she had long since stopped caring. *That's really what this is all about, isn't it Ren? Finding something to care about.*

"Hey Ren, you okay in there?"

Soren jumped at the sound of Brett's voice. "Yeah, yes, I'm…fine." She took one last look in the mirror and turned to open the door. Her eyes met Brett's questioning brown ones and she plastered a smile on her face. "Everything's fine."

Soren signed the final document and set the pen down wearily. "I had no idea it would be that much work."

Brett laughed, his voice deep and rich. "Oh just wait, this will seem like a cake walk compared to the mess you are getting yourself into. Remind me again why you are doing this? Savannah, Georgia is really an odd choice. I still can't believe you saw the house once and bought it, especially in its current condition."

Soren regarded Brett Kendrix thoughtfully. Not only was he her lawyer, he was one of her best friends. Along with his sister Jordan, the three of them had been best friends since grammar school. They were the three Musketeers, although they were more like frick and frack and one extra for good measure. They were inseparable and Soren's decision to move away had not gone over well with Brett and Jordan, not to mention Brett's wife Lauren and their kids. She tried to play off the severity of her leaving by telling them that once she had the house all fixed up, they could make the trek out for a big family vacation. Their sadness almost made her reconsider...*almost*. She considered his question. "Hell I don't know. It seemed like a good idea at the time. The house has history, more importantly history that isn't mine. All I know is that I have to get out of Nashville. I can't stay in that house anymore. Everywhere I turn a memory of Olivia plays out in front of me."

"You could have stayed with us awhile." Brett and Lauren had offered to put her up after she sold the house she and Victoria had shared and found a new one. Instead, while on an impromptu vacation in Savannah she'd found an older home in need of some TLC and put in an offer on it. Then she came home and dropped the bomb on all of them. That was two months ago. Today, she'd signed her life away, and hoped she would be saying goodbye to the part of her life that still left fresh cuts on her heart anytime she saw a little girl that reminded her of Olivia. "I know, but it's not just the house. It's the city. I look at every little girl that walks by hoping it's Olivia. I can't do that anymore. I need to move on. I think…I hope this move will help. Besides, I'm…I've been thinking of making my own album."

The shock on Brett's face was priceless and to his credit it only took him seconds to recover. "Ren, that's great! We wondered if you would ever write again." Soren had been a song writer in Nashville prior to the breakup, with quite a few of her songs making it to the top ten for artists like Martina McBride, The Dixie Chicks and numerous others, including eight number one's on the Billboard Hot 100, but hadn't picked up a guitar or written down a lyric for more than two years.

Soren smiled. "Except this time, it's for me. This will be my therapy. My last nod to the past and then hopefully I will be able to move on."

"So do Jordan and I get the first pressing?" Brett teased. "I can see it now—Soren Lockhart's first CD goes platinum and she wins Country Music's New Artist of the Year."

Soren laughed, swept along in Brett's fantasy. He'd always been the clown of the group, the one that left them all laughing, and most importantly had been her strength during this ordeal. "Woah, slow down tiger. I haven't even started writing yet. It could suck. Besides, I'm kind of leaning away from country." She watched his face, searching for his reaction to that.

When nothing more than warm encouragement registered in his eyes, she continued. "I always saw myself as more the singer songwriter type. Lots of great acoustic guitar and painful lyrics. The atmosphere of the house lends itself to dark and foreboding."

"Ren, I don't care what you write, sing, produce, whatever, I am just happy to see you back at it. I'm sure anything you do will be amazing…dark lyrics and all."

Soren beamed at the compliment. "Thanks Brett. You know you are the first person I've told. I haven't even said anything to Jordan yet." Jordan was the biggest country fan on earth and her music staple consisted of anything from Emmylou Harris to Carrie Underwood so the change in Soren's music would come as somewhat of a surprise.

"Don't worry about her. She'll be fine and if she isn't, Ali can make everything all better." Brett smiled when he talked about his sister Jordan and her partner Ali. The younger of the two by only seven minutes as she liked to remind him, Jordan had been the wild one of the group and didn't settle down until she met Ali Carothers five years before. Now she had a life partner, a house in Brentwood and child number one on the way. "One kiss from her and Jordan will forget everything else around her."

Soren shrugged. "You're right. And if she isn't fine then oh well." She winked slyly. "I mean this is all about me right?"

"Absolutely. I mean why else would you traipse across the country to a house in the middle of nowhere and leave us all behind?" He smiled to let her know he was teasing. "So are you really okay? This just seems so sudden. I just want to make sure you are doing the right thing."

Soren smiled ruefully. "Who knows? If not, when I come back you guys can throw all the *I told you so's* in my face."

Brett feigned innocence. "What are you talking about? We would never do that."

Soren rolled her eyes. "Right and I'm straight."

"At least come to dinner tonight so we can tie you up and stuff you in the closet so you can't leave."

"Oh God no, whatever you do I don't want to go back in the closet."

Brett groaned loudly, very used to Soren's lesbian jokes. "Just come by, okay? Lauren would shoot me if I didn't invite you and I refuse to get the wife mad at me."

"Far be it from me to be responsible for you being in the dog house...again. Lord knows you do that enough on your own." As a lawyer, Brett's long hours and late nights away from home didn't always sit well with his wife, Lauren. For the most part she was pretty patient, but on the days when their three kids wore her out, it was common knowledge Brett paid for it if he didn't make it home on time. "Besides if I come running home after realizing what a crazy idea this was I can't have you taking up the guest room."

Chapter Two

Soren stared at the forlorn looking house and for the first time felt the tendrils of fear starting to infiltrate her conscious thought. The eight hour drive from Nashville to Savannah had given her time to work through the feelings of uncertainty that had been present since she made the hasty offer on the house, but she'd never been afraid. Now sitting here looking at the house she'd hastily bought, she was honestly afraid that perhaps she had made the wrong decision.

She shook her head quickly banishing that thought and tried to smile. She focused again on the house, this time looking at the positives. She knew the house in its heyday would have been magnificent. It was in Wesley Ward on the corner of Habersham and East Gordon Street on Whitfield Square. The late afternoon sun cascaded softly through the thick foliage overhead and the overall effect was like an angelic glow. The 1870's Queen Anne had an old world charm that had grabbed her the first time she'd seen it.

It was a magnificent two story home with two polygonal towers topped with twin spires that flanked both sides of the home. A narrow widow's walk connected the two towers. A wide staircase opened onto a deep porch that surrounded three sides of the home and offered lovely views of the square and the gardens in the back of the home. Rows of large windows ran the entire length of the house. Decorative cornice molding finished off two large gables and halfcove shaker shingles tapered down to white—washed siding. The large front door was a deep oak color with decorative glass panel inserts. Soren breathed a sigh of relief. *Maybe it's not as bad as I remembered.*

Her relief was short lived. The trees and shrubs were badly in need of trimming and the white railing around the large porch could use some paint. She grimaced when she saw the black shutters were even more faded and off kilter than she remembered. The paint on the columns and wood siding was badly weathered and pealing. She took a tentative step onto the staircase, and felt the wood give under her weight. Her foot fell into the crack and she pitched forward. She dropped the bag she'd been carrying and threw her hands out to catch herself.

When she managed to right herself, she pulled her foot free and moved cautiously sideways until she felt the wood solid beneath her feet. Suddenly the enormity of her decision hit her and when the tears came, she could do nothing to stop them. *I think you may have just earned your first I told you so.*

#

"There has to be something you like about it." Jordan Kendrix said encouragingly. "You can start with just one thing."

Soren smiled picturing Jordan's smiling face. As always she knew Jordan would try to cheer her up. She had called in tears, ready to break down and come home, and she knew the one person that could talk some sense into her was Jordan. "Well the roof didn't cave in during the storm last night."

Truth be told, she had almost left the house and checked into a hotel several times, afraid the house was going to get blown over. Surprisingly enough the bones of the house were in incredible shape. Now she just needed to get the skin to match. She looked at the worn boards on the porch beneath her feet. Nothing a good sanding and a fresh coat of paint couldn't remedy.

Jordan's warm laughter came through the phone. "Well all right that's one thing…anything else?"

Soren took a quick sip of her coffee. "Honestly, it really is a beautiful house. I'll take some pics and email them to you. It just needs some cosmetic stuff." She was already feeling better about the house and a smile began to play at the corners of her mouth. "The realtor gave me the name of a really good contractor. They are supposed to be a little expensive, but worth the extra money. Something tells me that this house deserves to be treated with special care. She seems a little human almost." Her mind raced back to last night's storm. There were several times she awoke frightened and something had calmed her down, made her not feel so alone. And when she awoke that morning the novel she'd been reading before bed was open and she swore she'd closed it before falling asleep. She hadn't heard or seen anything or anyone for that matter, but she had sensed something. "It's almost like…"

"Almost like what?" Jordan asked curiously.

"Nevermind, it's silly." Soren responded then murmured softly. "Very strange."

"Tell me Ren. What is it?"

Soren frowned. "It's almost like someone is here. But that's just crazy, right?"

Jordan chuckled. "Ooh, maybe you have your own little ghost. An old lady of the manor. You better behave yourself. You don't want to spook the spirit."

"See I told you it was crazy." Soren replied sarcastically. "If you tell anyone I am seeing ghosts, I will come back there and kick your ass. Everyone already thinks I've lost my mind with this whole thing."

"No they don't." Jordan said sincerely. "You lost it way before that."

"Gee, thanks. Don't pull any punches." Soren stood up and tossed the remains of her coffee into the yard and sighed. "I guess I'm going to get off here. I don't know if I can take anymore abuse."

"Aww you know I only tease you 'cause I love you honey. If I didn't give you a hard time, who would?"

"Oh I don't know. Brett, Ali, Lauren…do I need to go on?" Soren smiled despite herself. She knew that Jordan did indeed love her. She'd proved that time and again. "Before I go though…how are Ali and the bun in the oven?"

Ali Carothers, Jordan's partner, was seven months pregnant with their first child and the pregnancy hadn't been the easiest on Ali. "Today she is doing pretty good. We've got another ultrasound tomorrow. Dr. Weller has been keeping a really close eye on her lately. She's been concerned with the small amount of amniotic fluid in the sack and she wants to make sure that Ali and the baby aren't under any unnecessary stress. So far she has let Ali keep working, although she has said that there is a possibility of putting her on bed rest. Keep your fingers crossed it doesn't come to that. Ali will be a bear to deal with if she is cooped up in the house. She'll go crazy!"

Soren laughed picturing Ali cooped up at home. She was a ball of fire and God help the person that gets in her way. "Fingers are crossed. Call me after the doctor's appointment and let me know that everything is okay."

"Oh I will. I may be begging you to come rescue me."

Soren felt a small rush of guilt. "I'm…I'm really sorry I won't be there through all this. I will fly back the second she goes into labor though. That's a promise."

"It may be safer if you wait until *after* the baby comes. She could go all *Alien* on us in the delivery room. It could get really ugly."

Soren laughed out loud. "True. Although we'd be a good match. You with an alien and me with a ghost." Rather than

15

dwell on feeling foolish for thinking she had a ghost, she made fun of herself instead.

"No doubt, fortunately mine will disappear pretty quickly. Yours might stick around. You may just get a new friend in that new town of yours. I'm sure the relationship would be rather transparent. You'd see right through her."

Soren groaned. "Wow, that was bad even for you."

"I wonder if she's hot. That may actually be kind of fun, in a kinky sort of way." Jordan opined.

"Seriously, stop it. That's gross." Soren said quickly.

"Hey action is action…and you could use some." Jordan paused suddenly serious. "I'm being for real. It's been a long time Ren. It's time to join the living again."

Soren winced at the painful reminder. Her heart didn't ache for Victoria. She'd been too hurt by her to have anything but anger in her heart for her. No, her heart broke for Olivia. She didn't think it would be right to jump into a relationship. She thought that signified giving up on her little girl if only in her own mind. Even now though she silently acknowledged Jordan's words, it was time to move on and that's exactly what she was planning to do. "How about if I concentrate on the rejoining the living part? I don't think I can pull off the whole Demi Moore *Ghost* thing."

"Fair enough, as long as you promise to at least open yourself up to any and every possibility."

Soren rolled her eyes and sighed. "Yes mother. Any more advice before I go?"

"Uhm, don't catch anything you can't get rid of with penicillin." Jordan said wryly.

"Ugh, goodbye Jordan." Soren said with a groan.

"Love you, see you later, bye!"

"Tell Ali hello, love you, see you later, bye!" Soren hung up the phone and set it on the small table beside her. She leaned back in the swing, rocking gently and studied the yard. The bricked patio was in good repair and would need only a few adjustments. The landscaping however was an entirely different story. The azaleas and hydrangeas needed trimming, wisteria had all but covered the gazebo and Spanish moss was growing from every branch on the large oak tree at the corner of the yard. Having been somewhat of a amateur horticulturist back home, she was no stranger to landscaping, but even she had to admit getting the yard back in order would require help. "That's one more person I'll be calling today."

The rocking motion of the swing calmed her and she closed her eyes, inhaling the scent of spring. She knew that the balmy temperatures would soon give way to the overwhelming heat and humidity that the south was infamous for. She knew she had better figure out a way to deal with the heat, and fast. Not that Nashville didn't have its share of hot summer weather, but she had always heard the stifling heat of southern summers made anything north of the Tennessee line seem cozy.

Soren's mind drifted to the summers she had spent with Brett and Jordan, the three of them growing up next door to each other and practically joined at the hip. For some reason she thought about the summer they had all turned thirteen. It was 1986, and also the summer they'd all discovered girls. Smiling she remembered the party where she had gotten her first kiss and realized the path she would take in life.

It was Brett and Jordan's birthday and as twins they did everything together, including party. They had set up the party in the basement where they could be as loud as they wanted, which was fairly loud given the fact that Brett's new present was a large boombox with two cassette decks. Ten of their friends, including Soren, sat anxiously around an empty Coke bottle and waited, with their breath held for the bottle to stop spinning. It slowed and stopped right in front of her. Soren looked up and caught the disappointed look in his eyes. He glanced nervously at Lauren then back at her. Soren raised an eyebrow trying to gauge his reaction. She gave up after a few seconds and stood up. She took one last look at the faces around her and followed Brett into the closet. Once her eyes adjusted, she could make out his face in the dimmed light that filtered through the narrow slats of the door.

Brett shrugged. "We could just pretend. We don't really have to do it."

His voice was barely a whisper and Soren strained to hear him over the din of voices coming through the door. "Are you sure? I mean we can…if you want." She swallowed the lump in her throat and prayed he would not want to. She wasn't sure why the thought of kissing him bothered her so much. They were best friends. They'd shared lots of firsts, why should this be any different? But it was. She honestly didn't want to kiss him. "You're sure we don't have to?"

Brett squared his shoulders. "Yeah, I'm sure. Besides, it would be like kissing my sister."

It did seem that way to Soren, except that the thought that crossed her mind was actually kissing Jordan. *Where did that come from?* Even more strange than kissing Brett was the thought that she wanted to kiss Jordan and that made Soren incredibly uneasy. "Yeah, gross. Like kissing your sister."

They burst out laughing and Soren punched Brett in the arm. "Shhh, we're supposed to be pretending to kiss."

Brett shut his mouth, but she could see his shoulders heaving as he tried in vain to control the laughter. Finally the laughter subsided and he regarded her thoughtfully. "I really wanted it to land on Lauren. She's really cute."

"Yeah she is cute." Soren slapped her hand over her mouth, fear and confusion flashing in her eyes. "I mean she's okay…for a girl." She tried to cover the comment, at a total loss as to why all of a sudden she was thinking about girls in a different way than she ever had before, like she was attracted to them. She wasn't sure what that meant, but was convinced whatever it was it was most definitely not good.

Brett didn't notice the slip at all. The shit eating grin on his face told Soren that his mind was elsewhere. "Do you think she would like me?"

Soren shrugged trying to be nonchalant. "I don't know. I guess. She could do a lot worse."

"Gee thanks a lot." Brett said rolling his eyes. "I wonder if she would go out with me."

"Where do you want to go?" Soren asked.

Brett rolled his eyes again. "Ha, ha! Real funny. You're such a dork. I meant be my girlfriend stupid."

Soren punched him hard.

"Ow! What was that for?" Brett rubbed his arm gingerly. "Why do you have to be such a tomboy?"

"That's for calling me stupid, stupid." She narrowed her eyes and smiled evilly. "Be nice or I'll tell Lauren you like her."

Brett's face blanched. "Okay I'll stop. Please don't tell her."

"Then how are you supposed to *go together* if she doesn't know you like her?" Soren asked sarcastically.

Brett's shoulders sagged momentarily then he looked up defiantly. "Gee I don't know stupid…"

He had no sooner gotten the word stupid out when Soren put her hand on the door knob and simultaneously opened her mouth to say Lauren's name. "Laur…ugh!"

Brett hauled her back into the closet. "Shut up Ren!" Lowering his voice, he pleaded with her. "Please don't say anything. What if she doesn't like me? I would die. Just keep it to yourself, will ya?"

Soren opened her mouth ready to tease him again when she caught the look in his eyes. "You really do like her, don't you?"

He shook his head hopelessly. "Yeah I really do."

"I'm sorry." Soren said sincerely. "Maybe you'll get lucky on the next spin."

"Yeah maybe." He tried to smile and Soren squeezed his hand reassuringly.

"Time's up!" Someone yelled and they both turned quickly.

"I guess we better get out there. Remember you gotta pretend we kissed…and promise you won't say anything."

Soren made an X over her heart with her finger. "Cross my heart, hope to die."

"Stick a needle in your eye."

Moments later it was Jordan's turn to spin. She held the bottle still glancing quickly around the room. Her eyes paused on Soren's for a second then she closed her eyes and spun the bottle. To Soren it seemed like it took forever to stop, spinning past her wildly. She counted the revolutions. *One. Two. Three. Four. Five.* Then finally the bottle slowed and stopped…directly in front of Soren. Jordan opened her eyes immediately looking at Soren and her face broke into a smile. Soren let out a breath and realized she'd been holding it the entire time the bottle was spinning. She met Jordan's eyes and her stomach jumped. They started to stand up when someone grabbed the bottle and handed it back to Jordan. "It can't be a girl. You have to spin again."

"Nuh-uh." Jordan said shaking her head. "Rules are rules…we gotta go in the closet." She stood and watched Soren, waiting for her to back her up. "Come on Ren."

Soren hesitated and looked around the room nervously. "I don't know Jordan. Maybe you should just spin…"

Jordan grabbed Soren's hand and pulled her up. "Come on chicken. We're doing what the bottle says." She literally dragged Soren into the closet and pulled the door shut behind them ignoring the shocked expressions behind them.

The girls were silent for what seemed like an eternity when Soren finally broke the silence. "Why didn't you just spin the bottle again?"

"I don't know." Jordan shrugged. "I guess I didn't want to. It's my birthday. I can do whatever I want, right?"

"Yeah I guess so." Soren glanced through the narrow slits in the door. "They're gonna talk about us you know."

"So who cares? Besides I didn't want to come in here with anyone else." Jordan's voice had lowered to a whisper.

Soren's stomach flip—flopped. *Was it possible that Jordan was thinking the same thing she was?* She shook her head. *No stupid, you're the only one that is a weirdo.* "How come?"

"I don't know." She was quiet for a moment. "I don't like anyone else…like I like you."

Soren cocked her head. "What do you mean? How do you like me?" Her stomach was fluttering like it had a million butterflies doing three—sixties.

Jordan studied Soren. "It's weird. It's like I want to go steady with you. Like boyfriend and girlfriend." She stopped talking and watched Soren, fear evident in her features.

Soren swallowed several times, unable to make her mouth work. When she was finally able to speak, her voice cracked and she laughed nervously. She licked her lips and tried to say something, anything in response to Jordan's admission. "Do you mean that?"

Jordan nodded her head slowly. "I wanted it to be you. I wanted to kiss you."

Soren's heart jumped. "When did you…I mean have you always felt this way?"

"For awhile I guess." Jordan's shoulders sagged. "I'm sorry, I shouldn't have told you. That makes me a freak, doesn't it? Please don't say anything to anybody. Just forget I said anything, okay?" She reached for the door knob, needing to put space between her and Soren. She had really messed up this time. As best friends, she thought she could tell her anything, but winced when she remembered the look of shock on Soren's face. Turning back around, she plastered a smile on her face. "Sike! I was just kidding. You should have seen your face. That was some funny stuff." She turned the knob, ready to run as quickly as she could when she felt a hand grip her arm tightly.

"Wait…please." Soren said softly. "I…I guess we are both freaks then." She leaned forward ignoring the shocked expression on Jordan's face and touched her lips to Jordan's softly. She wasn't prepared for the sweet warmth she felt or her heartbeat to skyrocket. She held her lips against Jordan's softly for what seemed like an eternity, relishing the feeling of exquisite rightness she found there. Suddenly all of her misgivings disappeared and she knew she was home. She liked girls, no question about it. Slowly she pulled away from Jordan and searched her face for her reaction.

Jordan rubbed her lips softly, a slightly dazed look in her eyes. "I knew it would be like that."

"Hello? Anybody home?" A deep feminine voice brought Soren back to reality. She looked up just in time to see a tall woman round the corner of the porch. The stranger pushed her sunglasses off her face and smiled crookedly at her. "Hey, sorry. I rang the doorbell…"

"That's my fault. I've been taking in the *beautiful* landscaping. Kind of got lost in it." She stood up and walked towards the woman, her breath catching when she saw her up close. She was tall, taller than Soren. She had to be almost six feet tall. Her long black hair was pulled into a braid that hung loosely down her back. Then her eyes captured Soren's attention. They were wide set eyes, hunter green with tiny gold specks that seemed to be looking into her soul. Soren ignored the slight catch in her breath and smiled.

"No worries ma'am. I figured I'd check around back when I didn't get anyone at the front …since we did have an appointment." She stuck her hand out towards Soren. "I'm Merritt Tanner…" She paused catching the blank look on her face. "The contractor. I believe you made an appointment with my secretary yesterday."

Soren shook her head. "I did…I was just…well I didn't…" She stopped suddenly embarrassed.

Merritt raised an eyebrow. "This is 409 East Gordon Street right?" She glanced at the clipboard in her hands and mumbled something unintelligible. "You are Soren Lockhart aren't you?"

"Yes, I am. I just, well I was expecting a man." She smiled apologetically. "You know with a name like Merritt I never expected a woman." Soren blushed.

Merritt let her breath out. "Okay, good. I was thinking I was going to have to head back to the office and beat some ass." She looked at Soren then added quickly. "Sorry, language I know. I'm working on it."

Soren laughed and waived a hand dismissively. "Don't apologize on my part. Save it for a real lady."

Merritt laughed and Soren noticed her whole face lit up when she did. She had mistakenly assumed she was quite a bit younger than she was, but the crinkles around her eyes led Soren to believe that she was somewhere around the same age. "Well Ms. Lockhart, shall we get started? It sounded like you had quite a long list of things you wanted to get done."

"Sure, but only if you promise to call me Soren." She said without a hint of reproach. "No Ms. Lockhart or ma'am or whatever other charming names you Southerners use." Her eyes twinkled and a smile was slowly creeping onto her face.

"I can do that, and by all means, please call me Merritt. No *Mister* Tanner here." She laughed at her own joke and her eyes crinkled again. "That's my father and I took over for him a long time ago. Deal?" She extended her hand again.

Soren laughed then shook her head up and down. "Deal." She took Merritt's hand and noticed immediately that her grasp was firm, which she thought said a lot about a person. She tried to ignore the slight elevation in her heart rate at the simple gesture.

Merritt held her hand a moment longer then released it almost unwillingly. "I guess we can start back here and work our way around. You just tell me what you are thinking and if you don't mind I'll just make some notes for now. If there is anything else I see that may need to be addressed, I'll point it out as we go along. From the looks of it I should have brought more paper."

"Don't remind me." Soren said wryly.

Merritt touched her arm and smiled. "Don't worry. She'll be beautiful again...given the level of dedication you have to the house."

"Dedication?" Soren asked confused.

Merritt grinned. "Yeah, dedication. That's my polite way of saying nothing is impossible...if money is no object."

"Ahh gotcha. Let's just say you worry about making her pretty, I'll worry about the money." She caught Merritt's raised eyebrow. "In other words, do whatever it takes."

"Good. I hate to do a job halfway." She ran her hand over the porch railing. "Besides she deserves the best."

They spent the next hour going over the repairs that Soren wanted. She had considered replacing the shutters, but Merritt insisted that they were still in good shape and since they were wood, could easily be refinished. She pointed out several things that Soren had missed, and agreed that the front steps should be redone completely. The shaker shingles were salvageable except for a handful of them.

Soren had nearly passed out when Merritt climbed a ladder and walked around the roof checking for holes or leaks. She mentally checked herself for staring at Merritt's shapely behind as she scaled the rungs. She was not here to meet someone, although she felt relief that for the first time in years, she was actually physically attracted to someone. It didn't help that Soren was an ass girl and Merritt *definitely* exceeded her expectations. She could tell that her legs were also muscular and toned beneath the cargo pants she was wearing. And she hadn't missed the fact that Merritt's arms were incredibly sexy either. *Really Ren, you are worse than a guy. Besides she may not swing my way. But I don't care right? I don't want her to swing my way, and it wouldn't matter…even if she did.*

She didn't breathe again until Merritt's feet landed safely on the ground again. It somewhat unnerved her that her concern went beyond the fear she would normally feel for someone. She shook the feeling off and listened as Merritt described the work that would need to be done on the chimneys. She would also need to do some minor work on the widow's walk, but other than that the roof had weathered well.

When Soren opened the front door and Merritt stepped into the large foyer, she gasped softly. "It's beautiful." She stared at the wide curving staircase that led to the second floor. She ran a hand along the dark wooden banister and let out a low whistle. "The wood is fantastic. Look at the detail. Whoever built this knew what they were doing. Aside from some stain in a few places, the staircase is immaculate."

Soren smiled, happy that Merritt wasn't immune to the beauty of the house. "The woodwork is like that all throughout. The detail in the trim is amazing. It had to have taken forever to do it."

"Probably so." Merritt acquiesced. "There was such a different mentality in the 1800's when someone built a house. Every detail was well thought out and done perfectly. They didn't cut corners or rush through things trying to save a buck. No pre-fab nightmares here…nope, nothing but pure reverence for the craft."

Soren studied Merritt closely. She felt drawn to her even though they had just met. She had to pull her gaze away from Merritt, despite the fact that being here with her made her feel suddenly alive and afraid at the same time. A tiny voice in her head screamed something about falling head over heals. Still she wondered what more they had in common besides truly appreciating the house and their shared desire to restore its beauty.

Merritt continued to be stunned by the house. They talked about the renovations to seven of the eight fireplaces and even asked if Soren would allow her carte blanch to refinish them. Even though they had just met, Soren knew in her heart that Merritt would treat the house like it was her own and she didn't hesitate to tell her she could take whatever liberty she wanted. Her only request was that she didn't want any of the wood painted or covered in anyway. Merritt smirked a little when she'd said that, as if she would be uncouth enough to ruin the home's integrity.

They had both agreed that the kitchen needed a complete overhaul. Merritt suggested knocking out the wall between the kitchen and the unused butler bar to maximize the space. She would install all new custom cabinets that were stained and trimmed to match the antique feel of the house, but with modern appliances that would make any gourmet cook jealous.

When they moved to the large living room just beyond the kitchen, Merritt discovered that the large double entry had pocket doors that had been sealed off sometime in the last hundred years. They both decided that needed to be changed. Soren also wanted the ugly carpet that had been laid throughout the house ripped up and the wood floors refinished. Just off the living room was a large study with floor to ceiling built--ins. Merritt had gone wild over those. She ran her hands along the shelves and made little noises every time her fingers found a small imperfection. "Wow, years and years of history here. I bet every little mark has a story behind it." She turned to Soren who couldn't hide the amused expression on her face. "Wouldn't you love to know her story?"

Soren shoved off the door frame and walked towards her as if some invisible force was pushing her. "I'm sure it's tragically romantic. A story of unrequited love."

26

Merritt winced. She knew all too well about lost loves. She was living with that pain daily. She smiled quickly. "Or perhaps a beautiful tale of love and laughter and family."

Soren hadn't missed the flash of pain in Merritt's eyes and she longed to reach out and comfort her, to hold her in her arms and take the pain away. Before she could, a loud noise made them both jump. They both turned in the direction of it. A large book had fallen off the top shelf and onto the floor, landing with a resounding smack. Soren glanced at Merritt and shrugged. "Must be a love story."

"With a tragic ending." They both laughed, but Merritt couldn't shake the feeling she had when she saw the same look of pain reflected in Soren's eyes and she wondered what her story was. What tragedy had taken the sunshine out of her life. She almost asked then remembered where she was…on the job. *Remember, it's not personal, it's business. Don't go getting yourself attached to the job.* She changed the subject quickly. "Well that about wraps it up down here, let's tackle floor number two…before any more books start falling on our heads."

Soren picked up the book, set it on the bottom shelf. "War and Peace…figures."

They walked up the wide banister, their hands somehow managing to brush together. Soren felt a jolt course through her body and she stole a glance at Merritt to see if she had noticed. She felt relief and disappointment when she saw that Merritt had been paying attention to the decorative trim on the wall along the staircase and had obviously been oblivious to Soren's touch. *Well at least one of us is alive.*

Merritt had to force herself to keep walking, the nearness of Soren making it difficult to breathe. She stopped at the top of the stairs and looked down the long hallway. "Lead the way."

Soren led her towards the three large spare bedrooms first and laughed when she heard her small grunt of disapproval. The doors upstairs had been painted just like the downstairs one. All that beautiful woodwork covered with layers of paint. "What is it with people and paint? I mean who looked at these doors and said *Gee, I think paint would be a great idea.* I just don't get it."

The last room that they looked at was Soren's bedroom. Although Merritt's presence in the bedroom was strictly business, Soren felt suddenly warm. The room, the closeness was all too much for her. It felt a little too personal, a little too intimate. She walked to the other side of the room and pretended to fuss with something on the nightstand, unable to stand close to Merritt. If she worried that Merritt noticed the subtle change, her worries were soon allayed. She either felt nothing or she was a damn good actress.

"Oh man, this room is amazing. I wonder if you know what a find this house is."

Soren glanced around the room. "It is, isn't it? I think this is what got me."

They both looked at the tall, arching ceiling that tapered to a point in the center of the tower. A beautiful crystal chandelier hung directly over the center of the room. The sun was cascading in through the large bay windows and a thousand tiny points of light bounced off the chandelier around the room. Her bed sat in the convex of the three corners of the tower. It faced a large fireplace with a deep wooden mantle that stopped just below the arch of the ceiling.

Merritt walked toward a door just left of the fireplace, opened it and stopped dead in her tracks. "Amazing…there's one room that's renovated!"

Soren chuckled and followed her into the bathroom. A large pedestal sink sat just inside the door, with a decorative mirror and two candle sconces framing it. There were built--ins on one wall opposite the shower. The layout of the bathroom had not been changed, at least to the best of Soren's knowledge.

"I don't think we will have to do much in here except maybe a coat of paint."

"God I hope not. I can't even imagine the price tag for what we've done so far. I think the bathroom would break me." Soren said wryly.

"Let's just say it will keep a roof over my head for another year." Merritt said and winked at Soren. She was surprised at how easy the banter between them was. *Cool it Tanner! Business remember...oh and you're taken.* She rolled her eyes thinking about how cruel the irony of that was. "Are you ready for the bad news?"

Soren winced. "Yeah I guess. It's like a bandaid...give it to me quickly."

"Don't worry, I'll kiss it and make it all better." Merritt jumped, appalled at her forthrightness. *Where the hell did that come from? Are you trying to flirt your way out of this job?*

Soren smiled cryptically, her eyes dancing like she'd just discovered the secret to eternal youth. "You promise?" *Well that answers that question and two can play at this game.*

"Scout's honor." Merritt said with a mock salute. "It'll only hurt for a second."

"You know it might take more than one kiss." Soren answered coyly. "I have a low tolerance for pain." *Okay Jordan, how's that for joining the living?*

Merritt swallowed hard. This teasing banter with Soren was the most action she'd seen in months, hell years. She knew it wasn't more than two attractive women flirting but it felt good. No, it felt damn good. She didn't want to stop but guilt got the better of her. ""Don't worry, I'm sure it will be painless...if you concentrate on the end product."

"Uh sure...okay." Soren sensed a sudden change in her demeanor and it bothered her more than she wanted to admit. "I guess you will be mailing the estimates."

"Nah, hang on." Merritt winked. "I'll be right back."

Soren watched her open the door and run to her truck. She opened the passenger door and grabbed a small bag. She watched her bound up the steps two at a time, expertly missing the broken ones.

Merritt gestured towards the bag and smiled. "Mind if I set up in the kitchen?"

"Yes."

"Yes?" Merritt asked puzzled. "Yes, I can't set up in the kitchen?"

Soren shook her head. "Yes, as in you can set up in the kitchen. You carry a laptop with you? I figured you would have to go back to the office to do that."

"Shucks ma'am this fancy thing?" Merritt said in her most affected Southern drawl. "This here contraption is brand spankin' new. Golly I haven't even figured out how to use the thing."

Soren rolled her eyes, but she couldn't help the slow smile that crept onto her face when Merritt winked at her. "Very funny...ha ha! I didn't exactly mean it that way." She watched Merritt pull a laptop out of the bag and place it on the table. She opened it, waited for it to boot up then started typing.

Soren fidgeted at the table until Merritt glanced up and raised an eyebrow. "Sorry, the ADD is kicking in. Can I get you something to drink?"

"Yeah, sure. Water is fine." She replied, her face already buried in the computer.

"Tea or lemonade okay? The tap water here is not the best and I don't have bottled water."

"Yep."

"Yep as in which one?"

Merritt looked up and smiled, her eyes holding Soren's captive. She wasn't prepared for the flutter in her stomach. "I'll have whichever one you are having...fair enough?"

"You don't make it easy on a girl do you?" Soren asked as she pulled the refrigerator door open. She didn't see Merritt smirking.

"Nope. But something tells me you are worth the extra effort."

Soren didn't mistake the intimate tone in her voice and it sent shivers up and down her spine. She didn't respond until she set a glass of lemonade down next to Merritt. "You may change your mind about that the longer you're around me."

"Hmm." Merritt sighed introspectively, her mind pulling pictures from somewhere else and flashing them against Soren. She found her eyes and held them for a moment longer. "No I think you would always be worth it." She wrenched her eyes away from Soren and back to the laptop screen, unable to breathe under the intensity of Soren's gaze.

Soren watched her closely trying to read the dark look that flashed across her eyes. Merritt seemed to enjoy flirting with her but something was definitely holding her back. She needed to clear her head, needed to break the connection that she'd felt with Merritt since she walked into her life. *Which if I'm guessing...* she glanced at the clock on the wall...*ugh! Is less than three hours ago.* She continued to steal glances at Merritt, whose attention now seemed focused solely on the laptop, and shook her head in amazement. *Ren, you're going to have to watch yourself around this one.*

Merritt looked up and smiled, sensing Soren's gaze. "Almost done. You got one of them new fangled fax machines in this place?"

Soren raised an eyebrow. "Yeah, sure. Why?"

"You'll see." Merritt smiled cryptically. "What's the number?"

"Hang on." Soren grabbed her purse and started rummaging through it until she found her date book. She flipped through several pages. "You ready?"

"Yep, lay it on me baby." She typed in the number then paused with her finger on the enter key. "Is it turned on? Got paper?"

"Yes and yes."

Merritt hit the key then jumped up quickly. "Where is it?"

Soren shrugged her head sideways. "In the makeshift office slash library."

"Be right back."

"Watch out for falling books." Soren teased.

Merritt feigned a look of horror and threw her hands over her head. "If I get knocked out, you have to do mouth—to—mouth on me."

"My pleasure." Soren mumbled to herself as she waited for Merritt to come back. *"It would be my pleasure."*

Merritt walked back in several moments later. She held the papers against her chest. "Before you look at this, I just want to remind you to focus on the end product."

Soren groaned loudly. "Yikes, now you're scaring me." She shoved off the counter and walked towards Merritt. She took a deep breath and steeled herself, more from the nearness to Merritt than the paper she was holding out towards her. She took several more deep breaths. "Okay, lay it on me."

Merritt smirked at Soren. "My, my Ms. Lockhart, we've just met. You're so forward for a lady."

Soren took a step closer and smiled at Merritt's sudden intake of breath. She saw her eyes darken to a smoky green before she backed up and pasted an innocent smile on her face. Merritt waggled her finger in Soren's face. "Uh-uh, no fair trying to get me to drop my price."

Soren snatched the paper away quickly and looked at the bottom of the sheet, stunned by figures. "Holy hell! There's eight numbers here…and six of them are in front of the decimal."

"Darlin', I'm worth every penny." Merritt purred suggestively. "But I guess there are some things we could cut out…"

"No, I don't want to do that. I want it done right. I just…wow! It's a lot to digest all at once."

"I could break it up over a year. We could do the stuff that needs to be done right away and then hold off on the smaller stuff." Merritt offered quickly. "But that would mean you'd be stuck with me and my crew a lot longer."

"Could we stretch it out over say three years and I just get stuck with you?"

"Mmm, tempting as that sounds, you may be ready to kick me out after six months."

Soren raised her eyebrow and grinned at Merritt. "Oh so you're moving in while you do the work? I have a big bed."

"Darlin', I think you have the potential to get me in a lot of trouble." Merritt said after a pause.

Suddenly the truth dawned on Soren. "Ahh, there's a Ms. Tanner back home. No, she probably wouldn't like it if you shacked up with me."

Merritt's eyes clouded over and her voice was bitterly sarcastic. "I doubt she would even realize I was gone."

Soren was again tempted to push for details, but she stopped. They had just met after all and she was the last person that needed to give relationship advice. She ignored the pang in her heart and smiled. "Far be it from me to stir up a snake's nest of trouble. I'll just say I would notice and leave it at that. So, how soon do you think you can get started?"

Merritt noticed the quick change of subject and she silently thanked Soren for not pushing. There was no sense in sharing the morose details of her life with someone she would essentially be working for. No, she knew better than to air her dirty laundry. She didn't need to drive another wedge between her and Kate. Lord knows, they had enough already.

Instead she sat down in front of the computer again. "Well let's just see, shall we?"

She pulled up her calendar and started looking for available days. Merritt had a habit of muttering to herself when she was trying to figure something out. It was all Soren could do to not laugh out loud and she had to cover her smirk with her hand. Finally, she couldn't take it anymore and had to speak up. "Do you know how adorable you are when you do that?"

Merritt looked up, confused. "Do what?"

"Talk to yourself."

Merritt laughed. "Yeah 'cause an insane crazy that talks to herself is always a good way to meet chicks. Works almost as well as using my little puppy Batman…that is *if* I wanted to meet women of course."

"Of course." Soren seconded. And as much as it scared her to admit, she had to acknowledge that it would take very little from Merritt to get her interested. All the physical longings she'd thought were deadened by Victoria were coming back to life and at a very alarming rate. *Ren you better get off that train of thinking and get off quickly or you'll be heading for a heartache just like Patty Loveless.*

"What are you humming?" Merritt asked breaking her reverie.

"What?" Soren asked confused. "Humming…oh, nothing."

"That's funny." Merritt smirked. "I could have sworn you were humming "Blame It On Your Heart" by Patty Loveless."

Soren looked at Merritt, an amused expression on her face. "That's ridiculous. Why on earth would I be humming that?"

"Exactly. Why on earth?" Merritt laughed. "I guess I must be hearing things. Just add that to my list of ways to pick up women. Of course, I'll be in a straight jacket…which may be entirely more acceptable than chained to a ball."

34

This time Soren laughed with her. Despite the hurt look in her eyes, Merritt seemed resigned to her situation so who was Soren to question it. Besides it helped to know that not everyone had the fairytale romance that she was lacking. "And not near as heavy."

Merritt snorted loudly. "True!" After a few more moments of laughter, she managed to get serious again. "Okay, it's looking like two weeks this Friday. How does that look for you?"

"Tomorrow would be better, but I guess I'm at your mercy so two weeks will have to work." Soren replied, adding the appointment to her Blackberry and smothering a laugh.

"What's so funny?"

"Nothing. I was just thinking I wouldn't mind being at your mercy...I mean you already have the chain." She stood up quickly catching the blush that crept up Merritt's face. "Buuttt, since that's not allowed just rewind that thought and delete it."

Merritt shook her head. "No can do. It's etched in my brain now." She shut the laptop and shoved it into her bag. "And by the way, flattery will get you everywhere. Might even drop the estimate to seven figures."

"Oh yeah, what will it take to get it down to six numbers?" Soren said suggestively. "A night of wild, unabashed sex?"

Merritt felt color flood her face and she looked away quickly, hoping Soren hadn't seen the way she flushed at just the mere suggestion of a night of wild abandon. She swallowed the hard knot that had formed in her throat and smirked. "I can see I am going to have to be careful with you, Ms. Lockhart. You don't pull any punches."

"I'm sorry." Soren said quickly, but her eyes twinkled and Merritt could tell she really wasn't. "You will have to forgive me. I've spent the last two years like a dead man walking. I guess I'm starting to wake up...finally."

Merritt held up her hand. "Don't apologize. It's the most action I've had in awhile. I just have to be sure I don't get too comfortable with it. Wanting something you can't have and all."

"Who says you can't have it?" Soren caught Merritt's sideways glance and smiled. "I'm kidding, I'm kidding. I'll have to remember you swing a bit more to the literal side."

"And you to the flirtatious side." Merritt teased. She reached into her back pocket and extracted her wallet. Opening it, she pulled out one of her business cards. "Here's my card. It has the office number and my cell. I'll call you a few days before to give you the definite times. It's always a little iffy when I am coming off another job. I'm never sure that everything will wrap up on schedule."

"That sounds perfect. I'll be looking forward to your call." She gestured around the kitchen. "I'm as ready as I can be to get this project started."

"And finished." Merritt smiled and her green eyes held Soren's until the silence was overwhelming.

Soren cleared her throat, trying to break the spell that had come over them. "Let me walk you out. The front door can be a little tricky." She skirted around Merritt and inhaled her scent. It reminded her of musky bergamot wafting on warm summer breezes, not too feminine and definitely sexy. It made her head swim. She had to get away from her, the nearness was almost too much.

Merritt followed several steps behind and caught herself watching the sway of her hips and the soft round curve of her buttocks. She imagined her hands cupping Soren and pulling her flush against her body. "*Shit.*" She muttered.

Soren stopped and looked back at her. "What?"

"Nothing." Merritt mumbled. "I stubbed my toe."

"On what?" Soren asked suspiciously.

"On my other toe." Merritt winced, even to her that sounded lame.

"Uh-huh, sure you did."

"Damn floor is uneven." Merritt grumbled and tried to ignore Soren's eyes. They had this annoyingly cute way of lighting up when she was teasing her. "Guess I'll have to add that to the list and up the original estimate."

"That is only acceptable if it means I get more time with you." Soren smiled sweetly. "As friends of course. Given that I just moved here, if I add you to the list that will total..." She looked at her hands and started to count out on her fingers. "...one."

"So you're saying you need me?"

"Yes, and you wouldn't want to leave me all by myself in this strange city, would you?"

Merritt swallowed, knowing the answer should be no, but she couldn't say no to those big blue eyes staring up at her like a lost puppy. "I'll be a big bad monster if I say no, won't I?"

Soren smiled confidently. "Yes. And I don't need a monster. I already have a ghost."

"Huh? Oh yeah, your ghost." Then Merritt smiled remembering the book mysteriously falling off the shelf. "Then far be it from me to say no. I'd be honored to be your friend."

"Ditto." Soren reached around and pulled the door open, pausing before she walked outside. "Then I'll get the friends and family discount."

"Hey wait a minute." Merritt suddenly realized she'd been had and followed her outside quickly. "I may have to rethink this whole friend thing."

"Uh-uh, too late."

Merritt begrudgingly admitted Soren had outsmarted her. Still the thought of having her in her life was appealing. She was fun and easy to talk to and it didn't hurt that she was easy on the eyes. "We'll discuss the friendship perks at a later date." She unlocked the door to her truck and put the laptop bag on her seat then pulled herself up into the cab and paused with her hand on the door. "It was a pleasure meeting you Soren."

"Likewise I'm sure." Soren waited while Merritt shut the door and started the engine. She didn't want to let her go, partly because she wanted the company, but mostly because for the first time in two years, she was starting to feel almost human. "Hey I meant to ask you…know any good landscaping companies?"

"As a matter of fact I do. Want me to make the call? I can have them come out tomorrow if you're free."

"Yes, that would be great. My schedule's open." Soren smiled. "Thank you."

Merritt pretended to tip her hat. "Shucks, weren't no trouble at all ma'am."

"Much obliged." Soren teased back. She watched as Merritt pulled away. Long after she'd turned the corner and driven out of her view, Soren stood rooted to the same spot wondering at the affect Merritt had on her and how she was going to deal with it.

Chapter Three

Merritt sighed loudly, unlocked the door and stepped into the kitchen. The unexpected, yet welcomed good mood that she'd been in since meeting Soren had dissipated the second she pulled into the drive. A sideways glance told her that Kate was home and from the number of empty bottles on the counter, she was well beyond sober. Merritt shook her head and wondered for the hundredth time, how they had come to this. This miserable co—existence that seemed to wrap around her like a constrictor, squeezing the life out of her a little each day. She knew it was because she had been cursed with a savior complex and that if she stayed around long enough, Kate would eventually see that she was enough to make her happy. She wouldn't need to drink just to cope or look outside their relationship to be happy. Although Merritt wondered even if Kate sobered up would she still want to be with her? Was she even still in love with Kate? Could she forgive her? Those were the questions that had plagued her for months. So far she hadn't allowed herself to acknowledge the answer because subconsciously she knew it was no and finally accepting it meant charting a course in treacherous waters, and Merritt wasn't sure she was ready for that.

Her thoughts were interrupted briefly when she felt something soft nuzzling her leg. She bent over and picked up the tiny Shih--tzu. "Hey Batman." She kissed the top of his head and smiled. "You still love Mommy, don't you? Of course you do." She rubbed his tiny black ears and laughed. She set him down and watched him scamper away, all twelve pounds of him. The only way he looked even remotely like Batman was the dark black mask that covered his ears and wrapped around his eyes like the caped crusader.

She rinsed the empty bottles out and threw them in the trash. The half—opened bottle of vodka she emptied into the sink out of spite. She cringed knowing that Kate and vodka didn't mix well. Tonight could be another ugly night. She fixed herself a glass of iced tea and went off to find Kate.

"Kate? Kate, where are you?" Merritt finally found her passed out on the couch in the basement. She picked up an empty glass that had fallen on the floor, its contents spilled on the carpet next to the couch. "Un—fucking—believable."

She picked up the melting pieces of ice and threw them into the glass furiously, the loud clinking noise not even phasing Kate. She didn't bother waking Kate up, she knew it would only be a matter of time until she slept off the current buzz and ventured out looking for more alcohol and probably a fight.

Merritt sat down in front of the computer and ran her hands through her hair, waiting for it to boot up. She spent the next twenty minutes updating the company system finalizing the details for Soren's renovations. Her mind wandered back to her day with Soren. Merritt had to force herself to not get lost in the deep blue depths of her eyes. Couple that with a great body and a sharp tongue and Soren was one incredibly tantalizing woman. If first impressions were any indication, Soren was definitely someone she would like to get to know better…if the circumstances were different.

Merritt couldn't recall how exactly she and Kate had arrived at this place in their lives and relationship. She recalled the first few years they had been together and smiled sadly. They'd met a little over five years ago at one of Merritt's softball games. She played third base for her company's rec league and in an unforgettable attempt to stretch a double into a triple, Merritt had careened into Kate, knocking her on her ass and Merritt head over heels. She'd fallen immediately for Kate's brown eyes and quick smile. They were the couple everyone wanted to be, young, successful, and in love.

But three years into the relationship, everything started to unravel. Merritt had taken over Tanner Construction and the long hours were taking their toll on their love life. To cope with that, Kate had started to turn to a few women she worked with and started drinking. At first, she was just a social drinker, a few hours at the bar and a few drinks to fill the void that Merritt's long hours had left. Soon Kate's loneliness turned to resentment and before she or Merritt knew what happened, Kate, in a drunken stupor, had stumbled into a one night stand. Overnight they'd transitioned from being a couple in love to two people stuck together in an emotionally toxic relationship. They both blamed Merritt for Kate's drinking and Merritt blamed herself for Kate's infidelity, yet neither one of them knew how to fix it. Merritt had hired more help and cut her hours way back. She tried to get Kate to go to couples counseling but to no avail. She'd done research, gone to a couple of Alanon meetings, even suggested going to AA with Kate. Kate had tried for a few months, but eventually slipped back into it making it clear that she didn't think she had a problem and didn't need Merritt's help or pity. The hardest part had been trying to forgive Kate, despite believing she was the reason Kate looked outside for intimacy. And she should forgive the affair since it was her fault, right?

The last two years of the relationship had been hell on both of them. Merritt hadn't let herself give up. That wasn't her style. She fought the feelings of unworthiness that had resurfaced when Kate started drinking. She tried to ignore the images of her father stumbling around drunk, or passed out somewhere. She knew all too well the feeling of being a failure, not good enough to make someone happy and the indelible images of Kate and another woman seared her brain, and hardest of all, her feelings of guilt. Most days she shouldered that and survived, but sometimes it was too much. Sometimes she felt like a child again, helpless and lost. Other days she felt unbridled anger with no outlet. And yet, she still kept trying, still tried to be Kate's savior, her own savior, somehow sure that was her penance for driving Kate to this dark place.

Hours later, Merritt awoke from a fitful sleep and saw Kate standing in the doorway. She heard ice clinking and knew that round two was in full swing. She tensed, not knowing if it was angry Kate or emotional Kate. "What do you want Kate? I'm tired."

"I missed you today." Kate said, her speech slightly slurred. "I thought maybe we could have had dinner together tonight. I waited for you."

Merritt sighed. "Tonight's gone Kate. I came home, you were asleep."

"I'm sorry Merr. It was a long day at work today. I was tired."

"You were passed out." Merritt mumbled. "At six o'clock. We could have talked about dinner then. Not now, I need to sleep."

"Fuck sleep Merritt. There's always going to be something more important than me, isn't there?" Kate's sarcasm cut through the night.

"Oh that's rich Kate. We've been through this a hundred times already. I can only apologize so much and I can only forget so much." Merritt threw the covers off and swung her feet to the floor. "Just go please, I don't want to fight with you."

"I don't want to fight with you either. How did we get here, Merr? What happened to us?"

Kate's voice was softer now and Merritt struggled to stay strong. She knew that tomorrow morning she wouldn't even remember this conversation. Things would be back to normal, well their normal anyway. She stood up and touched Kate's glass. "This happened, work happened, she happened, life happened to us." Merritt answered wearily.

"Will you ever let that go?" Kate sniffed. "I love you Merr. How did we let that slip away?"

Merritt tried to feel something, tried to find a small part of her body that could return those feelings. She wondered if she would feel differently if only Kate had said those words a year ago, six months ago even. She didn't know for sure, but probably not. "I guess it wasn't important enough to fight for." She could see a small tear glistening on Kate's cheek and she brushed it away. "I'm sorry Kate. I just don't know if we can fix this."

"Can we try? I'd like to at least try." She stepped closer. "Can I sleep with you? I want you to hold me."

Merritt stiffened. They hadn't been in the same bed for more months than she could remember. "Come on Kate, I've got a busy day tomorrow. I need to get some sleep."

"Please, Merr. Just hold me for tonight." Kate walked around her and got into bed. "Just like old times."

Merritt hesitated then climbed in beside her. She sat with her back against the headboard and Kate curled herself up next to her, handing Merritt her glass. Long after Kate had gone back to sleep, Merritt sat awake in the dark room, her eyes fixed on the night stand where she'd set the empty glass. "She's still cheating on me you know?" Her voice was barely a whisper. "She cheated on me with Devon, she's cheating on me with you. You're her mistress now and I can't fight you. I'll lose every time. I'm tired of fighting to hold on. I need to figure out how to let go. I have to accept I can't fix her, no one can...except you, Kate." She brushed a lock of hair off of Kate's forehead. "But you have to want too."

Merritt gently pulled her arm out from behind Kate and slid off the bed. She crept down the hallway into the second of their two spare rooms, hoping she could get at least a couple hours of uninterrupted sleep. The last thing she saw before she crashed was Soren smiling at her, silently drawing her away from her own reality.

Chapter Four

Soren jumped at the sound of the doorbell. She tucked the small leather bound book back in the box she'd found in the attack and started to stand up. She heard her knees crack and cursed gravity, getting old, sitting Indian style on the floor for so long and whatever other demons were responsible for her cracking bones. "That's what you get for sitting on the floor dumbass."

The bell rang again as the impatient visitor tried once again to let his presence be known. "Hold your horses, I'm coming." She threw the door open, not recognizing the newcomer. She was older than Soren with short blond hair, slightly grayed at the temples. She had tanned skin that had seen too many days under the hot Georgia sun without sunscreen and if asked, Soren would say just short enough and plump enough to be soft. Soren guessed her to be in her mid—forties. "Hello?"

"Howdy." The stranger said cheerfully. "I'm Gay."

Soren smirked. "Well good for you. So am I."

"Well darlin', aren't you a funny one?" The visitor winked. "Although that is very useful information. You're a beautiful, tall drink of water, aren't you? And being a lesbian just makes you even more attractive."

Soren had to laugh. The woman's southern charm made up for her candor. "So is it customary in your neck of the woods to go to random houses and come out?"

The woman burst out laughing. "Honey, you sure do beat all. My name is Gay. Short for Gayla…Cherry. And before you make a stripper joke, let me assure you I have heard them all."

Soren snickered. "Your mom didn't like you much, huh?"

Gay's twinkling eyes narrowed slightly. "She loved me all right, but the woman had a wicked since of humor. Damn near psychic too. Who would have thought she'd pick such a fitting moniker?"

"Very fitting." Soren teased. "Well Gay, short for Gayla, it's nice to meet you. What can I do for you?"

Gay pulled a business card out of her pocket and handed it to Soren. "Merritt called me yesterday."

"*Cherry Landscaping. We put the cherry on top.* Oh that's priceless. Could you be anymore gay?"

Gayla rolled her eyes, ignoring Soren's last comment. "Merritt did warn me you had a quick tongue. And she said you had a rather large landscaping project. She wasn't kidding on either account. Yikes…your yard."

Soren looked shocked. "What?! You mean this mess? I thought it was in great shape. I just want to touch up a few things."

"Honey I reckon that's like me saying I just want to lose a couple of pounds."

Soren laughed. "Stop it. You're cute…in a cuddly round sort of way."

Gay laughed with her, completely unphased by Soren's comment. "You know what? You're a funny gal. I reckon I like you. And if you ever decide you want a little cherry for dessert, you just let me know." She added with a wink.

"You know what Gay?" Soren responded with a smile. "I reckon I like you too."

"Well now that we have the pleasantries done, shall we get down to the nitty gritty? From the looks of the front yard, reckon we have our work cut out."

Soren snorted loudly. "If you think the front looks bad, just wait till you see the back. I'm kind of afraid of what we may find back there."

"That's why I have men working for me. A girl can only take so many spiders at one time." She tapped a clipboard very similar to Merritt's. "So tell me what you are thinking of for the front yard. And if you say trim my bush, be forewarned I have a dirty mind and I am fully prepared to take you figuratively."

"Funny girl. I suppose you are right. I should save that for the second date. I suppose I'll have to phrase it differently. I'd like to have everything in the front either taken out or trimmed way back. I don't want the yard to detract from the house. Just something clean and colorful, but understated. You know what I mean?"

"Sure do. You don't want your bush to outshine the house. And darlin' no one wants to get tangled up in overgrown bush."

"Something like that." Soren said with a groan.

Soren watched Gay do a rough sketch on grid paper. She wrote flower types and colors with the corresponding circular shapes. Soren could tell from the drawing that she was taking some of the existing foliage out and replacing it with plants and bushes that would bloom all summer. Soren followed her around the yard and studied her silently. She'd had a good feeling about the woman immediately. Based on first impressions, she definitely liked Gay. She was someone she thought she could be very good friends with and hoped that she felt the same. She was obviously a flirt and Soren didn't think she was the type that backed her words up, so she felt completely comfortable with their repartee. Oh sure, she could talk the talk, but when it came down to it, could Ms. Gay Cherry walk the walk? Probably not. She was certainly cute in a teddy bear sort of way. Warm and cuddly and innocent enough to make you feel happy. She also seemed to have an excellent eye for what Soren wanted and that counted for a lot in her book. She would have to thank Merritt for sending Gay.

A few moments later, Gay looked at Soren. "I think that about does it for the front. I'm fixin' to tackle the back."

Soren led her around the house to the backyard and smiled when she heard a small gasp.

"Holy overgrown nursery Batman! It looks like the garden center threw up." Gay said shaking her head. "You were not kidding. I wouldn't be surprised if we find a body or two."

"And I thought a few spiders were bad."

Gay pulled a pair of gloves out of her back pocket and slipped them on her hands. "Okay I'm going in…cover me."

Soren laughed out loud. "Send up a flare if you need to be rescued." She watched Gay amble past the gazebo towards the overgrown azaleas and hydrangeas at the back of the yard like a slow—moving bulldog out for an afternoon walk. Every few seconds, she heard Gay mutter an expletive reminding Soren of Jordan, who also had a mouth on her. She chuckled softly. "You okay in there?"

She heard a grunt, then Gay's throaty voice came from somewhere in the corner. "Run now! Save yourself. It's too late for me, but you've got your whole life ahead of you kid."

"I see you've met Gay."

Soren jumped at the voice. She turned to find Merritt standing beside her and smiled, her heart skipping a beat at her presence. "You could say that. She's…ahh…special."

Merritt laughed. "Yeah, she's special all right. By the way, I told her to take extra good care of you."

"Well that would explain her wanting to trim my bush." Soren said with a wink.

"That sounds just like her. Don't worry though, her bark is worse than her bite. She's harmless." Merritt added quickly hoping to allay any reservations Soren may have about Gay.

48

"I kind of figured. I like her though. Thanks for sending her my way." Then as if suddenly figuring out that her visit was unexpected, Soren regarded her quizzically. "So what brings you to my *Little Shop of Horrors?"*

Merritt smiled sheepishly. She didn't have a reason other than an overwhelming desire to be near Soren again. To see if the rush she'd experienced yesterday had been a fluke. Hoping that it was and she could go back to living in her small bubble. But no, she felt the same today. Loved the tingling feeling she got when Soren smiled at her. "I had some time to kill and I thought I would check and make sure that Gay had come by." She glanced towards the corner of the yard and watched Gay thrashing like a caged animal trying to extract herself from the flowers and pull Spanish Moss off her head at the same time. "I didn't realize I would get a show at the same time."

"Can it, Tanner." She walked closer and glared. "A little help, please."

Merritt laughed and pulled strands of vegetation off of Gay's back. "So how's my little cuz treating you?"

"I may be little, but I can still kick your ass." Gay said and punched Merritt in the arm.

"You're cousins?" Soren asked surprised. "I should have known. Does that mean I get the friends and family discount from Gay too?"

"I don't know about the friends and family discount…" Gay said with a lascivious grin. "…but I'm sure you and I can work out some…umm…type of arrangement."

"That'll do Cherry." Merritt teased, but there was an undeniable edge to her voice.

Gay opened her mouth to respond, but stopped quickly when she caught the look in Merritt's eyes. "Yeah sure thing Merritt." Turning to Soren, she smiled. "Please forgive me. I have a tendency to overstep my bounds."

"No harm, no foul." Soren needed to put the woman at ease. There was no way they could work together if there was an uncomfortable air between them. She had to admit that Merritt's rush to defend her felt good. "Besides Merritt obviously doesn't realize the extent to which you and I have bonded."

Merritt raised an eyebrow and regarded the two women. She had to admit the thought of the two of them together was sort of like watching an old Laurel and Hardy movie. "Well she is my cousin after all. One could only assume she has a way with women."

"Damn straight I do!" Gay seconded confidently. "I figure I have everything worked up out here. You want to go over the sketches and see if we are thinking along the same lines?"

"Yeah sure." She glanced at Merritt, a question in her eyes. "You gonna stick around?"

Merritt shook her head no. *Yes I want to stay. I want to be near you. But I want you all to myself.* Merritt tried to curb that thought, knowing she wasn't free to feel anything for Soren. At least her mind told her that was the right answer. She figured the warning hadn't reached her heart yet which was inexplicably yearning for Soren. She told herself she needed to put some space between them. "Nah, I have to get going anyway. Wouldn't want to delay the renovations to the castle." She punched Gay lightly. "Gay."

"What? Is it that obvious? It's the hair isn't it?"

"I could be wrong, but something tells me it's the *I Love Hot Moms* shirt you're wearing." Merritt answered sarcastically. "That or the fact that you look as queer as a three dollar bill."

"Well if that ain't the pot calling the kettle black. You're damn lucky Tanner."

"Oh yeah, why's that?" Merritt asked innocently.

"You're lucky that I won't kick your ass in front of a lady." Gay's voice had dropped to a conspiratorial whisper. "Sweet Soren just saved you."

Soren watched the exchange with amusement. She could tell that their familial bond was obviously strong and while they teased, she sensed that if the need arose, each would stand up for the other. They reminded her of growing up with Brett and Jordan and she felt a warm sense of home overtake her body. She felt parts of her heart that she thought long dead starting to awaken. In the few hours she'd spent with Merritt and now with the camaraderie she'd developed with Gay, she no longer felt the strong pull of hopeless desperation wield its tight grip on her. "You two are a mess. It's a wonder you made it this far without killing each other."

They turned to her with sheepish grins on their faces. Merritt pulled Gay into a headlock and gave her a noogie. "Aww, she knows I'm just messing with her. Isn't that what family does?"

"Only distant family." Gay retorted, pulling away from Merritt and trying to fix her messed up hair. "Something that first cousins once removed or second cousins or whatever we are wouldn't do."

"Whatever! You're just too short to get me in a headlock."

"Maybe, but I could clothesline you smartass." Gay pointed at her watch. "Didn't I hear something about needing to get out of here? Had to get to work or something like that? You need to head on down the road and stop messing up my chances with the lady here. Got it?"

"Yeah, yeah." Merritt rolled her eyes. "I'm leaving. See if I give you anymore referrals now." She turned to Soren, her green eyes held her blue ones captive. "So I'll call you?"

Soren swallowed and forced herself to breathe, realizing that she'd been paralyzed under Merritt's gaze. "Sooner than later I hope." She said breathily, realizing she must have sounded more intimate than she intended. She recovered quickly. "I'm dying to get started on the house."

Merritt took an unconscious step towards Soren and smiled, paralyzed by her nearness. "I hope so too. Goodbye Soren."

Soren merely nodded, unable to form any words. She felt an involuntary shudder penetrate her body and she was powerless to turn away, her gaze fixed on Merritt's retreating form. Again, she watched the road long after Merritt's vehicle was gone.

"Ahem." Gay cleared her throat loudly and Soren jumped, finally remembering where she was.

"Sorry. Got lost in my thoughts for a second." Soren apologized, the blush of embarrassment creeping over her face.

"She likes you." Gay said matter—of—fact. "More than a friend."

"No she doesn't." Soren replied dismissively then allowed her curiosity to get the better of her. "What makes you say that?"

"Because she's trying so hard not to like you."

Soren raised her eyebrow incredulously. "You got that from five minutes together."

Gay shook her head. "I got that from forty—five years together. I know my cousin. Her eyes will tell you everything. She's attracted to you and she's fighting it because she knows she's not free to act on it Although she damn sure should be. Plus she knows I flirt with everyone and she's never stopped me before. No, you're special."

Soren was silent a few moments. "Like you said, she's in a relationship so it doesn't really matter." She turned to go back up the steps to the back porch.

Gay followed her, all the while muttering under her breath. *"Why she stays with that fucking cheating bitch is beyond me. Buries herself in a goddamn bottle every night and then goes and fucks someone else. I just don't get it."*

Soren's mouth dropped in shock. "Wow, don't hold back. Tell me how you really feel."

Gay smiled wearily. "I'm sorry. I just get so pissed off when I think about how miserable Kate is making her. All the drinking on top of the…"

Soren put her hand up to silence Gay. "It's really none of my business. I don't think Merritt would appreciate me knowing the sordid details of her personal life."

"Hmmphh." Gay snorted loudly. "Maybe if someone else knew, she would realize what an ass she is for sticking around. She didn't make Kate pick up the bottle. She didn't make Kate cheat. I figure we're all responsible for our own actions. No one can make us do anything. In the end, no matter what anyone does to us, it's the individual that chooses how they react to that." She caught Soren's warning gaze. "I know, I know, I'll stop. You just don't understand. Merritt has been trapped in this black hole for too long. Forgive me for saying this, but I won't apologize for my very low opinion of Kate or for being happy that just being around you for five minutes makes her eyes come alive. If anyone needs that, I reckon it's Merritt."

#

Hours after Gay left, Soren was still thinking about what she had told her about Merritt. She had seen the pain in her eyes and felt a kindred spirit. They were both lost, broken souls in need of redemption, although she guessed they were both just figuring that out. Soren felt she had made progress in saving herself and hoped that one day Merritt would do the same.

She had the sudden urge to feel her hands on her guitar. To slide her fingers along the slender metal strings, letting every bit of her soul come out in the music. She pulled the guitar out of the case and touched it reverently. It was the first time she'd felt the sleek lines in more than two years and her fingers hummed with anticipation. This time would be different, every chord she played would be for her, every trembling vibrato a melancholy declaration sending the heartbroken parts of her soul winging to the heavens. And when her fingers strummed across the strings the first time, she wept.

She cried for herself and for Olivia, her lost baby. She cried for lost love and the pain that came with it. She cried for Merritt, and she felt a wall come tumbling down. And when she finished crying, she played. As the melodies tumbled over themselves like a fast—moving river overflowing its bounds, Soren started to heal.

Chapter Five

Soren was pulling into the driveway when her Blackberry started buzzing. She answered it on the fourth ring, trying to juggle her purse and two bags of groceries. "Shit. Hello."

"Soren?"

Soren recognized the voice immediately and her skin tingled. "Merritt, hi."

"Hi yourself. Everything okay?"

Soren smiled at the concern in Merritt's voice. "Yeah. I'm just suffering from not being born as an octopus."

"Huh?"

"Between my purse, grocery bags and the phone, it's got me wishing I had eight arms." Soren said quickly.

"Would you settle for two more?" Merritt asked. "I'm pulling up to your house right now."

"You are?" Soren looked in the rear view mirror and didn't see anyone behind her. "Where are..." She looked around her and smiled when she saw Merritt jogging around the side of the house.

"Right here." Merritt said as she hung up the phone and pulled Soren's door open. She gestured to the bags. "Leave those, I'll get them."

Soren took her outstretched hand and hoped Merritt didn't notice when she trembled slightly. When she stepped out, Merritt didn't release her hand. Instead she held it, her intense eyes captured Soren, immobilizing her.

"I'm glad you're home. I was going to run some paperwork by and figured I would just have to leave it in the box."

Soren's breath came in shallow gasps, her heart beating a mile a minute. Her gaze dropped to Merritt's beautiful mouth and her stomach heaved. "Paperwork?"

"Contracts and legal stuff." Merritt's voice was low and intimate.

Soren forced herself to look away from Merritt's mouth. She willed herself to take a step back and put some distance between them. "You could have faxed it."

Merritt didn't relent, taking a step forward. Soren felt her back touch the car and she looked into Merritt's eyes again, her heartbeat wildly erratic. "I wanted to see you. I…I missed you Soren."

Soren's breath caught in her throat. She shook her head, unable to speak. "Please."

Merritt sensed the desperate plea and took a step back, breaking the current that coursed between them.

Soren's head was spinning wildly, her brain trying to assimilate the enormity of what she was feeling for Merritt and desperately trying to quell the surge of emotions threatening to overwhelm her. "You shouldn't tell me that."

"I know, I'm sorry. I can't help it though." Merritt struggled for words. "It's like I'm not in control anymore and even though I tell myself it's wrong, some unseen force keeps pulling me back to you." Merritt rubbed her knuckles on Soren's cheek so lightly she could barely feel it, but it sent shivers through her body anyway.

"Please don't make me fall in love with you. I don't think I could take my world being ripped out from under me again." Soren stepped sideways away from Merritt. "I like you. I want to be friends. Can't we just leave it at that?"

Merritt's shoulders sagged, deflated. The last thing she wanted to do was hurt Soren. Though they had only known each other a couple of weeks, to her it felt like a lifetime. A lifetime of wanting something and knowing she would never be able to have it. She raised her eyes and met Soren's gaze. "Yes, yes we can." She hoped her tone sounded resolute, when she felt anything but strong.

"Thank you." Soren said quietly. There was a sadness in both their eyes, and she smiled trying to lighten the mood. "So where's that help with my groceries?"

Merritt smiled sheepishly. "Oh right, I guess I did offer my two arms." She reached in and grabbed the bags, then shut Soren's door. "Lead the way."

When they got inside, Merritt set the bags on the counter and held an envelope up. "This is the contract and some other legal stuff. I had my secretary put tags anywhere you needed to sign and date. You can look it over if you want, have an attorney read through it, whatever then just mail them back when you've signed everything."

"Will do." Soren was putting food in the fridge and couldn't see Merritt's face, but she could feel her watching every movement she made. She remembered something her mother had told her once about men liking to watch a woman walk towards them, but loving to watch them walk away and silently she prayed that Merritt was enjoying the view. She shouldn't have worried, when she turned around moments later, she saw Merritt's head snap up and her cheeks turn suspiciously red. *Oh yeah, she likes it.* She smirked and Merritt rewarded her by shrugging her shoulders as if to say what do you expect? I'm a lesbian. She felt an involuntary flutter in her stomach. "So when is the official start date?"

"On paper we have about four more days of work on the project we are on, then we start yours. So I'd say this coming Monday."

"That is perfect. As far as how long it will take to finish everything…" Soren inquired.

"For a job this size I would figure on ten to twelve weeks easy. Most of it will be spent in here."

Soren raised her eyebrows in a silent okay. "That's not too bad. I won't be here towards the end of it, but I'll give you a key anyway so you can come and go." Then feeling the need to explain, she continued. "My best friend and her wife are expecting their first baby the middle of July and I want to visit. I may be gone a week or so."

"Just remind me before you leave so I don't worry that something's happened, okay?" Merritt said quietly.

Again Soren was touched by the concern in her tone. "Don't worry. I'll say goodbye before I go and call every hour for status reports." She teased.

The corner of Merritt's mouth curved up slightly. "Okay, okay you're right. That did sound a bit girlfriend like. Maybe if you just call every two hours, I'll be okay." She shoved off the counter and stood with her arms crossed. "I miss you already…as a friend of course."

"Of course." Soren smiled. "Are you in a hurry to leave? I was just getting ready to make dinner."

Merritt glanced at her watch. "No, I've got some time to kill. What are we having?"

"You're gonna laugh. I'm having one of those cold weather cravings. Grilled cheese and vegetable soup." She stopped and looked at Merritt. "Unless that's not okay? I can make something else."

"No, that's fine." She took several steps towards Soren and put her hand on her arm, trying to ignore the flutter in her stomach. "Anything with you is more than fine." Her hand lingered briefly then disappeared with the briefest of movements. She shoved her hands in her pockets unable to control them otherwise. "What can I do?"

"Sit down and relax." Soren suggested. "Can I get you anything to drink? Beer? Wine?"

"No." Merritt answered quickly, her eyes clouding over. "Water or maybe some of that delicious fresh—squeezed lemonade you had the other day."

Soren had become all too familiar with the brief changes in Merritt's mood and thanks to the little that Gay had told her, knew what that cloud was. And just like before, she lightened the mood instantly. "Fresh—squeezed? That's funny. Try it's fresh delivered off the Schwann's truck." She added ice to a glass, filled it with lemonade and handed it to Merritt.

"Thanks." She took a big gulp and smiled. "Still taste fresh—squeezed to me."

"It's going to take me a few minutes…you can watch TV in the library if you want. The remote's on the table." Soren suggested, eager to put some distance between them. This cooking dinner with Merritt watching felt too much like home, too much like being in a relationship and she didn't need to feel that. Maybe some space would clear her head, let her forget that Merritt had come because she missed her. Let her forget that she missed Merritt just as much. She wondered what on earth she was thinking when she invited her to dinner, and how she was going to get through it. "I'll bring the stuff in and we can eat in there."

Merritt sensed the dismissal and wondered at it, but didn't question it. "Sure. Holler if you need anything." She stood up and left the kitchen, Soren's eyes following her as she sauntered out of the kitchen. She reminded Soren of a panther with long sinewy muscles, ready to pounce. She was fascinated by her and scared at the same time. Shaking her head, she went back to cooking.

Merritt wandered into the study. Her eyes rested on the guitar immediately and she couldn't help but smile. Her first thought was Soren playing the guitar and how incredibly sexy she found that. *God, what those fingers could do to me.* She shuddered at the sudden tingling heat between her legs. The thought of Soren's fingers bringing her to an orgasm made her knees weak and she had to sit down and take several deep breaths. *I am so in trouble!* Yet somehow, she seemed to welcome that thought.

Needing to focus on something other than Soren, she picked up the remote and surfed the channels. Before she knew it, Soren carried a tray into the room and handed it to her. She set the remote down and took the tray. "Thanks."

"You're welcome." Soren smiled and gestured at her glass. "You need a refill?"

Merritt glanced at her half—empty glass. "I'm good."

"Oh I'm sure you are." Soren said lasciviously. "But do you need a refill?"

Merritt blushed. "Cute. No, I have plenty to drink right now, thank you though."

"'Kay, be right back."

Merritt's eyes followed Soren as she left the room, admiring the gentle sway of her hips and her deliciously cute backside. Soren, sensing she was being watched, looked back and met Merritt's eyes. She saw the raw hunger there and knew it wasn't for the grilled cheese she'd just brought her. Soren felt captive to an unseen force and she was certain that Merritt could hear her heart pounding from across the room, drowning out the deafening silence that screamed all around them. She knew if she let herself go, those green eyes would be the death of her. She smiled nervously and wrapped her palm around the door frame, knowing that would be the only way she could keep from walking back into the room and taking what Merritt's eyes were silently offering her.

Merritt finally pulled her eyes away and broke the force that threatened to tear her in two. Nothing in her small world could have prepared her for the undeniable yearning that she had to possess and be possessed by this woman. It was unmatched in its fury and so completely and totally overwhelming that Merritt knew her life would never, could never be the same and that was something she wasn't ready to deal with.

When Soren returned moments later, she noticed a change in the air. It wasn't a physical change she could touch, it was just that the air no longer hummed around them,

60

charged with unspoken desire. They fell into an amiable silence and ate, their attention somewhat diverted by re—runs on HGTV.

Several moments later, Merritt let out a contented sigh. "That was delicious!"

Soren smiled. "Yes, Campbell's does have a way with vegetable soup. Did you get enough? I can make you another sandwich if you want."

"No, that was plenty. Trying to watch my girlish figure, you know."

"Whatever. You are in great shape." Soren winked. "Besides I may have fresh pecan pie with vanilla ice cream for dessert…if I can tempt you."

"Darlin', you tempt me every time I see you." Merritt teased. "And yes, I would love to have your pie…your pecan pie, I mean."

"You're incorrigible." Soren said with a laugh.

"Guilty. But you like me anyway." Merritt stood up slowly, balancing her tray in one hand and her drink in the other. "I'll help you get it."

Soren set her tray on the counter and grabbed the dishes off Merritt's tray. She started to wash the few dishes they had and was surprised when Merritt took the soapy dishes from her, rinsed them and towel dried them. Soren answered her question before Merritt had a chance to ask. "The bowls and plates go right there and the glasses in the cabinet to the right." She didn't feel the need to tell Merritt she didn't really have to help, Soren could handle a couple of dishes. No, she relished being around someone who didn't have to be prodded to help. Again, she felt like it was all so easy, so comfortable being around Merritt. They could be that way as friends though…couldn't they?

Merritt's voice broke through her musings. "Big slice or little slice?" She turned from the sink to see Merritt holding a knife poised above the pecan pie.

She held her thumb and forefinger a couple of inches apart. "A medium—size piece."

Merritt's eyes ran the length of her body and back up again. She wiggled the knife at Soren. "You're a might too skinny. I think a big slice and a double scoop of vanilla is in order."

"And you're trying to send me into a sugar—induced coma, why?" She teased, her tone slightly sarcastic.

"Me?" Merritt said innocently. "You're the one that is feeding me pie and ice cream. First dinner, now dessert. If I didn't know any better, I'd say you were trying to get into my pants."

"Nonsense. Besides, they'd be way too long."

Merritt rolled her eyes. "Oh hardy, har, har. Just for that…" She moved the knife over two inches and sliced into the pie, cutting out a piece that was close to a quarter of the pie. "Coma here we come."

Soren's eyes widened. "There is no way I am eating all that."

Merritt shrugged. "Guess we'll have to share then, won't we?"

"Guess so." Soren countered. She pulled open the refrigerator door and pulled out a bag of coffee. "You want some decaf?"

"Sure then I really should get going." Merritt said. "Gotta get home and give Batman some attention." She laughed. "He's probably feeling quite alone and neglected locked away in his bat cave."

"Poor Batman, he needs a Robin. Or at the very least an Alfred." Soren said with mock seriousness.

"Him and me both. Or at least an Alfred who cares." Merritt changed the subject abruptly. "Ice cream scooper?"

Soren grabbed it out of the drawer to her left and held it towards Merritt. When she reached for it, she let her hand linger briefly enjoying the rush she felt at the contact. "Thanks. Two scoops, right?"

"Better make it three, since we're sharing. I have a thing for ice cream."

"What else do you have a thing for?" Merritt asked coyly.

"Puppies, chocolate, music, tall, dark and sexy brunettes. Although not necessarily in that order." Soren said softly.

Merritt didn't look up, pretending to concentrate on the ice cream, but she didn't have to. Soren had seen her hands tremble and she knew her words had affected Merritt. How long could they keep up this front of cool, unaffected reserve? She wondered which would hurt them more. Giving into passion or forever denying themselves the possibility of one great love? She shrugged, unable to answer the question that bothered her more and more every time they were together. Instead she grabbed two mugs. "How do you like it?"

"Huh?" Merritt asked confused then saw the mugs in Soren's hands. "Oh, black please. I like my coffee like I like my women."

"Black and strong?"

Merritt threw back her head and laughed. "Rich, smooth and strong."

Soren poured the coffee into the mugs then stirred half—and—half and sugar into her cup. She took a small sip and moaned appreciatively. "I like my coffee like I like my women. Sweet and creamy." She walked out of the room leaving Merritt standing with her jaw wide open. "Don't forget the spoon."

Merritt followed Soren into the study a minute later, her mouth full of ice cream and pecan pie. She groaned softly. "You seriously have the best pie ever."

"You have no idea." Soren said in her most suggestive voice. "Now are you going to share or do I have to get my own?"

Merritt stole two more bites before handing the plate to Soren. She scooped up a large bite and shoved it in her mouth. When she finished it, she laughed softly as a thought hit her. "Same spoon huh? It's like we're making out." She handed the plate back to Merritt.

The smile that danced on Merritt's face was replaced by simmering desire and her eyes held Soren's, penetrating deep into her soul. "Rest assured, that's not even close to making out."

Soren felt heat searing her body, the flames of passion igniting all over her. She touched a hand to her lips and they felt swollen as though Merritt had actually ravished them with her own lips and not just with her eyes. The air crackled between them, punctuated with smoldering desire. She fought hard to break the spell, not sure what invisible magnetism had bewitched her heart and soul. Her heart raced and she felt heat pulsating between her legs. She could see Merritt's pulse hammering at the base of her neck and she longed to kiss the small spot. She swore she could feel invisible hands pushing her from her chair and she gripped the arms, her knuckles white with exertion. She felt herself standing dangerously close to the edge of a precipice. Somehow she closed her eyes and mentally pulled herself back before her body tumbled headlong into Merritt and carried her heart along as an unwilling captive. God, she wanted this woman, maybe needed this woman. But even so, she wouldn't let herself fall in love with Merritt.

Merritt could sense the change in Soren without a word even being spoken. She'd seen the veil that passed over her eyes, clouding the desire that had just been there. She could see Soren's desperate plea to change the subject and put emotional distance between them. Unfortunately, as much as she wanted to just take Soren into her arms and kiss her, she knew that that decision would damage the blossoming friendship they had and hurt Soren in the process. She would not do that. She pointed the spoon towards the guitar resting on a stand in the corner. "You play?"

64

"Yeah a little." Soren finally answered, not sure how much she would tell Merritt.

Merritt sensed her hesitation. "A little?"

She had a warm smile on her face that made Soren feel comfortable. She felt an overwhelming urge to tell Merritt everything. "Okay maybe a lot. It's sort of my job. Well it used to be anyway."

"You were in a band?" Merritt asked around another bite of pie. "I bet you are sexy when you play."

"Nothing that cool and definitely not sexy." Soren said as she swiped a napkin across her mouth and set the empty plate on a small end table. "I was a songwriter in Nashville."

"Country music?" Merritt wrinkled her nose distastefully. "Not much of a fan of that…no offense."

"None taken." Soren replied with a laugh. "I suppose it's like caviar, it's an acquired taste. It's funny really. I never saw myself as a country music writer, but living in Nashville I sort of gravitated towards that."

"I'm guessing you must have held your own up there. Write anything I would know?"

Soren named off several of the more well known and was pleasantly surprised when Merritt not only knew them, but reluctantly admitted she may have liked them…a little. "Wow, you are really good then. Got anything you want to try out on me?"

Soren smiled. "No, just bits and pieces. Some melodies, one or two bridges, no lyrics yet. I'm actually working on my own stuff this time. Some self therapy, if you will."

"Therapy?" Merritt stood up and grabbed Soren's mug. "Refill?"

"Sure, thanks." She picked up the empty pie plate and followed Merritt into the kitchen. She set the plate in the sink and took the proffered mug, adding cream and sugar. Merritt leaned back against the counter and sipped the hot liquid slowly. "So what happened to you that requires therapy?"

Soren leaned back against the counter and felt her hip graze Merritt. She crossed her arms and let her mug rest against her left arm. "Life I guess. Just got thrown a curve ball and I'm finally dealing with it."

"Care to elaborate?" Merritt prodded softly. "I'm a really good listener."

Soren shook her head. "Not really. It's not something I like to discuss."

Merritt cocked her eyebrow and watched Soren out of the corner of her eye. "How can you write about it if you can't even talk about it?"

"I feel like I've talked about it till I'm blue in the face." Soren sighed loudly. "Brett and Jordan, my best friends back home, got to hear me cry in my beer for more than two years."

"Maybe telling it to someone with a fresh perspective will help you heal." She nudged Soren's shoulder softly. "That's what friends are for right…to be each other's sounding boards."

Soren looked into Merritt's eyes and saw none of the pity she had grown used to seeing with her friends back home. It wasn't that they didn't care or she didn't appreciate having their support, she just got tired of them feeling sorry for her, she felt enough of that herself. There was only the look of warm encouragement and gentle strength. "I have a daughter."

If Merritt was surprised by the announcement, she didn't show it. "Mmm, the pictures in the study and your bedroom. What's her name?"

"Olivia. My daughter's name is Olivia." Her voice was tinged with such sadness that it broke Merritt's heart. "The pictures you saw are the last ones I have of her. She was four. She's six now."

Merritt knew in her heart that someone else must have banned Soren from her life. She knew that she was not the kind of person that would choose to not be in her daughter's life. "What happened?"

When Soren answered, the words tumbled out. She didn't hold back anything, feeling compelled to share this intimate piece of herself with Merritt. She told her about she and Victoria's life together in Nashville. Their decision to have a child together. The day when Victoria had told her she was leaving her for a man and taking Olivia with her. "I felt like she'd ripped my heart out. I wanted to die that day. I begged her to at least let me still see Olivia, but she didn't want to have to explain who I was. The thing that hurt the most was her telling me not to worry about Olivia, that she would forget about me soon enough. If it hadn't been for Brett and Jordan, I am not sure what I would have done that day."

Merritt's arm had found its way around Soren's shoulders and she leaned into her, feeling strength and comfort in her arms. Merritt rested her cheek on Soren's head. "I don't believe for a second that she has forgotten you. I'm sure you will always be in her heart."

Soren smiled. "Thank you, that helps."

"So was that day the last time you saw her?"

"No, I used to go to the park we'd always taken her to just to see her. One particularly bad day I tried to get close, hoping she'd see me and come running. I just wanted to hug her. Victoria saw me and she filed a restraining order against me. I hired an attorney and he basically told me that as Olivia's birth mother, Victoria had all the rights. It didn't matter that we were married, since Tennessee didn't recognize gay marriage. Basically, I was fucked. I tried one more time to see Olivia. Victoria had me arrested for violating the restraining order. The only saving grace was that she used her one good deed of the year on me and decided not to press charges."

"How nice." Merritt said icily. "Isn't she wonderful?"

"She had her moments." Soren said quietly, listening to the even cadence of Merritt's breathing, amazed at how comforting something so simple was to her. "It's been a rough couple of years. I miss Olivia everyday and there have been moments when I was sure I couldn't go on. The thing that keeps me going is the hope that one day I may get to have Olivia in my life again."

"So that's where the therapy comes in." Merritt said gently.

Soren reluctantly pulled away and met her gaze. "It's part of it. The move was the big part. My agent talked me into coming here and staying with her for awhile under the pretext of getting away and relaxing. I think it was her trying to kick my ass in gear. Two years is along time to go without working."

"She lives here?"

"Nope, vacations here. You do that when you're a rich agent type. See what my fifteen percent has gotten her." Soren said with a smile. "Anyway, long story short, I saw this house for sale and called the listing agent. He showed me the place thirty minutes later. I think he saw the sucker written on my forehead."

Merritt laughed. "Well I didn't want to say anything but…"

"But what?" Soren narrowed her eyes and glared at Merritt.

"The place was on the market almost a year. You were probably his first bite." Merritt teased, and pulled Soren into a one—armed hug before releasing her. "He saw you coming a mile away."

"Figures. And what is the cut for him referring business to you?"

To her credit, Merritt blushed at the question. "Maybe he gets a really nice Christmas basket and someone might sponsor his company holiday party."

Soren punched her in the arm. "You turd, I should have figured."

"What?" Merritt feigned innocence. "It's not like I made you buy the house." Her smile faded, suddenly serious. "But I'm glad you did, or I wouldn't have met you."

"I feel the same way." She stepped away, putting distance between them. Having a friend will definitely help. In addition to getting back to writing. This time I'm doing my own album. I'm writing my own story, not someone else's. This house, you, music, that's my therapy. It's how I'm figuring out how to move on. Hanging on to the past left me going through life as a shell and I don't want to do that anymore."

"Truer words have never been uttered. Maybe one day I'll figure out how to take that advice." Merritt shoved away from the counter and stretched her arms over her head, yawning loudly. "So is that all the figurative ghosts that you have in your past?"

Soren laughed. "No more ghosts, skeletons maybe…" She stopped suddenly, her mouth dropping open. "Oh my goodness, that reminds me…guess what I found the other day?"

"Oh lord, do I even want to know?" Merritt asked wryly.

Soren grabbed her by the wrist and yanked her hard. "Follow me." She pulled her back into the study and pulled a soft, leather bound book off of one of the shelves. "Look what I found."

"Ahh yeah, Soren, it's a book." Merritt said as though it were obvious. "It's a study, that's what you find in them…books."

Soren rolled her eyes. "Funny smartass. I know it's a book…well a journal actually, but I didn't find it in the study."

Merritt watched her confused, not sure where Soren was headed with this. "So you found it in the…?"

"The attic. I was standing at my bedroom window looking at the widow's walk when I realized the small window behind it doesn't face into any of the rooms. I thought it may have been a blind dormer but when I started checking it out, I realized it was a small window in the attic. I figured I would wait and see what you thought about opening it up, but…" Soren hesitated.

"But what?" Merritt asked suspiciously.

"Have you ever had a feeling that you had to do something? That some unseen force was pulling you towards something?"

"Everyday since I met you." Merritt teased. "But yes, I guess I know."

Soren acknowledge her comment with a sad smile. "After I realized there was an attic I had this overwhelming desire to see what was up there. Which let me tell you was not the easiest thing to do by myself."

"Why didn't you call me silly? I would have helped you."

"Oh sure…*Hey Merritt, I know we just met and all and yes this does sound incredibly crazy, but I need to get up into the attic. Think you could swing by and help me?* Me lugging the ladder up the stairs was comical enough, but add in the soft spots in the floor where I almost fell through and it was absolutely hilarious."

"I would have come if you had called me." Merritt said softly.

"I know you would have." Soren smiled and laid her hand on Merritt's arm. "Thank you. So now do you want to know why this is such a big deal?"

Merritt took the journal from Soren and turned it over in her hands. "Sure."

"Okay, I found it in a box with some old newspapers from December 1941. I wasn't sure what significance they had until I started reading the journal. It belonged to Samantha Shaw, the daughter of Robert Shaw, who

70

according to her journal built the house in 1890 when she was seventeen years old. She writes about moving here from Macon and her father running the Savannah Times."

"So you found a little piece of history. That's cool. She would have been around when Savannah was really starting to grow. Did you know that Juliette Gordon Low, the woman who started the Girl Scouts was born here? I blame her for my addiction to Thin Mints." Merritt asked with a wink. "So what else did you find out about Ms. Shaw?"

"I haven't read too much further into except I did read the last excerpt."

"Oh, you're one of those."

"One of what?" Soren asked slightly confused.

"You read the last chapter of a book so you know how it ends before you read it." Merritt said sternly, her eyes twinkling. "What would James Patterson think of you?"

"No I'm not." Soren responded sheepishly, but she knew that Merritt could tell she was fibbing. "Okay, maybe a little. Anyway, do you want to hear about our heroine's tragic love story or not?"

Merritt straightened her shoulders and pursed her lips. "Yes, Ms. Lockhart."

Soren laughed at her sing—song classroom voice. She flipped the journal open to the last page. "Here it is. It's dated November 28, 1941. *My journey on this earth is nearly finished. I can feel myself getting closer and closer to death everyday. It is only a matter of time before my soul leaves the confines of this earthly shell. My life has been a good one and I have but one regret.* Listen to this." Soren's voice was low and throaty as if she were lost in a trance, watching a scene unfold somewhere other than here. *"To fall in love is a wonderful feeling, to be loved in return the most amazing thing that could happen to me. It is only with enlightened wisdom that comes from age and experience that I am able to look back and know with unflaggling certainty that I did not live my life as my heart intended. Perhaps, as society* dictated, but at what expense? *My dear James passed on believing that he was my one true love, but in truth, my heart has always belonged to another.*"

"So little Samantha Shaw cut out on her hubby? Even back then, huh?" Merritt snorted.

"No, she didn't." Soren continued reading. "*I was never unfaithful in my devoted marriage to James, but there was a part of me that he could never have. My darling Nina has always and will always be my heart's true mate. It is only now on death's door that I am free to admit what I have felt for more than fifty years.*"

Merritt whistled loudly. "Wow, so she was in love with a woman. I bet that was hard. There is no way society would have accepted them. No wonder she married James."

"I know isn't that horrible? I couldn't imagine being in love with someone for over fifty years and never getting to be with them." Soren found her spot again and held her finger there. "There's just a little bit more and this part nearly broke my heart. *My dearest Nina, my heart weeps for you hourly. I felt myself die inside the very moment I said goodbye to you. Our hearts are entwined today and forever. I feel my soul will not rest until the fates smile upon us once more and our love finds a home.* She died two weeks later. The newspapers were the ones with her obituary. It's all so tragically romantic. Do you think they ever found each other?" Soren asked in a serious tone.

Merritt raised her eyebrow. "Oh don't tell me you believe her soul stayed around after she died looking for Nina."

"Why not?" Soren asked pensively. "Strange things have happened to me since I moved in. Things that I can't explain…feelings that I have. I don't know, it's hard to explain. I think she's here in the house. Maybe not like a ghost, but her essence. She can't let go until fate brings love to this house. It's the universe's way of keeping balance."

Merritt laughed and starting whistling the theme to *Ghostbusters*. "Soren you are starting to sound like the locals…Savannah's full of ghosts. I didn't take you for someone that believes in the gobbledy gooks." She waved her fingers in the air and made a low eerie sound. "They got to you pretty quick huh?"

"Maybe. There are lots of unexplained phenomena. Is it out of the realm of plausibility that Samantha is hanging on waiting for Nina? Besides, despite what I've gone through I am a sucker for a tragic love story."

Merritt chuckled. "You almost believe it enough to convince me. Of course, if she is here, she's not going to be happy come next week."

"How's that?"

"Cause we're about to make a whole lotta noise."

Soren laughed. "True. Maybe she's hard of hearing."

"I hope so." Merritt's phone buzzed and she pulled it out of her pocket. She glanced at the screen and frowned. "I guess I better get going…duty calls. And I've probably worn out my welcome."

Soren shook her head. "You could never be unwelcome here."

"Thank you for dinner and for the company. This has been the nicest night I've had in a while. Keep me posted on Samantha." She walked towards the back door and pulled it open. "What about our story?" Merritt asked in a low voice. "Have you read the last chapter of ours? Is it tragic?"

"I think our story is just beginning. I don't want to know how it ends if it ends tragically." Soren said softly, her eyes finding Merritt's face. "You know being just friends with you is going to be nearly impossible."

Merritt rested her palm on Soren's face and smiled, her eyes filled with sadness. "I know…I'm sorry." She pulled the door closed behind her. Soren raised her hand to her cheek, wondering if her story would end up just like Samantha's.

73

Chapter Six

"Where the fuck have you been?"

Merritt laid her keys on the counter and glanced up wearily. Tired eyes met Kate's furious glare. "Work."

"The fuck you have. I called the office…you left two hours ago." Kate's anger was fueled by the bottle in her hand. Tonight's battle between the duplicitous nature of Kate was won by the angry Kate.

"I stopped and had a bite to eat. I knew you wouldn't be up for dinner." Merritt set her bag on the counter and pulled a bottle of water out of the fridge. She realized that she probably shouldn't try to get under Kate's skin, it would only make matters worse. "I had my cell. You could have got me on that."

"What and interrupt your date with the flavor of the month?" Kate said sardonically. "What's her name Merritt? You owe me at least that much."

"I think you're confusing me with yourself." Merritt answered derisively. "Aren't you the one that stepped out on me Kate?" She bent over and picked up Batman, who had scampered into the kitchen attracted by the loud shouting. She squeezed him lightly and scratched him behind the ears, relishing the small bit of calm that she got from him.

Kate stumbled into the kitchen and pointed her finger in Merritt's face. "If you paid half as much attention to me as you do that damn dog, maybe I wouldn't have looked for intimacy someplace else."

Merritt sighed. "Yes Kate, it's all my fault. Everything is my fault. The drinking, the cheating, everything that happened between us is only on my shoulders. Isn't that argument worn out? I'm sorry Kate, sorry that work was too important, sorry I couldn't make you happy. But I didn't make you pick up the bottle. I didn't make you fuck another woman. We've been together five years Kate, why couldn't you talk to me? If you were unhappy and I was the cause, why couldn't you just come to me and tell me?"

"I was miserable and you were too busy to notice." Kate wasn't shouting anymore, but her eyes still flashed. "Everyone else noticed."

"Kate, I'm not a mind reader. Of course those people you work with, *your friends*…" Merritt sneered. "Your friends noticed because you talked to them." Merritt set Batman down, unable to talk without gesturing her hands. She put her hand on her chest. "But you didn't talk to me. The one person that you needed to talk to most of all you shut out."

"You were never around to talk to…did you ever think about that? Do you think I liked going out all the time?"

Merritt shrugged. "I thought you did. How am I supposed to know any differently? The whole going out thing started long before you and I had issues."

"Did it? Or is it just convenient for you to think that so you don't feel so guilty?" Kate mocked.

"Whether or not you were unhappy because of me is beside the point. What matters is that you cheated on me Kate. That's never okay, no matter what the reason. I am still trying to put that behind us, partly because you asked me to and partly because yes, I do feel some responsibility. I'm having a hard time with this Kate."

"It's been over two years Merr. Don't you think you can let it go? I've forgiven you for checking out of our relationship." Kate's voice was syrupy sweet and it grated on Merritt's already raw nerves.

75

Merritt's blood hummed and she could feel a new surge of resentment. "You think time is all it takes? You think after awhile my brain just won't remember? Even if it forgot, my heart still remembers. Haven't you noticed that we no longer sleep in the same bed? I haven't touched you in months. I can't because every time I do, I see her with you. If anyone should have a drinking problem it's me." She could feel her whole body shaking with anger. "Do you know why I've stayed this long?"

Kate shook her head, but didn't say a word.

"Because you're broken and the part of me that does feel somewhat responsible won't let me abandon you to face the world alone. I keep thinking that I can ride in on my white horse and fix you." Merritt's eyes pleaded with Kate to understand. "But I can't fix you, you have to fix yourself, but first you have to want to."

"You didn't say you stayed because you loved me." Kate said quietly.

Merritt looked at the floor. "I don't know anymore Kate. I wonder if I do or if I am just holding on to what we had."

"I'm still in love with you." Kate pleaded.

"Are you Kate? How can we be in love and fight all the time? I don't see how you could scream at someone you love. This thing we have isn't love. It's dysfunctional cohabitation."

"Please don't say that Merr. I'll do anything, just tell me what you want me to do." Kate swiped at a tear.

"That's just it. I don't know that you can do anything. I think we need to step back and take a look at what we've become." Merritt said softly.

Kate's head jerked up and her eyes flared. "You're just saying that so you can screw someone else. Or have you already?"

"No Kate, I haven't." Merritt's voice sounded tired and she realized that the past two years had taken a major toll on her. "I think we need to discuss this when you're sober. I can't keep ignoring that you have a problem. Just because we haven't talked about it and I turn a blind eye to it, doesn't mean it isn't there. It's always going to be there and I just get more and more resentful each day that I don't say something. I've been silent for too long Kate. I think I'm finally ready to do something about it."

"Oh so now that you are ready we all have to cater to you. How high do you want me to jump Merr? What hoops are you going to make me jump through?" Kate asked acerbically. "We're a couple remember. We have to make decisions together, not you dictating what happens and me following blindly."

"You mean like *we* made the decision to become an alcoholic and *we* made the decision to sleep around? Nice try Kate." Merritt's voice remained calm. She was long past fighting, long past screaming. "That's the problem. We ceased being a real couple a long time ago and we haven't been able to make decisions that were in the best interest of us as individuals. Wants and needs change all the time, and maybe if we step outside of the situation we can finally realize that what we had five years ago isn't what we want now. I think we need to put some space between us. That is the only way that you and I will figure out what's best and how to work on our own issues. Certainly you can see that."

"You mean my drinking I assume." Kate stated sarcastically.

"Yes, you're an alcoholic. You need help, help that I can't give you." Merritt held up her hand. "Before you attack me, I have things I need to work on. Right now I have things about myself I don't like. I'm not any good to either of us or to anyone else for that matter. I need to take some time to work on me."

"Great! You're leaving me alone to sort through this. You're not even going to support me?" Kate responded in an accusatory voice. "That's rich. Tell me what you think I need to fix and then you don't even stick around to help. I can't do it alone. Or do you even care?"

"Of course I care. But we both know that even if we started working on our problems, seeing each other everyday is just going to bring us right back around to where we are now. Are you happy Kate? I'm not and I can't remember the last time I was. We both deserve something better."

Kate rolled her eyes. "And you think someone else could make you happy. Isn't that what this is really about? You don't want space, you want out."

"I'm not saying anything more than you and I need to figure things out for ourselves. Maybe it is over. I don't know. I don't know how I feel anymore other than miserable and I know you feel the same way. I don't know that when we get past this I will feel anything for you. I can't make promises because I just don't know. I'm lost Kate, just as much as you are. I don't know who I am anymore. I'd like to get the old Merritt back and I can't do that when we're together."

"I think we both know that once we go our separate ways, there is no going back." Kate's eyes were sad. Some of her earlier buzz had worn off and part of her knew that what Merritt said was true. She was unhappy, but also terribly afraid of being alone. "I'm not ready to say goodbye. Are you?"

Kate's voice was low and the look in her eyes almost broke Merritt's heart. A small part of her felt like she was abandoning Kate and that wasn't fair, but she knew that this was something she needed to do if she wanted to find herself again. "I have to be. It's the only way."

Merritt saw the brief flash of painful acceptance in Kate's eyes. She covered the small expanse between them and gathered Kate into her arms and they cried. They wept for what they had been together, what they had become and most importantly, to the endless possibilities of the future.

#

Gay flipped on the porch light and looked through the peep hole. The corners of her mouth turned up as she undid the deadbolt and pulled the front door open, Merritt standing there with a large duffel bag slung over her shoulder, Batman tucked under her arm and a sheepish grin on her face. "Well lookey here what the cat drug in. If it ain't my good for nothing cousin. What brings you to my humble abode at *one—thirty* in the *AM?*"

"Been a long time since we had a slumber party. Figured tonight was as good a time as any." Merritt stepped inside and shut the door behind her. "Do I need to chill down here while you sneak your latest conquest out the back door?"

Gay burst out laughing. "Hell no, you know I'm celibate."

"Couldn't con anyone to come home with you huh?" Merritt teased. "What's that make it now? Two days celibate."

"One and a half, but who's counting?" Gay said quickly.

"Don't tell me...the chick from Starbucks?" Merritt handed Batman to a blushing Gay and dropped her bag on the floor.

Gay looked shocked. "What? I can't help it I'm irresistible."

Merritt snorted. "That's one word to describe you."

"Hey now!" Gay retorted. "You oughta be a little nicer to the girl who's putting you up. And speaking of that, why are you here again?"

"Kate and I are going to try things apart." Merritt answered quietly and took Batman from Gay. She followed Gay into the living room. "I was kind of hoping you could put us up for awhile."

Gay smothered a grin. *It's about fucking time!* That's what she wanted to scream. She wanted to know why Merritt had stayed as long as she had, but respected that her cousin

79

had reasons she would rather not share. Instead, she put on her concerned face. "You okay?"

Merritt rubbed her chin, quiet in thought for a moment. "Yeah, you know what? I am okay. I feel like a weight has been lifted off my shoulders." She flopped down on Gay's couch with a sigh. "Don't worry, I'm only gonna crash here a few days. Batman and I will be out of your hair as soon as I can line up an apartment." She scratched behind his ears and was rewarded with a warm tongue on her hand.

"Shit!" Gay said slapping her leg for emphasis. "You know you're welcome to stay as long as you need too." She gestured towards the kitchen. "You wanna beer or something? We can talk if you want."

"Nah." She stretched her arms over her head and yawned. "I'm way past tired. If it's okay I think me and the superhero are just going to crash. I'll be ready to talk about it in a couple of days. Gotta let the purple haze wear off, you know?"

"That's cool. I have to get back to my beauty sleep anyway." She watched Merritt drag herself off the couch and pick up her duffel bag with a loud groan. "Think maybe we could talk about Soren?"

Merritt glanced at Gay. "What's to talk about…you interested?" Merritt asked suspiciously.

Gay waved her hand in the air. "Naw! But I think you are."

"I'm in no kind of condition to start anything with Soren. Attracted or not, I gotta lay low for awhile…do some renovations to myself." Merritt said quietly. "Besides she deserves someone better than me, and I'm not sure I can be that person right now."

Gay put her hand on Merritt's arm and laughed softly. "I hear your head talking Cuz, but I see the way y'all look at each other. I wonder how long you can fool yourself before y'all realize coming into each others' lives may just be the best thing that's ever happened to you."

80

Chapter Seven

Soren awoke with a start, not sure what had aroused her. Perhaps the sound of papers fluttering, but that could have been a dream. She stared at the chandelier overhead and for the briefest of seconds thought she saw some type of apparition. She bolted up and stared in that same spot, this time seeing nothing but the rainbows the crystals were casting about the room. She rubbed her eyes with her fists and shook her head. *A whole bottle of Reisling...great idea Soren.*

She spent several more moments gathering herself then tossed the covers aside. She spun around and put her feet on the floor, hands braced to push herself out of bed when something caught her eye. The journal lay open on her nightstand, the same journal that she was certain she'd closed the night before. Panic struck her briefly as she contemplated the thought that perhaps she really was losing her mind. She didn't think so, at least not yet. She was only thirty—six. "No. I know I closed it last night." Wine or not, she was lucid enough to remember closing it before she turned out the light beside her. *Just wait till I tell Merritt, she'll think I've fallen even further off my rocker.* "Oh well."

She picked up the journal and immediately realized the entry that had been marked was three years after the last one she'd read last night. "Interesting." Rather than flip back, Soren decided to read from that point. Obviously, Samantha wanted her to see this. "You get your wish Samantha."

September 15th, 1895.

*I've met the most amazing woman today. Miss Nina P.
or Miss P. as her students refer to her. She is a first--grade
teacher. She is fresh from a French finishing school in
Baltimore and so beautiful and refined and definitely
modern. So very stern—looking in her school mistress attire,
but with so charming a twinkle in her eyes that I can't believe
she could not be a tiny bit mischievous. She dined with us
tonight on the auspices of convincing Father to write a series
of articles in the Times. She is a student of philosophy and so
utterly radical that I couldn't help but laugh as she explained
to Father her desire to establish schools for the poor, all the
while waggling her index finger in this face. I am most
certain he was not at all prepared for the enchanting Miss P.
I wonder that I have never met anyone who I find so
completely amiable. She has so completely fascinated me and
I believe we are soul mates of a sort. I must confess I am
quite smitten with the enigmatic Miss P.*

"Well, well. well. It does sound as though our little
Samantha has gotten her first crush." Soren said teasingly
and was not surprised when she heard a small giggle, or at
least she thought she had. She set the journal back on the
nightstand, stood up, and stretched like an alley cat waking
up from an afternoon nap. The words that Samantha had
written seemed familiar like she had read them before, or
maybe it was that she'd experienced them herself. *Isn't that
what I feel like with Merritt? I'm smitten.* She thought with a
genuine smile. She wondered who Nina P. was and if she'd
been so completely enamored with Samantha after their first
meeting. That part she may never know, but with a little
research she planned to pin down the identity of Samantha's
one true love. Figuring out what she would do about her
possible ghostly visitor was another thing.

82

She decided to forgo a shower this morning since she'd taken a hot bath the night before. Besides, Merritt and her crew should be there any minute. Her stomach fluttered at the very thought of Merritt and she wondered perhaps if she hadn't skipped intense like and gone straight to smitten. *Do not pass go, do not collect two hundred dollars.*

She tried to force her mind off of Merritt and succeeded only in thinking about her even more. *Argh! Get a hold of yourself.* She threw on a pair of cargo shorts and a short sleeve Tennessee Vols shirt. Not her alma mater, but she loved the ladies basketball team. She pulled her hair back in a short ponytail and slipped on an old pair of Keens. She surveyed the results in a full length mirror and decided she was wearing a very sensible outfit for some serious historical fact finding.

Soren had just brewed a fresh pot of coffee when she heard a knock at the front door. She set her mug on the counter and went to answer it. She thought she had prepared herself for seeing Merritt again, but nothing in her life could have readied her for the intense sexual desire she felt in that one brief moment. She felt her knees tremble and could only hope that Merritt could not read the naked hunger she felt. If she did notice, any reaction stayed hidden behind the dark sunglasses she was wearing.

"Hey." Soren said in a voice that sounded to her own ears incredibly shaky. She struggled to keep her eyes off of Merritt's breasts which were straining against the white tank she wore underneath a loose button—down shirt. Struggled not to look at the faded pair of Levi's that hugged her toned body. Struggled to focus anywhere but her full lips that she wanted to kiss. It was a struggle that was becoming more difficult everyday.

"Hey yourself." Merritt said with a smile. She pushed her sunglasses up and her green eyes held Soren's captive. "How are you?"

Soren swallowed all the things she really wanted to say. *Going crazy! I want to kiss you. I'm trying not to fall for you. Can't you see how you make me feel?* "I'm good...how are you?"

Merritt glanced away shyly. "Better now." She loved the serene feeling that came over her anytime she was in Soren's presence. As much as she liked the surge of desire she felt at just thinking about Soren, she craved the peace too and didn't question the ambiguous range of emotion. She just ran with it. "I'm always better with you." She answered sincerely.

Soren's heart jumped at the naked confession. It was made so nonchalantly that one could have mistaken it for a token of friendship, but Soren felt connected to Merritt and knew that her eyes didn't lie. She felt the same way. Healed, and on the path to being whole again. Somehow, she made everything seem right again. "You wanna come in?"

Merritt shook her head no, although her face said otherwise. "My guys are going to be here soon. I just wanted to let you know we were getting ready to start. If you have any running to do, you may want to get your car out of the garage now. We're going to park the trucks back there."

"Nope, today I think I am going to make use of some free transportation."

"The express shuttle?" Merritt asked.

"Uh—uh. The Trek shuttle." Soren said with a grin.

Merritt scrunched her eyebrows together. "Trek shuttle? Did Samantha tell you about some top secret transportation I don't know about?"

"Yes, but I misplaced my broom." Soren laughed when Merritt rolled her eyes. She put her hands out as though she was riding a bicycle. "Taking the bike out today. Trek 7100 Hybrid...strong enough for the trail, but PH balanced for the road."

"Funny. In case you need to do some off—roading here in Savannah." She teased. "So where might your travels be taking you today?"

84

"That my dear depends entirely upon you." Soren smiled cryptically.

"How so?" Merritt raised her eyebrow, not sure how she was involved in the decision. She cocked her head sideways and listened for a moment. "By the way, the guys are a block away. Sure you don't want the car?"

"Nope, I'm good. I've got two good legs…"

I'll say you do. Merritt thought to herself and smothered a grin.

"…a comfortable bike, great weather and plenty of time. And did I mention a really cool basket that fits on the handlebars in case I need to carry anything?"

"Right." Merritt said sarcastically. "And do you have a banana seat too?"

Soren punched her lightly in the arm. "Funny. It just so happens it's a black metal basket. Not girlie at all." She caught the wry expression on Merritt's face. "Okay, so maybe it is a little girlie, but it's very useful."

"No doubt." Merritt teased. "So how do I figure into this excursion equation?"

"First, promise you won't call me crazy."

"I promise…" Merritt said and held three fingers to her forehead in a scout salute. "…crazy."

"Ooh, you are cruisin' for a bruisin' Tanner." Soren growled playfully.

"Or you could spank me." Merritt responded playfully. "I have been a bad girl."

Soren's mind immediately went to Merritt naked in front of her, down on all fours, begging to be punished. She could feel her hand spanking then caressing her firm bottom. Each strike making her more and more excited, wet with anticipation, begging her to take her. Soren felt heat pool between her legs and she blushed wildly. She swallowed trying hard to slow her erratic heartbeat. "Maybe I'll just leave that to your girlfriend." Her voice suddenly somber.

Darkness flashed across Merritt's face briefly and then it was gone just as quickly. "I guess so." Somehow right now didn't seem the time to correct Soren and tell her that she didn't have a girlfriend anymore. "So where are you looking to go on your trek today? Pun intended." She teased.

Soren once again tried to ignore the pain she saw in Merritt's eyes. She could pry information out of Gay, but it really wasn't her place. If Merritt wanted her to know her life story, she would tell her on her own terms. "I want to go to a library."

Merritt looked bewildered. "A library…how come?"

"Uhm, to read." Soren said sarcastically. "Actually, I'm going on a treasure hunt so to speak." She registered Merritt's continued look of confusion. "And here's the crazy part."

Merritt craned her neck and watched the first of two large trucks pull around the corner, loaded with scaffolding. "Looks like there's no going back now. The wrecking ball is here." Merritt teased. "Guess we better wrap this conversation up so we can get to demolition."

Soren tensed then visibly relaxed when she saw Merritt's eyes dancing mischievously. "That's cool. I'm eager to get started anyway." She paused, and licked her lips, the movement causing a rush of desire to hit Merritt in the stomach. "I want to do some research on Samantha Shaw and her mystery lover. I know you aren't sold on the ghost thing…yet, but I'm starting to believe in the hereafter. When I woke up this morning I heard papers rustling and I felt like someone was in my bedroom with me. And even crazier, Samantha's journal was open. I know I closed it, and even if I didn't, the entry was one from three years past where I had stopped reading the night before."

"It could have been the wind. Maybe it blew it open." Merritt suggested sagely.

Soren shook her head. "Uh—uh, all the windows were closed. I think Sam opened it to that one on purpose. She's trying to tell me something...I just know it."

"Darlin', I think it's just your mind playing tricks on you. Don't let the folklore of the town corrupt you." Merritt teased. "I'm sure there is a rational explanation for what has been happening."

"Boy you are a negative nelly, aren't you?" Soren joked. "Who pissed in your Wheaties?" She winked at Merritt and was rewarded with a sarcastic smirk.

"I normally skip breakfast." She replied drolly. "I'm sorry, I'll try to keep an open mind...for you."

"Thank you." Soren said smiling sweetly. "Anyway, the entry was one from September 1895, on the day she met Nina. She writes that Nina, or Miss P. as her first grade students called her, had come to dinner at her house." She paused for effect and Merritt jumped on it.

"And?"

"Sam was taken with Nina quite from the start. I'd say it was her first crush."

"How do you know? What did she say about her?" Merritt asked quickly.

"Oh, I thought you weren't interested." Soren teased.

Merritt shrugged nonchalantly and winked. "I'm feigning interest for you."

"Liar!" Soren retorted with a smile. "You want to know just as bad as I do. Admit it. You're hooked."

"Just call it morbid curiosity." Merritt said. "Hang on." She turned towards several men walking around the corner. "Hey guys, give me a sec would ya? Then we can get started."

"Sure thing *boss*." One man responded then they ducked back around the corner, muted laughter wafting onto the porch.

"Oh great." Merritt said and expelled a breath. "I'm gonna hear about this later. They just love to see their boss wasting time talking to hot chicks."

Soren waggled her eyebrows suggestively. "Oh you make it a habit of spending time with lots of hot women?"

Merritt blushed. "Yeah, that's me…got one on both arms at all times."

"I don't doubt that for one minute." Soren joked. "Guess I better get in line."

"Rest assured…" Merritt said quietly, her eyes dark with desire. "…you are at the front of a very short line." She held Soren's eyes captive, amazed at the electricity that passed between them. She knew if she only let herself go Soren would reach inside her and capture her soul. Her breathing came in short, ragged gasps and she felt herself being drawn closer to Soren. The gap between them narrowed dangerously, several more inches and Merritt knew she wouldn't be able to stop herself from kissing Soren. With strength she didn't know she possessed, she pulled herself away and put several feet between them. "Library. You wanted to go to the library." She said lamely.

Soren finally let out the breath she'd been holding. She acknowledged the raw emotion that had passed between them during the moments before. She admitted sadly that too many of the moments had passed between them and knew she needed to get a grip. "Yes." *God yes!* She answered with a raspy voice, a silent yes to the many unspoken questions that she'd seen in Merritt's eyes. "Got any suggestions?"

"There are several public libraries in the city, but if you want to do some sightseeing on your way, there's a branch on Bay St, up near the river. Ask for Nancy and tell her Merritt sent you. If there is any information out there on Sam *and* Nina, she'll know. Then if you're up for it, Historic River Road is just a block further. Lots of little shops and places to stop for lunch. You can actually park the bike and walk."

Merritt's tone had lost the intimacy from before and Soren had to smother a giggle at how much she reminded her of a tour guide. "Perfect!" She clapped her hands together excitedly. "And how Madame Atlas, might one get from here to there? And don't say on a bike."

"Nonsense...besides a car is way faster." Merritt said with a wink. She sidestepped Soren's arm and barely missed another punch. "I'm just kidding. It's a pretty straight shot up Habersham. Once you get to Bay St, turn left, it's a couple of blocks down the street."

"Thank you." Soren said sweetly. "Now I guess I should let you go. Duty calls."

Merritt groaned. "Yeah, it does...lady that owns the company is a damn slave driver." Her eyes twinkled as she sauntered down the steps, two at a time, jumping off before she hit the broken one. "You know Ms. Lockhart, I think you might find the illusive Miss P. after all."

Soren smiled. "I fully intend to Ms. Tanner. And I am going to tie you to a chair and give you all the details." She winked mischievously.

"Tied to a chair?" Merritt asked lasciviously. "At your mercy? Be still my heart." She smiled one last time and disappeared quickly around the corner, leaving Soren to her own sordid thoughts about chairs and handcuffs.

"Argh!" She muttered to the sky.

Chapter Eight

Soren peddled slowly, taking in block after block of some of the most beautiful examples of architecture she'd ever seen. Greek Revivalist mansions with grand columned porticos, Italianite buildings with large arches and cupolas, stately Queen Anne's with long porches, decked out with ornate shingles and asymmetrical roof lines, large Victorians, huge English style castles, and any number of other magnificent buildings fashioned after some famous time, place or what's his name. Placards on most houses stating it was the so—and—so house, built in eighteen hundred and something. *One day Soren.* She thought she might declare hers the Shaw House...built in 1890. It did have an upper crust ring to it.

A loud horn broke through her ruminations and she swerved closer to the curb to let it pass. Rather than go around her, it slowed and began honking obnoxiously. She motioned with her arm for it to go around then finally annoyed, pulled onto the curb and stopped quickly, waiting for the car to go around and leave her alone.

Soren was unpleasantly surprised when rather than continuing on, it slowed and finally stopped beside her. Thinking it was someone who might be lost, she got ready to tell them she would be no help either...unless they were looking for a library. She broke into a grin when a round, tanned face peered at her out of the truck. "Gay!"

"No, but I sure do love women!" Gay teased back.

Soren laughed and shook her finger at her. "What are you trying to do, scare me? Sneaking up on a girl like that."

"You call that sneaking?" She nodded towards the cemetery. "I reckon I woke up half the dead in Colonial Park. The streets will be crawling with mummies before you know it. Probably try to steal your bike."

Soren propped her arm on the door and balanced her bike expertly. "Point taken, but you were damn close to getting the finger for a sec. If you hadn't popped your cute face up I was fixin' to get rough." Soren said sternly, unable to keep a smile from pulling up the corners of her mouth.

"Darlin', I reckon you can get rough with me anytime you want. You'll get no refusal from me."

"But will you scream?" Soren asked feigning seriousness.

"Like a stuck pig." Gay said loudly. "You shore are somethin' special honey. I hope she grabs a hold of you and doesn't let go."

Soren frowned. "I don't think she's in any kind of position to grab anything."

"I wouldn't be so sure of that honey." Noticing Soren's quizzical expression, Gay continued. "Let's just say I've had a couple of house guests since Thursday night, with no sign of leaving on the horizon."

Soren tried to hide the surprise on her face. Thursday was the day that Merritt had stopped by and had dinner with her. Part of her hoped she wasn't the reason for the change in status quo, but part of her felt unexplained joy at the development. *Oh stop it Soren. It isn't like she's running to be with you. She didn't even tell you she'd broken up with her girlfriend.* "I don't see how that affects me in anyway."

"Y'all are so mixed up…don't know daylight from dark. I've seen the two of you together. The way y'all look at each other is hot enough to get my knickers in a wad. I just hope y'all realize it before it's too late."

Soren shook her head. "Oh Gay, there's nothing to figure out. You just witnessed two adults with healthy sexual appetites is all. That could happen to anyone. Besides right now I am sorting myself out. A distraction, no matter how hot she is, would just throw a wrench in the gears."

"Well darlin', from the looks of you, I'd say a good shakin' up might do you a world of good." Gay shrugged her shoulders and laughed. "But what do I know? This aging lesbian's opinion is about as useful as gooseshit on a pumphandle."

"Woman, you are not right." Soren reached in the truck and slapped her forearm playfully.

"Ooh foreplay. Now you're talking my language." Gay teased. "If Merritt doesn't wise up, I am fixin' to throw my hat in the ring for you."

Soren knew she was only teasing, the older woman had no interest in her beyond friendship and that is what made her so comfortable around Gay. "So what are you doing today besides driving around picking up women on bikes?"

Gay laughed. "Guilty as charged. Although I didn't expect to run into a stunning beauty like yourself."

"Why thank you, ma'am." Soren couldn't keep the blush from creeping into her cheeks. Any woman would have a hard time not reacting to Gay's engaging flirtation. "I'm sure you say that to all the girls though."

"Nah, just those that I have a vested interest in. I'm wooing in the name of another." Gay winked. "How'm I doing?"

Soren smiled brilliantly and Gay could see what had drawn her cousin to this woman. "I'll give you a ten for effort."

"A ten?" Gay wrinkled her nose. "I can see I'm going to have to turn up the charm. Speaking of, I was actually on my way to your house to work on some of its charm when I saw you and figured I'd pester you first. No need to thank me. Merritt said they were starting today, so I figured we'd sorta work in tandem. I'm fixin' to make a mess and let her haul it away." She said with a mischievous grin. "So what are you up to on this fabulous summer morning?"

Soren hesitated, not wanting to reveal too much information. If Gay noticed, she showed no reaction. "I'm headed to the library to get some mindless reading. There's a perfectly inviting swing on the back porch that I haven't made good use of yet." She pointed at her basket. "And maybe a little shopping. Merritt suggested a library on Bay Street and sightseeing on Old River Road."

Gay cocked an eyebrow. Merritt had suggested the library where Nancy worked. *How interesting...and so out of character for her. She must really like you.* "Yeah, I saw the basket...wow, it's...ahhh...nice." Gay managed to keep a straight face...mostly. "Do you have a little bell on the handlebars too?"

"What is it with you guys? It's not like I'm riding around on a hot pink cruiser." Soren said defensively. "You're just jealous that you don't have as cool a bike."

"Yeah honey, that's it." Gay said with a smile. "I reckon I've annoyed you enough. I shan't tarry any longer."

"'Kay." Soren pushed off the truck. "Maybe I'll see you later."

Gay winked. "If I'm lucky and you're careless." She put the truck in gear. "Hey sugar. Ride a little slow so I can get a good look at that beautiful backside."

Soren rolled her eyes and waved. As she rode off, she stood up and waggled her behind, inciting a new round of honking before Gay waved and turned a corner in the opposite direction.

Fifteen minutes later Soren was at the checkout counter of the Ola Wyeth Public Library inquiring after Nancy. Several minutes later Soren turned to see an attractive sexagenarian striding confidently towards her. She had short salt and pepper hair that was cut in a stylish bob that framed her kind face. As she approached, Soren could see her eyes were the same beautiful green shade that Merritt's were and she suspected that Merritt had sent her to see her mother. She smiled brightly and introduced herself. "Hello dear, I'm Nancy. How can I help you?" She was every bit the epitome of a well—bred Southern Lady.

Soren smiled and took the proffered hand which grasped hers in a surprisingly warm, yet firm handshake. She was immediately drawn to the motherly woman and could see where Merritt had gotten her stunning beauty. "I'm Soren Lockhart. Merritt said to tell you that she referred me. She said that you might be able to help me with some research."

"Ahh my darling Merritt. And how is my daughter?" Nancy asked with a smile.

Soren pictured Merritt, not sure how to respond. All of the things she wanted to say seemed highly inappropriate to share with one's mother. "Well she's…fine I guess. I really don't know her well enough to say. She's just, well she's doing some work on my house." Soren sputtered.

Nancy did not miss the blush that crept onto Soren's face, nor did she fail to notice that this was the first woman her daughter had ever sent to see her. *Oh no my dear, she may be just working on your house, but it seems the fates have been working on you too as well.* "It is a pleasure to meet you Soren Lockhart. Any friend of my daughter's is most certainly a friend of mine. Please tell my daughter that I've had to resort to asking someone else how she is. She needs to visit her mother more often." Her twinkling eyes belied any harshness to her words.

"Yes ma'am." Soren said softly.

"Please call me Nancy." She put her hand on Soren's forearm. "What topic are you interesting in researching?"

"I'm trying to find out some information on the family that built the house I am living in. The Shaw's."

"Robert and Dalia Shaw?" Nancy asked quickly. "That should be easy enough. He ran the Times so we should have information on them." Sensing that Soren was holding something back, she gently encouraged her. "Anyone else dear?"

"Well actually yes. I don't have much information to go on for the other person. All I know is her first name and last initial and that she was a first grade teacher. It's Nina P. She would have been good friends with the Shaw's daughter, Samantha. They met in 1895. I don't know if that is enough to go on though."

Nancy cocked her head and regarded Soren quizzically. "If I may ask, how did you come by that information?" Nancy's curiosity was peaked even with the limited details that Soren was able to provide.

Soren decided she would share everything with Nancy, just as she had Merritt, minus the ghost part. "I found a box of old newspapers and a diary in my attic." She could see Nancy's eyes light up and she knew she was as hooked as she had become. Merritt had done well in suggesting her mother to man the search. "The diary belonged to Samantha Shaw. It begins when her father built the home in 1890 and ends several weeks before her death in 1941."

Nancy clapped her hands together excitedly. "My dear, do you realize what a find you have? I would love to see the diary sometime…that is if you don't mind sharing."

"Of course not. I could bring it by sometime if you would like." Soren suggested.

"That would be wonderful!" She started walking towards the back of the library. "Now why don't we try to find out the name of your mystery woman. Fortunately, in the late 1890's, there weren't many schools set up yet. It is possible that we could find records for the ones that were in existence. It's a long shot, but definitely worth a try. The other possibility is copies of the Times from around that period. Perhaps it will have an article about her." She paused and looked at Soren. "Is there any other detail you can remember that may help?"

Soren thought for a moment then her face lit up. "Samantha did mention that Nina had just returned from a French finishing school in Baltimore. And she wanted Robert Shaw to do an article in the Times to promote her idea of opening schools to teach the poor." She looked at Nancy expectantly, hoping this new tidbit of information would prove useful.

Nancy beamed. "Oh that helps tremendously...if he did write the article. From what I read about him, he was very set in his ways and wrote several articles bemoaning the fools who promoted equality in women. It's possible that he refused. Did Samantha mention anything further about that?"

Soren looked chagrinned. "I'm sorry, I didn't read any further. I was so excited to find out who Nina was that I came here right away. Perhaps she mentioned it." Her chin dropped. "I could come back...after I've finished reading it."

Nancy had her hand on her chin, deep in thought. "No dear, let's just do some searching and see what we find. We could very well find it on our own." She took a key ring from her pocket, selected one, and opened a door marked private. "We keep all the old newspapers in here. We transferred most of them to microfiche about ten years ago. Unfortunately, anything dated prior to 1900 we were unable to transfer, so we kept the original copies on hand. That will make it a bit more tedious to look through the editions of the Times around the period of 1895 and after. They are all catalogued by year so that will make it a little easier." She led Soren to a long row towards the back of the room and stopped in front of several bankers boxes. "Now the Times was not published daily in 1895. There were only weekly editions."

"That should help, right?" Soren asked hopefully.

"Yes and no." Nancy replied. "It means less to look through, but also less chances for Robert to run a story on Nina." She slipped her glasses on and began running her finger along the dates listed on the sides of the boxes. "Aha.

1895. We'll start here. There's a good chance that Nina was from a prominent family if she went to a finishing school in Baltimore. That wasn't a luxury that most people could afford." She started to pull the heavy box off the shelf when Soren stopped her.

"Please let me." Soren implored. "At least let me do some of the work."

Nancy laughed and stepped back. "Oh but you will, my dear. As eager as I am to find out who Nina is, I have to get back outside. I'm leaving you to do the dirty work. Reading through hundred year old papers isn't going to be a walk in the park."

"Oh my!" Soren said with a grunt as she lifted the heavy box off the shelf. She waited for Nancy to indicate where she should set it and was relieved when she pointed to a table not more than ten feet away. "They must have published a book a week. These are quite heavy for a year's worth of newspapers."

Nancy chuckled. "Good guess. They did actually make them rather lengthy. They also used a thicker paper at that time so it added to the weight of it." She glanced at her watch. "Well I'm going to leave you to it. If you need anything, just come get me. Otherwise, enjoy your search."

"Thank you." Soren opened the lid carefully. "Nancy?"

Nancy paused at the door. "Yes dear?"

"I really appreciate all your help."

"No trouble at all." Nancy said sweetly. "I think you'll find I enjoy a good mystery just as much as the next girl." Soren watched her walk out the door then pop her head back in the room. "Good luck."

Nancy shut the door behind her and leaned against it. She pulled her glasses off and smiled again. She liked Soren Lockhart, really liked her and being a good judge of character, she could tell that Soren was a truly good person. *And if I know my daughter at all, she is quite taken with her as well.* Nancy had long ago stopped giving Merritt advice, but secretly she hoped that this new development signaled a changing of the guards. Perhaps Merritt was finally going to end her relationship with Kate. Even if she didn't end up with Soren, which Nancy supposed might happen given the way Soren had blushed when she talked about Merritt, she wanted her away from Kate. She wanted to see her daughter happy again. She turned back to the door and whispered softly. *"Perhaps you are just the woman to make that happen."*

Chapter Nine

Soren smiled into the Blackberry, excited to hear Brett's voice on the other end. It had been a hectic week. From coming home Monday and finding her entire home surrounded by scaffolding to the noise and constant foot traffic of Merritt's crew as they worked on her home, she was mentally exhausted and hadn't had a chance to talk to anyone back home in over a week. She hadn't really had a chance to see Merritt either, much less talk to her other than thanking her for suggesting her mom. She didn't think she'd been purposely avoiding her and with the excuse of being incredibly busy, Soren hadn't had to contemplate how she would have felt if that were the case. By Saturday morning she was ready to relax.

"How's it going sweetie?" Brett asked in his ever present chipper tone.

"I'm good Brett. How is everything back home?" Soren asked with a slight tinge of sadness. Most days she was fine with the distance and not being surrounded by her family and friends, but there were fleeting moments like this one, when she experienced a feeling of homesickness.

"Everyone's good. Lauren and the girls are enjoying their summer. They still miss you at the pool. At least they have their new cousin to look forward to. Keeps them occupied. When they aren't swimming, they're buying the heck out of Baby Gap. The doctor put Ali on house arrest and

I think Jordan is ready to pull her hair out." Brett said with a laugh.

"So they finally put Ali on bed rest huh?" Soren asked, sorry she was missing the last few weeks of Ali's pregnancy, if only to offer moral support to Jordan. "Have they pushed up her due date at all?"

"Not yet. I think their doc really wants the baby to bake the whole nine months." Brett paused for a second then changed the subject quickly. *"So are you really doing okay down there? I understand if you're not. Are you getting out and meeting some new friends?"*

Soren thought immediately of Merritt. Whether meaning to or not, she'd blown past Soren's barriers and left a lasting impression on her very being. She thought about the way Merritt's green eyes captured hers and told her everything she wouldn't let herself say. The intensity of those unspoken words caused Soren's blood to surge. "I've made one...or two friends." She said breathily.

Brett could hear Soren's ragged tone over the hundreds of miles and his curiosity was peaked instantly. He figured he better play it cool if he wanted any information from her. *"Oh yeah, tell me about them."*

What could Soren say that could possibly capture Merritt? She didn't think there were words to describe the woman that she was trying desperately not to fall in love with. Anything she said would seem pale in comparison to the real deal. "Well the contractor who is handling the renovation to the house is really nice. Her name is Merritt. I met her mom Monday when I went to the library to get some reading material. And her cousin is my landscaper. She's an entire conversation in itself. But I think you would like her."

"Oh you met the mother already?" Brett teased. *"She must be special."*

You have no idea how special. Soren thought longingly, the empty feeling in her stomach a nagging reminder of how much she had missed her this week. Suddenly she felt the need to tell Brett how she felt so he could remind her of what an idiot she was being for falling in love with someone she'd just met and who for all intents and purposes was not available. "I'm screwed Brett."

"How so?"

"Merritt is special. She's smart, funny, and absolutely gorgeous. She makes me feel alive for the first time in years. When she looks at me I melt. I have had to physically restrain myself to keep from jumping her. And I have to tell myself every time I'm with her, don't fall for her. She makes me forget that I did not come here wanting this. I came here for me. To heal." Soren took a deep breath. "God, Brett, tell me I'm crazy. Tell me that I've fallen off my rocker."

"Lord, Soren, don't hold back." Brett laughed softly. *"Honey, I can't tell you you're crazy though. That's how I felt the first time I saw Lauren."*

"Yeah but you got the girl, and I'm afraid all I'm going to get is hurt." Soren replied quietly. "I don't think I can handle my world getting ripped out from under me again."

"I'm sure she's nothing like Victoria." Brett said with a disgusted tone. *"If she's making you feel as crazy as you do, I'm betting that the feeling is mutual, whether she is ready to act on it or not. And obviously, your heart isn't concerned with what your head's plans are. Have you talked about it?"*

"Kind of." Soren sighed. "We agreed it would be in our best interests to just be friends. We might as well have agreed to stop the sun from shining."

"I wouldn't give up hope Soren. I'd say you concentrate on you and take the offer of friendship...for now. You're both adults. I'm sure you can figure out how to deal with the urge to jump her bones."

"And if I don't?" Soren asked cautiously.

"If you don't...I hope you both jump at the same time." Brett teased. *"All right, I guess I'll let you go. I know you didn't want to spend your Saturday morning talking to me. Keep me posted on your BFF."*

"'Kay." Soren paused. "Brett? Thank you."

"Anytime."

Soren had just set her phone back on the table beside her when she caught a blur of moment out of the corner of her eye. She turned in time to see a small black and white fur ball scampering towards her. He stopped at her feet and sniffed, familiarizing himself with this new person. He must have decided he liked her because he allowed her to pick him up. He showed his approval by licking her face. His owner rounded the corner seconds later and broke into a grin. "I think he likes you."

Soren looked away from the ball of fur in her hands and smiled at Merritt, her heart racing at their nearness. The previous days before when she'd barely seen her melted into the past. "I think so."

"Obviously, he gets his good taste from me." Merritt teased and sat down beside Soren on the swing, her stomach fluttering. It never ceased to amaze her that her body could react so violently just from seeing her. She again wondered if being close to Soren was what heaven felt like. If only she were ready to let herself go and take what her soul longed for. Desperately she tried to quell the rising hunger in her body. "This is Batman."

Soren held him up in the air and gave him a thorough once over. "Hi Batman. It's a pleasure to make your acquaintance." Batman yipped in response. "I'm glad you've come to visit me."

Merritt took her sunglasses off and looked at Soren. "Just Batman?" She held her breath willing Soren to look at her and say yes, not sure how she would handle it if she did.

Several seconds passes before Soren returned her gaze. "You know the answer to that." The air hummed around them, the only sound Soren could hear was the unsteady beat of her heart, which seemed to match her shallow, uneven breaths.

"I need to hear you say it." Merritt pleaded breathlessly. "Please."

Soren's heart melted and she fell hopelessly into green eyes. "I'm...glad...you're here. I...missed...you."

Each word came out on a ragged breath, punctuating the aching in Merritt's heart. She couldn't understand why she tortured herself this way, but she felt like she would suffocate without hearing it, the weight of expectancy piercing her heart. "I missed you too."

Soren swallowed, trying to relieve the constricting grip of desire she felt in her throat. "I thought you were avoiding me."

Merritt winced, wanting to look away. The hurt in Soren's eyes cutting deeply. "I was...I needed to."

Soren tore her gaze away, unable to look at Merritt and see the raw pain mingled with naked hunger she saw there. "Why?"

Merritt stood up and paced back and forth. She pinched the bridge of her nose. She finally met Soren's eyes. "Because every time I look at you, I come completely undone."

Merritt's admission seared through Soren's body like white hot heat. Every nerve in her body was alive. She was glad Batman was on her lap or she would have kissed Merritt, unable to think of a better response. "I know the feeling." She said quietly.

Merritt closed the gap between them, standing at arm's length. "What are you doing to me?" She whispered weakly. "I am losing every shred of control."

"Is that such a bad thing?" Soren took a step forward. The last remaining barrier between them tucked in her arms. Batman looked back and forth between the two women, waiting for attention.

At that particular second, time stood still and in the quiet bubble that surrounded them, Merritt could think of no reason why it was a bad idea. How easy it would be for her to capture Soren's trembling lips against hers. She felt her body move of its own accord, closing the distance between them, feeling Soren's soft skin brush against hers. She saw fierce passion in Soren's eyes and knew it matched her own hunger. Merritt felt weightless, heady with emotion. She could feel Soren's warm breath on her face and her scent was intoxicating.

Soren's body was racing, electricity coursing through her veins. She hadn't felt an unquenchable thirst for anyone in her life and this surge of emotion ripped through her like an out of control typhoon, wreaking havoc on her senses. Every inch of her skin was sensitive and alive. Merritt's skin felt like flames dancing against hers. She felt her knees tremble and a moan escaped her lips. She held Merritt's gaze a millisecond longer, then closed her eyes in surrender.

"Yip!"

Soren opened her eyes in time to see a tiny black and white face peering at hers. She was too stunned to react when he licked her face. She laughed nervously, the romantic tension displaced briefly. "Well I have to admit when I had dreams about being licked, I really wasn't thinking it would be Batman."

Merritt looked dazed, hers eyes completely unfocused. She felt as though she had been violently ripped back to reality and the glaring reality of what she'd almost done hit her squarely in the face. *God get it together. You're acting like a teenager in heat.* She pulled Batman out of Soren's arms, ignoring the small yelp he let out at being separated from his new best friend. "Lord Batman, it's your first date. Try to save the kissing for later."

"Aww poor Batman, his mommy's being so mean." She scratched his head. "You just wanted us to pay attention to you."

"We were actually hoping that we could get you to come out with us on an adventure. That would give you plenty of one—on—one Batman time." Merritt said hopefully. She saw the diary on the table and a small frown played at the corners of her mouth. "That is if we aren't interrupting anything."

"Not at all." Soren said shaking her head, willing her heart to stop pounding. "And even if you were, it would be a welcome interruption."

"Find out anything new? Mom said you didn't have much luck at the library."

"Not a name yet, but definitely more about the relationship between the two women and Sam's feelings for Nina." She picked the diary up. "What were your plans for us today? I could fill you in on the way." What she really wanted to do was spend the day exploring Merritt's inviting lips and find out where that kiss would have taken them. But she would settle for spending some quality time with her. "That is if today's activities allow for reading."

"They almost require it." Merritt said cryptically.

"Do I need to bring anything?" Soren asked, intrigued at the day that Merritt had planned.

Merritt shook her head and smiled. "Nope. Just you, sunglasses, comfortable shoes and an appetite."

"Let's see." Soren said as she patted her head searching for her glasses, checked her shoes and assumed her Teva's would do just fine. "Check, check, double check and some reading material. I'm good to go."

They walked down the stairs and around to the truck, their almost kiss put on the back burner, but definitely not forgotten. No matter what happened between them, both knew if they couldn't be friends and get along for a whole day together, anything romantic between them didn't stand a chance.

When they got to Merritt's truck, Soren glanced in the bed and saw a large picnic basket. "Ooh, a picnic?"

Merritt smiled and opened the passenger door, taking Soren's hand, helping her into the truck. She welcomed the familiar tingle she felt just touching Soren and held on a little longer than necessary. "We thought today was a perfect day to enjoy a picnic."

Chapter Ten

Soren watched her stride around the truck confidently. She definitely exuded sex appeal, and so far it had all found the mark in Soren. She didn't think she could be immune if she tried. Soren watched as she strapped her seatbelt on and started the engine. Every movement was automatic and fluid, Merritt's strong hands held her attention, her mind picturing them splayed intimately against her body and a new surge of longing hit her. She decided to *attempt* to focus on the adventure ahead of them.

She was curious as to their destination, but it occurred to her that the mystery added to the allure. She raised her hand on the door frame and felt the wind rush around and over it. Since the day she'd met Merritt, she felt more alive than she had in years, more aware of her surroundings. She smelled the warm, humid air, felt the sun kiss her skin, the heat of Batman in her lap, all things she would not have given little more than a perfunctory acknowledgement to a month ago. She watched Merritt's profile until sensing she was being watched, Merritt turned and smiled. "What?"

"You're beautiful." Soren said the only conscious thought in her head at that moment, and the rewarding blush on Merritt's face made her smile. "You favor your mother."

Merritt's smile widened. "I'll take that as a compliment."

"Please do. It was intended as one." She turned back towards the open window, inhaling the warm salty air and watched the salt marshes fly by as they cruised along. Judging from the direction and the briny smell of the air, she figured they were heading for the coast. The thought of a day at the ocean with Merritt pleased her greatly. Too bad a swim in skimpy bathing suits wasn't on the agenda. Soren knew that underneath the jeans and work shirts, Merritt had a body to die for.

"Penny for your thoughts."

"Huh?" Soren asked.

"I was just wondering where you were." Merritt said softly.

"Here…mostly." Soren responded with a laugh. "A little bit back home."

Merritt reached over and captured Soren's hand in hers, surprising them both. "Tell me more about Olivia."

Soren felt warmth effuse her body. It touched her deeply to know that Merritt appreciated her need to hold onto Olivia and that talking about her lessened the hurt of losing her. For some reason, Soren's mind went back to her first birthday party. How happy they'd all been then, or at least it seemed. She shook her head, vowing not to dwell on the negative. "God, Olivia is the most beautiful little girl I've ever seen, and I'm not just saying that because I'm her mom either."

Merritt laughed softly and squeezed her hand. "Of course not! You can see that from her pictures."

"And she is a ball of energy. From the moment she gets up in the morning until she conks out at night, she is always on the go, tearing through the house. From six months on, we could barely keep up with her. She was crawling everywhere and then god help us, she walked at ten months and it was all over." Soren groaned. "It was all Victoria and I could do to keep up with her."

"I bet." Merritt replied and tried to keep the steely anger she felt out of her voice. She didn't even know Victoria, but despised her anyway. She couldn't imagine how anyone could be as heartless as she had been. She clenched and

108

unclenched her jaw several times, feeling anger for Soren. "I was a handful for my mom and dad and I didn't walk until I was fourteen months. I have always been a little slow on the uptake, but I always end up where I need to be."

"So my house will be finished four months after your original estimate." Soren teased. She knew she was talking about her milestones as a child, but somehow she felt they hinted at a promise of their future and it comforted her. She caught the evil look Merritt was giving her and winked. "Ahh you know I'm just kidding."

"Yeah, yeah, I know. Now let's get back to Olivia and dispense with the jokes about my innate procrastination." She growled, her voice tinged with laughter. "Tell me about her first birthday."

"Wha…" Soren stilled, her mouth open in shock. "How did you know?"

Merritt looked confused. "Know what?"

"About her first birthday. That's what I was thinking." Soren said quietly.

"I don't know." Merritt crinkled her brow. "I guess that's the first thought that hit me. I saw you with her."

Soren contemplated her words. Somehow and she didn't know how, Merritt knew her, could read her thoughts, had gotten inside her head. Her sixth sense picked up on the subtle, intangible thoughts that were bouncing crazily around her head, and that made her feel less alone than she had in months. This bond with Merritt eclipsed the physical and emotional boundaries she'd built. She felt connected in a way she couldn't give a name to and she wanted to capture that. She wanted Merritt to feel what she was feeling. She wanted to be inside Merritt's heart and her head like she had done to her. Soren suddenly knew what it felt like to crave someone so much it hurt and she welcomed the ache. She squeezed Merritt's hand silently sending a prayer to the heavens and hoping someone was listening.

"Olivia's birthday is March 21st. I think that's what caused my little breakdown and buying the house. Some people drink...I shop." She saw Merritt cringe and it hit Soren what she had said. "Oh my God! Merritt I am so sorry." She stopped suddenly, even more embarrassed. She wasn't supposed to know about Kate. "I'm making a monumental mess..."

"Soren stop. It's okay." Merritt assured her in a soft voice. "I know my cousin has a big mouth. She never liked Kate and she's only looking out for me. I'm actually glad she told you. It's kind of hard for me to talk about."

"I'm here...if you ever want to."

"Maybe one day, just not right now. Right now I want to talk about Olivia and enjoy the day. Okay?" Merritt asked quietly.

"Of course. Besides I think we both need to focus on the positive." Soren smiled at Merritt and squeezed her hand reassuringly. "Anyway Olivia's first birthday was memorable to say the least and not because of the cake fiasco."

"Cake fiasco?" Merritt asked.

Soren chuckled, memories of that afternoon playing in her head. "Yep, the cake fiasco. It was a mess. Victoria went all out since it was Olivia's birthday. Invited tons of people, had a full meal catered, and ordered the biggest cake I've ever seen. I think it was more her party than Olivia's. That should have been my first warning that image was everything with her. Oh well, lesson learned right?" She paused answering her own rhetorical question before continuing. "When the cake was delivered, we knew right away that it was the wrong one."

Merritt raised an eyebrow. "Wedding?"

"Even better." Soren replied shaking her head. "It was a birthday cake for some guy that was obviously a huge Elvis fan. It even had a miniature pink Cadillac on one of the tiers."

"*One* of the tiers?" Merritt asked incredulously. "Just how big was this cake Victoria ordered?"

Soren blushed with embarrassment, acutely aware of how incredibly ostentatious the entire celebration had been. She wasn't that person, but had allowed Victoria to make her that way. She remembered that she had suggested a small party with just the three of them and a homemade cake and Victoria had scoffed at the idea. "It was big...too big. I think it was supposed to feed over one hundred people. That's a lot of Elvis cake."

"So what happened...they took it back and brought the right one, didn't they?"

"Hmm, well not exactly." Soren said cryptically, turning her attention to the road for the first time in several minutes.

"Ooh, not exactly doesn't sound so good." Merritt said as she slowed the truck and negotiated US—80 as it turned right and ran parallel to the water. Soren read a signed that welcomed them to Tybee Island and she smiled. The low, wet marshes were replaced with ocean style homes and restaurants. The streets were littered with people decked out in beach attire shuffling slowly as they browsed the main strip of Tybee Island. She inhaled the warm ocean air and listened to the nearby screech of the seagulls. She loved to people watch and she struggled to pull her eyes back into the truck and answer Merritt's question. "No, not exactly was bad. As the guys were loading it back up, Ferrus, our eighty—five pound German Shepherd came bounding around the corner. She'd picked up the scent and before any of us could react, she clipped one of the guys in the leg and..."

Merritt groaned. "Oh no, don't tell me."

"Oh yes, it was man down. Elvis crashed." Soren joked. "He never got to leave the building."

Merritt snorted loudly. "Okay, that was bad...even for you. So what did you do?"

111

"I laughed." Soren answered. "What could I do? No amount of yelling or crying was going to bring the cake back."

"What about the other cake…the one that was really yours?"

"The guys tried to call and get that one, but since we had ruined the one we got in the mix—up, I felt bad and told them to just let them have it. I kept the Cadillac though…for Olivia of course." Soren said slyly.

"Of course." Merritt echoed. "So no cake at the birthday party huh? Bet Victoria was none to happy about that."

"Oh man, she was furious. I think more so with me for not demanding the other cake. Olivia couldn't have cared less. She was one, what did she know? She had her cousins there, her *favorite* Aunt Jordan. She was in heaven with just that."

Merritt cocked her head. "Why the tone on favorite with Jordan?"

"Because that day I think the only one that liked her was Olivia. I wanted to wring her neck when she showed up."

"What happened?" Merritt turned left onto Atlantic Avenue towards the beach.

"She showed up at the party ripped. She had made the mistake of falling for one of her clients, her married clients. Jordan owns her own pool cleaning company and she met Ali while she was cleaning her and her husband's pool. Months of flirting led to a one night stand and the day of the party Ali had told Jordan that even though she loved her, she was staying with her husband."

"Ouch." Merritt said as she maneuvered into a parking spot on the boardwalk.

"Tell me about it." Soren agreed. "She spent the entire first half of the party crying and cornering unsuspecting guests warning them not to fall in love with a beautiful woman. She'll only break your heart and the second half carrying Olivia around singing Happy Birthday at the top of

112

her lungs." She paused, picturing Olivia's blond curls catching the breeze every time Jordan swung her around and her blue eyes lighting up with excitement. It seemed like an eternity ago and only yesterday at the same time. "So, long story short, the cake fiasco and the Jordan episode made the event quite interesting."

"And memorable." Merritt said with a laugh. She got out of the truck and walked around the back to open Soren's door. She took Soren's hand as she stepped out of the truck, squeezing it then releasing it quickly.

"Yeah, it was definitely not a day I'll forget." Soren watched Merritt grab the picnic basket from the back. "What can I help with?"

Merritt set the basket down, reached in front of Soren and pulled a large umbrella from behind their seats. "This."

Soren took the umbrella and let the weight of it pull her arms down to the ground. "Oh man, I don't know if…I…can…car…ry…this…my…self. It's…so…heavy."

Merritt rolled her eyes. "Real funny. You can carry my keys too." She dumped her keys in Soren's hand unceremoniously, smiling at the easy way they teased each other. "Come on Batman. Let's go for a walk."

Merritt slowed her stride down for the shorter woman and Batman who was stopping to inspect something every six inches. Several times Merritt had to coax him to catch up. "Jordan and Ali are together though right?" She asked hesitantly, not sure she remembered that from their earlier conversations.

Soren smiled easily. "Yes, it would seem that Jordan got under her skin just as much as she had with Jordan. It wasn't but a few months after Olivia's birthday that Ali had moved out of her house and in with Jordan, and had filed for divorce. Of course I did take every opportunity to tease Ali and remind her what a blubbering mess Jordan had been."

"Well I would have done that too." Merritt slowed down and turned to Soren, a question in her eyes. "Jordan doesn't drink like that all the time, does she?"

Soren almost laughed at the hilarity of the question, but the look in Merritt's eyes stopped her. She shook her head no. "That was a one time thing. Aside from a drink or two sometimes, Jordan isn't much of a drinker."

Merritt nodded her head, a silent acceptance of Soren's words. She started walking again and Soren fell in step beside her. "Merritt?"

"Yeah?"

"Thank you for letting me talk about Olivia with you."

Merritt touched Soren's arm softly. "I promise you can always do that with me."

Chapter Eleven

Soren stuffed the last bite of chocolate brownie in her mouth with a moan of appreciation. "I'm going to marry the woman that made that. Sure it wasn't you?"

"Sadly no." Merritt said with a rueful smile. "I wish it were. I'm not the handiest person when it comes to cooking. You have Cheryl at Back in the Day bakery to thank for this…and her husband might have something to say about you marrying his wife."

"Well I suppose I could settle for you." Soren winked. "If you bring me this same spread every day." She thought she might have to figure out how to not eat so much the next time. Soren had eaten half a Caprese sandwich stuffed with tomato and mozzarella and seasoned with olive oil and balsamic vinegar, and half of a Madras Curry Chicken sandwich, fresh fruit and two chocolate brownies. Stuffed didn't even begin to describe how she felt. "Maybe just half of it would be okay."

"Yeah I have to admit I've never seen that much food go into one person like that. I'm impressed." Merritt chuckled appreciatively. "I may have to get a second job though. If this is what it will take to get you to marry me, I'll go broke in the first year."

"I could scale back to once a week…" Soren suggested. "…if that's what it took to get you."

"Darlin', if I were with you I'd work three jobs to keep your cute little stomach happy."

"Silly Merritt, don't you know?" Soren asked coyly. "All I need to be happy is you."

Soren's admission was rewarded with a fierce blush that crept high into Merritt's cheeks. She turned her attention to clearing away the remains of lunch and breathed a sigh of relief when Soren started playing with Batman, mercifully letting the subject drop before they had an embarrassing intimate moment in front of hundreds of other beach goers. "Leave the scraps. Batman is eyeing them like a caped crusader ready to pounce on a super villain."

Merritt laughed without looking up. "Got to you huh? He has a way with the ladies." Batman came over to Merritt and laid on his back and let her scratch his belly. "Don't you boy? Already got Soren eating out of your hand…or vice versa I guess. Player."

"He knows a sucker when he sees one." Soren said ruefully then laughed when Batman abandoned the belly rub and gobbled down the bite of sandwich Soren held out for him. She watched him scarf several bites down and laughed even louder when he scampered off on his short legs to chase seagulls.

She pulled her legs up against her chest, resting her arms across them. She stared out over the water. Fishing boats cruised along the water, vacationers and seasoned fisherman sharing the teeming waters casting lines into the crystal blue water hoping to catch the big one. A flock of pelicans cruised low over the waves occasionally diving down to scoop up a mouthful of water and fish. The Tybee Island Light standing guard and the Cockspur Light a tiny dot in the distance. She watched the children building sand castles along the beach, thinking how much Olivia would love the ocean and wishing she'd had the opportunity to take her there.

As if reading her thoughts, Merritt scooted closer and spoke quietly. "Do you ever think about having any more children?"

Had she thought about it? Sure, but not specifically. Merritt was the first person she'd wanted to be with since Victoria and Soren saw that as a major step in itself. She hadn't even begun to picture having a family together. "Oh sure, but never more than a fleeting thought. I haven't found anyone I wanted to share that with. Besides, thinking about it opens old wounds and sometimes those hurt too much to even think about putting myself in the same situation again."

"You could do it by yourself." Merritt suggested. "Lots of people do."

"I know. I guess that has just never been something I wanted. Part of having a son or daughter is getting to share such an amazing gift with someone you love. Besides it's much easier to corrupt tomorrow's youth with two warped minds." Soren winked.

"True. Although I am sure you could do that pretty well on your own." Merritt teased and pulled back quickly to avoid the fist coming towards her.

"Turd!" Soren said with a growl. "What about you lippy? You ever want kids?"

"Sure." Merritt shrugged her shoulders. "Just never been the right time...or the right person. But I'm always hopeful. Remember I always get places I need to be I just..."

"You just take a little longer than most." Soren finished with a laugh. "So I guess we're about the same on this. We are just waiting for the right person and the right time."

"Exactly." Merritt eased herself down on the blanket and closed her eyes. "I think I could fall asleep right here." She cocked one eye open and squinted up at Soren. "Read me a bedtime story."

"Okay." Soren picked up the diary that Merritt had tucked inside the basket and flipped gingerly through the pages until she found the one she was looking for. "So I am finding out that Sam is a little sporadic in her writing. It seems she only writes every so often and only long entries on the days she sees Nina, so there is a lot of time between passages. I'll read you this one. It's from spring of 1896 so almost nine months have passed since her first entry about Nina. It's April 28th." Soren stretched out on her stomach, supporting her weight on her elbows with the diary tucked between them.

"Father let me take the carriage out today. It is a beautiful spring Saturday and I told him I wished to go on a picnic in the square. I'm not sure which square she is talking about." Soren interjected. *He and Mother did not join me as Mother's spring time cold has flared up this morning. She has spent the last three days sneezing. Poor thing.*

I had Ms. Cook prepare lunch for me and I am certain she made enough to feed half of Savannah. Imagine my surprise and delight when I ran into Nina P. on Habersham Street enjoying the day on foot. I invited her to share my carriage and my lunch and she was much obliged. I had a hard time managing the horses and am obliged to say that it is fortunate that they know the way to the square as I could not take my eyes off Nina. She is heartbreakingly beautiful in my eyes, especially when she speaks about her students. Her eyes light up and I believe I could spend the rest of my life listening to her speak. How very odd!

"I know how she feels." Merritt said quietly. "It's too bad she didn't know what she was feeling was falling in love."

Soren nodded her head. "Not at that moment I don't think. But she figured it out, just didn't figure out how to live with it." She found her place and continued.

All the young men that we drive by wave and beckon us to stop. They even joined our lunch party without so much as an invitation. They are all starry eyed and fidgety around us. I had to hide behind my hand several times so as not to be unladylike and laugh at their attempts to woo us. I had the

*strangest feeling thinking of Nina with a suitor. I wished to
be a man so I could be her beau.*

*I invited her back to my house so I could show her my
watercolors. I've not shared my paintings with anyone before
but I had an overwhelming urge to let Nina see the most
private part of me. She said that I was a wonderful artist and
would I let her hang some of them in her classroom. I think I
would give Nina anything she wished for.*

*As we sat on my bed deciding which ones she should
take our hands brushed together and I had the oddest flutter
in my stomach. When she left that afternoon I hugged her
against me and felt my heart pounding out of my chest. I
stood pressed against her, the heat of her breath on my
forehead, her lips brushing ever so softly against my cheek. I
wanted to kiss her just like Father kissed Mother, but that is
wrong. Oh but heavens, my body longed for her to touch me
like a husband would. She must have sensed it and knowing
so made her uncomfortable. She shuddered in my arms and
ran from the room, shaking her head, her pleading no's
ringing in my ears.*

*I don't know what spell Nina has cast on me but I am
bewitched. She makes me think all of these thoughts that I
have never had before, not even when Father's young
employs join us for dinner in an attempt to win my hand. I
don't want them. I want to be with my friend. I don't need a
husband, I just need Nina. I will hide what I feel for I do not
want to scare her away like I did this afternoon. I will pray
for these new feelings to go away so I don't have to ache for
her the way I do.*

"Wow." Merritt said with a whistle. "She's got it bad.
Wonder if she realizes it's not one—sided."

"I know." Soren agreed. "Nina wasn't shuddering
because she thought it was wrong. She was feeling the exact
same thing Sam was."

Merritt sat up and leaned on her elbows. "As hard as it is now, over a hundred years later for two women to be together, can you imagine what it would have been like back then?"

"Sam would say it was ghastly." Soren replied with a laugh. She looked at Merritt and smirked. "So much for your nap."

Merritt grinned and plopped back down, shutting her eyes. "Uh-uh, read me some more." She cracked open her eyes and caught Soren looking at her askance. "Please." She said smothering a smirk with her hand.

Soren flipped the page, skimmed the first few lines then flipped to the next one. She did this for several minutes and Merritt wondered if she'd forgotten she was supposed to be reading out loud. "Soren?"

"Shhh!" She said and held her hand up to silence Merritt. "Oh my God!"

Merritt shot up. "Oh my God what?" She tried to grab the diary out of Soren's hand but she swatted her hand away. "Come on Soren. What is it?" She pleaded in a childlike voice.

Soren's mouth was open and she looked as though she'd seen a ghost. She turned the diary towards Merritt, her finger holding a yellowed piece of newspaper down. Merritt's eyes found the words that had dumbfounded Soren and her jaw dropped accordingly. "Holy shit! It's her."

She stared at a sepia photograph of a tall, dark—haired woman surrounded by several children. She read the caption again, muttering the words under her breath as she read. *"Miss Nina Anderson Pape stands amongst the first group of students attending the newly organized Pape School.* I'll be a son of a bitch."

"We found her." Soren said quietly. "We finally found out who Nina is." She held the diary close to her face and studied the picture again. "Well I guess I can see why Sam said she was beautiful to her. She's, umm, well she does have pretty eyes."

Merritt snorted loudly. "Oh hell, why don't you just say she's ugly?"

"No, I'm not doing that." Soren retorted sharply. "Beauty is in the eye of the beholder and that's all that matters. Maybe it's just a really bad picture. Besides, who knows what Sam looks like."

"I'm sure she's gorgeous." Merritt said with a laugh. She pushed herself up off the blanket and stretched her arms over her head. "Now that the mystery is solved you wanna go for a stroll? I think Batman could use something new to chase."

Soren tucked the diary back in the picnic basket and held her hands out towards Merritt, who grabbed them and tugged her off the ground. She pulled hard enough to propel Soren towards her and she had to stop her with her own body, the move forcing their bodies together. Their arms pressed between them, their faces a breath apart. Merritt held onto Soren's hands, keeping their bodies pressed together, her eyes locked on Soren's. Soren licked her lips and Merritt swallowed, a knot of desire almost knocking her legs from beneath her. She stepped back quickly releasing Soren's hands and shoved her own in her pockets. She saw her control spiraling into oblivion and it scared the shit out of her.

Soren had seen the look of desire mingled with something else. Fear. She suddenly realized it wasn't fear of Soren at all, it was fear of hurting Soren that reflected in her eyes. *I don't want to hurt you.* It all made sense. Merritt was blaming herself for the demise of her relationship with Kate and she mistakenly believed she would do nothing but hurt Soren. She wanted to scream *I trust you Merritt. I know in my heart of hearts you would never hurt me.* But she didn't, she kept it hidden just below the surface. She knew she couldn't tell Merritt that and everything would be okay, Merritt had to believe that for herself. She needed to trust herself before she would ever let go and open up to Soren. She also knew that she was willing to wait. All great things are worth the wait she thought.

They began walking up the beach, weaving in and around sunbathers and sand castles. Batman ran up and down the beach, chasing the waves as they retreated back to the ocean growling to proclaim his superiority over the waves then scampering away as quickly as his little legs could carry him when the waves came rolling back in to challenge his authority. They laughed as the Dark Knight barked ferociously daring the waves to come any further then ran yelping in the opposite direction when they washed over his feet.

"Batman is not really a fan of water. You should see it when I try to give him a bath. It's ugly." Merritt laughed as he turned his attention to a flock of gulls scattering them like grains of sand in the wind. "Don't tell him I told you though, he thinks he's pretty tough."

Soren chuckled. "Hmm, like mother like son. You guys are like two peas in a pod. A tough exterior hiding a little softie."

"Hey!" Merritt objected. "I'm tough. Okay well I can be tough when I need to be." She said sheepishly when Soren fixed her with a sideways glance.

"Uh—huh." Soren countered sarcastically. "Like it or not, you've got a heart of gold."

Merritt shrugged nonchalantly. "Maybe so. What about you?"

"Gosh, I don't know. Probably a little of both. Sometimes I think life makes you hard, circumstances harden your heart and you wonder if it will always be that way." She paused trying to figure out how she felt at this precise moment and finally smiled up at Merritt. "Although I'm finding I am developing a bit of a soft spot recently."

Merritt knew she was referring to her and she couldn't keep the grin off her face. "Yeah Batman has a way of doing that to the ladies."

"That he does." Following Merritt's cue she changed the subject quickly. "What were you like as a kid?"

"Interesting question." Merritt chuckled. "Let's see what was that word you called me? Incorrigible? That is me now and that was me growing up. God, I had Gay as a role model. I don't think I could have been anything but."

"We're you as devastatingly beautiful then too?" Soren asked quietly.

"Unfortunately no!" She answered quickly then laughed. "I was tall and gangly, glasses and a horrible overbite. The worst acne you could possibly imagine and clumsy as all get out."

Soren shook her head. "I don't believe that at all. Tall and thin maybe, but no way on the other stuff."

"Scouts honor." Merritt said with her hand to her forehead in a salute. "I didn't grow out of my awkward phase till college."

"And that's when you became a lady killer." Soren teased. "Merritt Tanner wreaking havoc on a sorority full of women."

"Not exactly." Merritt said with a rueful smile. "I was a shy kid and I didn't get over that till…well I guess I still haven't. I didn't even have a girlfriend until I came back to Savannah and started working for my Dad."

Soren looked surprised. She couldn't put her head around the idea that Merritt was anything but outgoing with a long history of girlfriends, so the admission surprised her. "I have a hard time seeing you as shy."

"Painfully so." Merritt steered them towards the boardwalk. "The only times I came out of my shell was playing ball and with Gay. I was different then, in my element I think. I felt comfortable then and I shed some of my timidity." She turned and made sure Batman had followed them out on the boardwalk. "Gay was always outgoing and growing up I tried to emulate everything she did. I wanted to be just like her, bold, flirtatious, fun. She could talk to anyone. I mean she never had a problem with that."

"No surprise there." Soren smirked, amused at the tone of awe in Merritt's voice. "It's no wonder she always gets the girl. She's incredibly charming and debonair."

"That's how she's always been. Every one I knew had a crush on her." Merritt laughed suddenly. "But for every bit of charm she had, Gay has a little mischievous streak in her too."

"I'm sure there were lots of people with crushes on you." Soren teased.

"I doubt that." Merritt said with a self—deprecating smile. "Remember dork with braces."

"I hear what you are saying, but until I see proof, I don't believe it. Nope I think you've always been gorgeous."

"Ever the optimist huh?" Merritt joked.

"I'm certainly trying to be." Soren said sincerely. "It hasn't always been easy."

"Tell me about it." Merritt said ruefully.

Soren stopped at the end of the boardwalk and stood in front of Merritt. "So you were a tall, nerdy ballplayer who only talked to her cousin and wouldn't have realized a girl was interested in you even if she was standing right in front of you?"

Merritt hung her head smiling sheepishly. "Guilty."

"Well let's hope for my sake, your vision has improved." Soren said flirtatiously.

Merritt blushed and stepped closer. "Rest assured my vision is quite good and I am thoroughly enjoying the view." She backed away slowly, her penetrating eyes never leaving Soren's face. She rested her arms casually on the railing and smiled lazily.

124

Soren's pulse raced at the intensity of those green eyes, watching her, reading her. Her breathing was heavy as she gulped to get air in around the desire that gripped her throat. Her eyes pleaded with Merritt. "Talk about something, anything. Distract me please, before I kiss you."

Merritt's eyes clouded over and she steeled herself. Suddenly, everything around them had faded into the background and she found herself dangerously close to ignoring Soren's pleas and accepting her kiss. Nothing else seemed to matter except this woman and this moment. She cupped Soren's face against her palm, her eyes apologizing and begging her to understand. She blinked, trying to clear her head, praying for some innocent thought to penetrate her one track mind and calm the flames of desire that burned through her body. Soren parted her lips and Merritt shuddered with unbridled desire welcoming the new familiarity of it. *Oh God, what am I doing?*

They stood frozen, paralyzed by desire, connected to each other with a force neither one of them knew how to handle. Tiny voices warned them that this was crazy, but they welcomed the insanity of it. Both knew their first kiss wouldn't be here no matter how badly they wanted it, no that magic would wait, but this fire, this intensity could no longer go unquenched. They'd stepped past reason, gone beyond all rational thought. No amount of restraint would stay the insatiable force that pulled them together. And with strength she didn't know she possessed, Merritt lowered her hand and stepped away, releasing the breath that she'd been holding for moments that seemed to her like an eternity.

Merritt turned to the water and rested her elbows on the railing, her chin propped up on her fists. She stared out over the ocean, her breathing ragged, achingly aware of the woman standing next to her. She felt the need to explain why she was not good for Soren. "I ended things with Kate."

Soren who had reached down to pick up Batman looked at Merritt surprised by the admission. She hugged him against her and waited for Merritt to continue.

"Honestly, Kate and I were finished a long time ago. We should never have stayed together as long as we did, but I don't think either one of us knew how to move forward. I won't share the details because…well because I don't know that they matter as much as how we felt because of them. Or maybe how what we felt led to them. Am I making any sense?"

Soren didn't turn to Merritt but shook her head affirmatively. "I think so."

"I failed Kate, and I failed myself in the process. I'm not saying I'm the only one to blame, just explaining my hand in everything. I don't know if it would have mattered if I did things differently. The outcome may have been the same no matter what. I carried a lot of anger around for too long, but now being on the outside looking in, I think I can understand Kate's side of it." She was silent for several moments, lost in thought. "The main reason I left was because I wasn't in love with Kate anymore. I'm sure she wasn't in love with me. We had become very different people than when we first got together and I didn't like who we were. We both had some things we needed to work on and being in that relationship wasn't allowing us to focus on ourselves anymore. Everything was about the mess we were together. I spent so much energy trying to save Kate that I ignored the fact that maybe we both needed to be saved from ourselves. I couldn't save her when I was drowning myself." Merritt rubbed her temples. "I probably sound like a complete and total idiot."

Soren put her hand on her arm and squeezed it gently. "No, you don't. I think I understand you better than you think. In a way, it helps me understand myself a bit more. That's hard to do when you're in the trenches."

Merritt studied Soren for several long moments. "The reason I fight so hard against us is because I'm still figuring out how to fix myself. I'm broken Soren. And I can't let myself love you if there's a chance I'll hurt you."

"I'm an adult Merritt. That's not a choice you can make for both of us." Soren said defiantly.

"Damn it! I know that." Merritt snapped. "I'm sorry, I didn't mean that."

"I know you didn't. Don't you think I know how hard it is for you to keep fighting this?" She held her fist against her heart. "I know Merritt. I know because I'm on the other end of this. I tell myself everyday I'm going to respect your decision, keep my distance, but I gotta tell you…I'm dying here. So instead of making the choice that you think is right for both of us, let me make it with you."

Tears welled in her eyes. "I can't, I can't. Not until I'm whole again. I won't break you like I did Kate."

#

Soren watched Merritt drive away from her house. She swallowed the knot in her throat and fought the tears that threatened to well up in her eyes. This afternoon had certainly not ended anywhere close to how she had pictured. The weight of guilt that Merritt carried from her failed relationship with Kate was monumental and Soren wondered just how long she would be burdened by it. The fact was in most relationships every one messed up. Welcome to imperfection! She also knew from the look of raw pain in Merritt's eyes that she was still battling those demons. What she didn't know was how long Merritt would struggle.

Merritt believed she was broken, which couldn't have been further from the truth. She was as Soren liked to say a work in progress. But isn't everyone? She wasn't broken, she was human and God help her, Soren loved her for all of it. Yes, love. Somewhere between lunch and Merritt's confessions of failure, Soren had plunged head over heels.

Unfortunately, if this afternoon were any indication, she was going to be facing that dilemma alone—for a while anyway.

She smiled as she stepped back into the house and shut the door. "Well Sam, it looks like we have our work cut out for us. It may be a little bit longer before you can rest." She smiled again at the small chuckle of laughter she heard, not sure if she imagined it or not.

Chapter Twelve

"You want to what?" Soren stared at Gay incredulously. Gay's plan to sneak into the new subdivision of retirement condos where Nancy lived and commandeer several large rocks for Soren's landscaping sounded about as ridiculous as sneaking into the Library of Congress and taking the Declaration of Independence. "Please tell me you are joking."

Gay smirked and shook her head. "Nope. Seriously though, how bad could it be? They are at the back of the subdivision and they obviously aren't using them. We just sneak in, sneak out, we're done."

Soren crossed her arms and looked askance at Gay. "Gee I don't know. How about it's a bad idea, trespassing, stealing, and did I mention it's a bad idea? We can't just go to a store and buy some and have some nice man in a big truck bring it here and drop one off. That would work just as well."

"No! Where's your sense of adventure?" She grabbed Soren's hand and pulled her off the porch steps. "These are *the* perfect rocks and I need them to finish the flower beds in the back...and besides I'm cheap."

Soren reluctantly followed Gay to her truck and flopped onto the passenger seat ignoring the smug smile of satisfaction on her face. "If we get caught and arrested, your ass is so posting my bail."

"Oh pshaw!" Gay said with a dismissive wave of her hand. "Merritt will bail us out."

A cloud passed over Soren's eyes. She plastered a smile on her face, but it stopped short of her eyes.

"What's wrong?" Gay asked in a voice filled with concern, a frown on her round face. "What has my cousin done now?"

"Nothing." Soren's chin trembled and Gay could hear the quiver in her voice. She sighed softly. "It's not what Merritt did, it's what I did."

"Honey, tell ole Gay about it and I'll decide if it's as bad as you're making it out to be."

Soren studied Gay's face, surprised at the gentle sincerity and decided that she may be the best person to talk to about her *issue.* "I did what I promised myself I wouldn't do. I fell in love with Merritt." She paused, waiting for the off—the—cuff remark she'd grown accustomed to with Gay.

Gay's eyes held the road and she rubbed her chin thoughtfully. "Darlin' if my cousin is not half way in love with you herself, I'm not Gay. And that's a major feat in itself considering that's what my birth certificate and half of Savannah's rec softball league say I am." She winked mischievously. "Seriously though, I reckon she's just about as smitten as you are."

"That seems to be our problem." Soren said wearily. "Right person, wrong time. I'm a patient person, but this aching need for Merritt and knowing I can't have her is killing me."

"Darlin', there are ways to get rid of that ache…" Gay raised her eyebrows suggestively.

"You are not right." Soren teased. "Besides, we would be the mismatch made in heaven."

Gay frowned. "You say that now, but I would grow on you."

"Oh yeah, definitely." Soren laughed wickedly. "Like any great fungus you'd be all over me."

"Ouch." Gay replied with a groan. "I'm retracting my offer. Besides, I really don't think you could handle this. I'm

130

a machine. Stronger women than you have broken under this tongue."

Soren burst out laughing. "Thanks Gay. You're exactly what I needed today."

"Yeah that's what most women tell me." Gay said with a smirk. "Now listen, I'm going to be serious for once. Merritt's always been the type who doesn't wear her emotions on her sleeve. She keeps them locked up tight. And the last few years have been the worst I've seen. She's been closed off and distant, and the little bit she shares with me is that of someone who blames herself for everything that happened between her and Kate."

"But I don't believe that." Soren interrupted. "Every relationship is two—sided and that includes the blame when things go wrong."

"You know that and I know that, but it's been a hard lesson for Merritt to learn. Even growing up, she took the heat for everything…when really I was the trouble maker. She's got thirty—nine years of behavior that's engrained in her and that's a tough thing to let go of. I'm not saying she can't, I'm just saying she struggles."

Soren nodded somberly. "I know the feeling. I've had my own ghosts to contend with and I'll admit it hasn't been easy."

"But she's changing, albeit slow. When you came along and started to chip away at that lock, it scared her." Gay flipped the signal on and turned off the main road into a newly developed subdivision. "She lights up when she talks about you whether she realizes it or not. I haven't seen that in years, and she's afraid of letting herself love you because she fears hurting you. That's why she fights it."

"I know." Soren responded quietly. "She told me. But here's my thing, she has to understand that the decision she's made for herself to remain friends only isn't allowing me any input in the situation. I've been hurt before and I healed…or I'm healing anyway. I trust Merritt and I know she won't hurt me, at least not on purpose. I also know that's a risk you take in any relationship. I'm an adult. I know there are no guarantees. If there is any lesson I've learned it's that one." She paused, her eyes meeting Gay's and holding them. "Be honest with me Gay. You're her cousin. Do I fight for her or let it go? I just can't see living my life without her."

Gay smiled. "Fight, but go into it prepared. She's stubborn and foolish sometimes. It may take awhile, but I think you know it would be worth it. I like you and something tells me you are just what the doctor ordered." She pulled the truck half way around a cul—de—sac and stopped, her eyes finding a large boulder about a hundred yards away. "That's it."

Soren spied the rock and shook her head. "I just don't understand how you can be so smart one minute, and the next minute so incredibly Gay."

"Cherish it darlin'." Gay said with a smirk. "It's not too often I straighten up."

Soren snorted loudly. "If ever!" She opened the door wearily. She trudged through the knee—high weeds, following Gay closely and grumbling the whole time. "There better not be snakes in here."

"There are...big poisonous ones." Gay said seriously. "No worries though, just zig—zag back and forth. They won't catch you."

"That's alligators you moron." Soren said sarcastically.

"Okay, well I guess you could just shovel it to death...I got one in the truck. Course you gotta steer clear of the head...it can still bite you for a couple minutes even after the snake is dead."

"Oh great!" Soren said rolling her eyes. "This just keeps getting better. I'm going to the truck." She turned to go and Gay grabbed her arm.

"Come on chicken. Would I steer you wrong?" She asked innocently.

"Ahh yeah, probably." She stopped suddenly almost bumping into Gay. She stared at two large rocks. They were granite, one a deep blue gray and the other a brilliant mix of reds, purples, blacks and a sprinkling of white quartz. They would compliment the landscape perfectly. "They're perfect…but I'm sure we could have bought two just like it."

"But they're free." Gay said smugly, ignoring Soren's eye roll. "That's me, always trying to get you a good deal. I figure Merritt's gonna hose you so I do my part to counter that."

"And get me killed in the process." She bent over and tried to roll the larger of the two rocks. It wouldn't budge. "Okay smarty pants, how are we supposed to get this to the truck? It has to weigh a couple hundred pounds."

Gay looked around and spotted a pile of construction trash. "Got an idea." She made her way to the pile and pulled a large piece of cardboard out and waved it at Soren with a smile. "Reckon we can roll it on this and just drag it back to the truck."

Soren cocked an eyebrow and looked at Gay incredulously. "Please tell me you have a better idea than that."

Gay set the cardboard down next to the rock. "Come on. This will work fine."

Soren rolled her eyes and came around beside Gay, bending over and putting her hands on the rock.

"Okay, on three." When she said three, both women pushed hard trying to roll the large rock onto the cardboard. When it only budged an inch, Gay looked at Soren exasperated. "You gotta put your weight into it."

"You put your weight into it." Soren retorted quickly.

"For God's sake Soren, if you put as much energy into pushing the damn rock as you do making fat jokes we might get this." Gay said sternly, but couldn't keep the corners of her mouth from turning up. "You need to get that scrawny ass of yours behind it and bear down."

"Oh you'll see scrawny ass if you keep it up." Soren punched her in the arm. "You'll see my scrawny ass walking back to the truck and hightailing it out of here."

Gay shook her head and snorted loudly. "I've got the keys darlin'." She grinned evilly then planted herself against the rock, squaring her broad shoulders and planting her feet firmly. Soren thought she looked like a bull ready to charge and had to stifle a laugh. "This time, push!"

"Like I wasn't before." Soren muttered sarcastically, but positioned herself like Gay, readying herself for the attack. "On three?"

Gay nodded. "On three."

This time when they pushed, they grunted loudly, putting all their weight into it. It started to rock and within minutes the momentum carried it squarely onto the flat piece of cardboard.

Soren stood up and dusted her hands off. "My work here is done."

"You just keep getting funnier." Gay said sarcastically. She threw her head over her shoulder towards the truck. "Now for the fun part. We're gonna drag this to the truck."

"Yeah fun. Why are we doing this again?"

"We're saving money. It's a chance to bond. They're the perfect rocks." She caught the look that Soren gave her and smiled mischievously. "You needed an adventure. I'm here to ensure that you get your daily dose of fun. Besides when was the last time you got out and did something crazy?"

"Well aside from the one time in summer camp with two other counselors, it's been awhile." Soren smiled and shook her head when Gay cocked her head questioningly. "Uh—uh, that story is reserved for telling only after a few beers."

"That's a good thing to remember. I'll ply you with alcohol the next time I'm trying to loosen your lips." Gay teased.

"Oh please, like I haven't already let the cat out of the bag and confessed everything to you anyway." Soren blew a stray hair out of her eyes. Again she acknowledged that Gay made her comfortable…comfortable enough to talk to her about Merritt. She wondered if she might get to keep Gay even if things with Merritt didn't pan out. She hoped she ended up with both.

"Please darlin', you're easier to read than a dollar poker player with a bad tell. I'd have known whether you told me or not." She laughed quickly. "But I'll buy you a beer anyway…since I am putting you through the wringer this afternoon."

"Darlin'." Soren said with an affected Southern drawl. "For this, you're buying me dinner."

"Fair enough." Gay bent down and grabbed a corner of the cardboard. "You ready?"

Soren groaned then bent over and grabbed the other edge of the cardboard. "Can I just mention again this is the most ridiculous thing I've ever done? Seriously, we can still just buy the rocks, have them delivered, save my back."

"Just pull." Gay gripped the edges tightly. It started slowly at first then gathered momentum, the cardboard scraping along the gravel loudly. She knew they were a sight to see, two women hunkered down dragging a boulder across a hundred feet of rocky, overgrown terrain. "Man I'm glad no one is watching this." She huffed loudly.

Ten feet later, Soren stopped and flexed her hands. She glanced over her shoulder at the ninety plus feet they had left to go and she groaned loudly. "I think this thing weighs a ton." Yet somehow Gay's insane enthusiasm was growing on her and she planted herself next to Gay, and got ready to pull. They had managed to drag it another thirty feet when Soren stopped suddenly, watching three men walk down the street towards them. "Why are those guys walking this way?" She asked alarmed.

Gay shrugged. "Maybe they are coming to help us."

"Or maybe they work here and they are coming to stop us from stealing."

"We're not stealing. This is obviously where they pile all the junk they dig up when they are grading the lots. We're helping them out really. Taking the stuff off their hands."

Soren continued watching them, getting more and more alarmed by the minute. "No seriously, they're coming this way." She was ready to cut out when they veered off and headed into one of the only two homes finished on the street. "Oh sure, don't come help us." She let out and exasperated sigh. "The least they could have done was helped instead of staring the whole damn time."

Gay shook her head. "There's just no pleasing you, is there? First you don't want them to come this way and now you want them to help?"

Soren rolled her eyes and grabbed her corner. "Let's just hurry up." They pulled together again, their hands aching from holding on so tightly that they had to stop every ten feet or so and readjust. The sheer ridiculousness of it all hit them both and they burst out laughing. They looked at each other, and laughed even harder. Soren was doubled over and still trying to pull her corner, when the old paper finally gave out and ripped in half sending her stumbling backwards. She stopped, her giggling making it impossible to even talk.

Gay studied the ripped cardboard and shrugged. "I think we can carry it the last fifty feet."

"Are you sure?" Soren asked, wiping tears of laughter off her cheeks.

"Yeah." Gay answered confidently. "Between the two of us no problem."

Soren paused, hesitant to try to lift the boulder. She saw the look of determination on Gay's face and knew there was no talking her out of this either. "Fine, we'll try it. Make sure you lift with your legs." Soren advised knowledgeably as she knelt down to get a firm grip.

"You ready?" Gay asked as she got her hands positioned under the rock.

"Ready." They lifted, both women grunting loudly. "Oh my God, this is heavy. Okay just don't drop it." They scooted sideways, taking small steps like a crab scurrying across the sand. Gay saw an exposed man hole cover and she directed them towards it, heaving it onto the metal just as Soren's grip broke and she fell away laughing hysterically. "I am so glad you had that. I had to drop it. I almost peed my pants."

Bent over at the waist, Gay's shoulders trembled with laughter. "That was so close." She stood up smirking. "It's all fun and games till someone loses a foot."

"I'm going to get the other one. I think I can carry that one myself…that way there's no chance of you dropping it on my foot." Gay said with a wink. "Then I think I have an idea." She jogged back to the pile of construction garbage and tested the weight of the other rock. Satisfied she could muscle it back, she bent over and picked it up, heaving it towards her hips for stability and started walking quickly back to Soren. The rock slipped from her fingers about ten feet away. Determined not to let the rock win, she rolled it the rest of the way.

"Not as light as it looks, huh?" She was panting hard and Soren couldn't resist teasing her. "Still thinking this is a great idea?"

"Maybe not, but it's fun." Gay smiled sheepishly. "I think it's time for plan B." Gay walked back to the truck, lowered the gate and pulled out two shovels. She handed Soren one of them. "Here's the plan. We just have to roll the rock onto the shovel then we can drag it to the truck."

"Great." Soren said sarcastically. "Then how are we supposed to get it onto the truck?"

"We're gonna lift it up there."

"Right. 'Cause that was easy." Nevertheless Soren stuck her shovel under the smaller of the two rocks and rolled it onto the shovel with a grunt.

Gay snorted loudly. "Okay, well I'll get the heavy one then."

"Hey, your idea." Soren smiled smugly and started dragging her rock back to the truck.

Gay pushed the rock off the man hole cover and it landed with a loud thud. She looked at Soren and waved her hand nonchalantly. "Don't worry. I'm okay. I've got five other toes."

Soren ignored her and kept walking. She kept turning around behind her and checking the ground so she didn't trip on anything. She got to the edge of the field and had to maneuver the shovel over two small humps. She assessed the small area and finally chose a narrow path to pull the shovel through. She tugged and the shovel slid over the bump, scraping along the concrete curb with an annoying grate that reminded her of nails on a chalkboard. She walked triumphantly towards Gay who was fighting with her boulder, having to stop every few feet and roll it back onto her shovel. Soren stifled a laugh. "Let me do it. I figured out the magic way to do it."

"Have at it." Gay stepped back from the shovel and dusted off her hands.

Soren grabbed the handle and started to pull, not surprised when it toppled off again. "See you don't have it on here right. You need to put the heavy end towards the back of the shovel and then if you tilt it just right, it won't fall off."

"You just work your magic, witchy woman." Gay grabbed the smaller rock that Soren had already taken to the truck and hoisted it up into the truck bed with a loud grunt. She picked up the shovel and headed back into the field where she had seen several smaller rocks that would accent the smaller beds nicely. She loaded three of them onto her shovel and headed back to the truck, passing Soren who was struggling to work her magic on the rock. She chuckled loudly.

Soren looked over at Gay's three small rocks and scoffed loudly. "Hey!"

Gay shook her head. "Sorry, you got the magic touch."
She whistled pulling the shovel with one hand. The scraping
sound of metal against rock echoed loudly around them and
she looked around half expecting someone to come run them
off. It was a Sunday afternoon and while the builders didn't
generally work on Sundays there were occasionally sub—
contractors that worked off hours. Thankfully, aside from the
guys earlier, she hadn't spotted anyone *yet.*

Gay contemplated helping Soren who had continued to
struggle, but decided she'd rather sit and enjoy the view.
Soren may have been a bit skinnier than she normally liked,
but she did have a cute ass.

When Soren got to the small humps right before the
curb, she stopped and repositioned the rock, making sure it
was just like she wanted it. She found the same path that
she'd taken for the first rock, braced herself and pulled hard
against the rock using all her weight. The next few seconds
happened in slow motion as Gay looked on helpless.

Soren bent at the knees and pulled the shovel towards
her. It hit a snag and the rock fell forward, sending Soren
flying backwards into the street. She landed with a thud
underneath the open gate of the truck. The look of shock on
her face was priceless as she realized she was flat on her butt,
staring up at Gay who was trying hard not to laugh. She
looked like she didn't know whether to laugh or cry.

"Oh my God, are you okay?" Gay held her hands out
and pulled Soren to her feet. "I won't laugh anymore till I
know you're okay."

Soren burst out laughing. "I don't know what happened.
That's the same rut I went through the first time. It just got
stuck." She looked down at her forearm which was sporting a
pretty nice concrete burn.

"Oh yeah, you got the magic touch all right." Gay
snorted loudly, unable to control her laughter anymore. "You
should have seen it. You flew threw the air. And how you
ended up under the truck is beyond me."

"Oh man, that hurts." Soren rubbed her butt gingerly. "This is the last time I let you talk me into an *adventure.*" She checked her arm again for bleeding. Satisfied it was okay for now, she threw her shovel into the truck. "Let's hurry up and do this."

They didn't exactly hurry, but several minutes later they had managed to load the rock and leave the scene of the heist, laughing hysterically.

Hours later they sat on the swing, surveying the results of the day's activities. The afternoon sun cast soft rays over the landscaping, the quartz glistening brilliantly. Gay had positioned them all with her own *feng shui* techniques and Soren begrudgingly admitted that they were indeed aesthetically pleasing. Gay smiled smugly. "I told you they were perfect."

Soren took a swig of her beer. "Hmm."

"Hmm, what?" Gay asked quickly.

"I don't know." Soren replied slowly. "Didn't they seem bigger to you when we were hauling them back to the truck? Looks kinda small for something that felt like it weighed five hundred pounds."

"My back might disagree." Gay groaned loudly.

"Well dumbass why didn't you lift with your legs and not your back?"

"I couldn't." Gay smiled sheepishly. "I don't know how to lift with my legs."

Soren held her arm up in front of Gay's face. "I guess your sore back just makes us even."

Gay nodded in agreement, chuckling softly. "I reckon that's true. I'll admit in retrospect my idea *may* have been a tad over ambitious. I'm not thirty anymore."

"A tad?" Soren asked incredulously. "Try incredibly insane." She pushed her foot and put the swing in motion. "In retrospect, I'll admit your idea may have been a little bit fun."

Gay smirked. "I knew you were loving it." At Soren's admission, they both started laughing again and couldn't stop. Finally, Soren managed to settle down, inhaling deeply. "You were right. I needed some adventure."

"Well smack my ass." Gay slapped her knee loudly. "I'll be! Soren is admitting I was right." She said, addressing no one in particular. "Write that down."

Soren giggled, the effects of the alcohol making Gay's infectious personality even more irresistible. She wondered why she was still single. "Gay, how come you never settled down?"

"Lord darlin', there ain't a snowball's chance in hell I'd let some woman tame me. I'd feel like a tornado trapped in a henhouse." Gay laughed wickedly. "I reckon I just haven't met the woman yet that I want to tame me. Many have tried, but I figure it's going to take someone special…and since your heart's already spoken for…"

Soren smiled. "Ahh as sweet as you are Gay, I know you're just teasing me. Have you really never been in love?"

"Not that I can recollect." Gay rubbed the label on her beer bottle distractedly. "I've been in lust more times than I can count. It just never went any further."

She smiled to cover that up, but Soren picked up on the melancholy tone. "Did you ever want it to?"

Gay shrugged and emptied her drink. "Maybe, once or twice I reckon. If you want to know if I wished I were co—habitating with someone, I don't know." She shrugged nonchalantly. "Can't really miss what you never had, right?"

Soren was silent for several moments. "You can't?" She asked quietly.

Gay put her hand on Soren's arm and laughed. "Don't be sad for me honey. I'm happy…really. I'm where I chose to be. Some of us are nesters and some of us like to rattle the cage. I'm a rattler. Plain and simple. Now don't think that I'm not a romantic at heart though. I'm pulling for you two kids."

Soren laughed softly. "You're just like Merritt, a big softie masquerading as a tough guy."

"Hey!" Gay frowned. "You take that back."

"Nope." Soren shook her head. "I've got your number missy. Deal with it."

Gay stood up slowly and yawned. "I think I better get going. Can't sit around all night and let you impune my honor."

Soren laughed and Gay saw the magic in her face that had captivated Merritt. For a brief, a very brief, moment she wondered what would have happened had Soren fallen for her. She dismissed it just as quickly, acknowledging that she wasn't quite ready to give up her wild side. There were just too many women left in the world she hadn't met.

Soren walked her out to her truck. "Thanks for the adventure and the pizza. You really know how to show a girl a good time."

Gay started the truck then stuck her head out. "At least that's what it says after my phone number on all the bathroom stalls."

Soren heard her laughter ring out in the night as she pulled away. She rubbed the scratches on her arm absentmindedly and once again thought that this move may have been the best thing for her.

Chapter Thirteen

"Hello?" Soren tucked the phone under her chin and continued to dead head petunias. Gay had done a fabulous job on her landscaping, leaving Soren with not much more than simple upkeep. Her favorite part of all of it was the large stone fountain in the middle of the backyard. She could swing on her back porch and let the soothing sounds of the trickling water gently soothe her. She would be forever grateful to Gay for the phenomenal change from when she first moved in.

"Soren?" A pleasant elderly voice asked sweetly. *"Hello dear. It's Nancy."*

Soren smiled. She'd only met Nancy once and talked to her a handful of times, but already she felt a strong familial attachment to the woman. She reminded Soren of her own mother, who she reminded herself she had not called in a couple of weeks and owed her a phone call. "Hi Nancy. How are you?"

"I'm wonderful dear. Thank you for asking. And yourself?"

Soren wanted to tell her she was okay, but not great. It had been a week since she'd talked to Merritt, really talked to her. She'd been at the house with her crew, but the conversations were always meaningless drivel about the weather, or the business, or how good something looked now that it had been renovated. Nothing of importance and certainly nothing more of them after last Saturday's very personal confession at the beach. By Wednesday, Soren realized just how much she'd come to need Merritt's presence in her life. She felt like she was drying up emotionally without her. But she couldn't share that with Nancy, no that was something she needed to keep to herself, no matter how seemingly easy to talk to Nancy had been. "I'm doing well. Finally experiencing a true southern summer. It's like walking into a sauna anytime you go outside." Soren stepped inside and felt the rush of cool air welcome her. She made her way to the kitchen and pulled a bottle of wine out of the fridge and found a glass.

Nancy chuckled on the other end. *"Get used to it dear, that is Georgia weather for you. And what about the house? How is it coming along? I haven't spoken with Merritt recently. Is she meeting your expectations?"*

Not yet. Soren thought somberly. *But I have high hopes she will.* "Oh yes, the renovations are coming along just fine. Merritt and her crew are incredibly talented." Soren said appreciatively. "She's stayed true to the original architecture. I think you'll be very proud of her." Soren tucked the phone back under her chin, grabbed her glass and the bottle and went into the library.

"I always have been proud of my Merritt. From an early age, she followed her father around watching him like a hawk, studying everything he did so one day when she took over the business she would know everything he knew. They are two peas in a pod those two. She may look like me, but she is her father in every other way."

Somehow just hearing Nancy's voice and picturing her made Soren feel closer to Merritt. That was something that had never happened with Victoria's mother. She'd been distant, almost cold from the very beginning. If anything, Victoria's mother had pulled them further apart, rather than helping strengthen their bond. Like mother, like daughter Soren thought bitterly. But Nancy was the complete opposite. Warm and caring, not a cold, unfeeling bone in her body.

Merritt may have been a lot like her father, but Soren could already appreciate the qualities she had inherited from her mother. "I think she's picked up a few of your finer qualities as well."

Nancy laughed softly. *"Why thank you my dear. I'd like to think so."* She paused and Soren could hear papers shuffling in the background. *"And now for the purpose of my call. I managed to track down quite a wealth of information on your Nina Pape."*

Soren's heart leapt and she had difficulty containing her excitement. "Please don't leave me in suspense. What did you find out?"

Nancy was silent except for several hmm's as she found what she was looking for. *"First of all, we were correct. She did come from a prominent family in Savannah. Why her grandfather was the mayor of Savannah five times. She was also a distant cousin of Juliette Gordon Low."*

"The woman who started the Girl Scouts." Soren interjected. "Of course, I only know that because Merritt told me. Otherwise, not so good in history."

"That's right." Nancy corroborated. *"Juliette actually started the Girl Scouts based on a girls' group that Nina started much earlier. Nina was also instrumental in the creation of kindergartens in deprived neighborhoods."*

"Wow!" Soren was in awe.

"Just wait. There's more." Nancy flipped through more pages. *"You mentioned she started the Pape School, which went on to become one of the nation's most respected college prep schools. In 1898, she founded the Tybee Island Fresh Air Home as a retreat for underprivileged children. By all accounts, Nina was a woman to be reckoned with. She would likely qualify as one of the first woman to push for equal rights. She is an integral part of Savannah history. That diary that you have is a major historical find."* Nancy couldn't contain the excitement in her voice. *"Whatever amount of information we can glean from it regarding Nina*

will be an important contribution to Savannah and I hope you'll be inclined to share."

"I'm realizing more and more just how special Nina was." *To Sam especially.* "I'd like your advice on who the best candidate will be, but rest assured Nancy when I am finished with the diary and with Sam and Nina, I would be more than willing to donate the diary."

Nancy breathed an audible sigh of relief. *"That's wonderful! I'm going to hold these books out in case you wanted to do some reading on your own. You can pick them up anytime."* Nancy offered generously.

"That would be wonderful!" Soren exclaimed excitedly. "Nancy, thank you so much for all your help. I must admit I am thoroughly enjoying this treasure hunt, and I couldn't have asked for a better person to help me."

"Oh stuff and nonsense." Nancy poo—pooed the praise. *"It's been my pleasure. I would like it very much if my darling daughter would bring you around to dinner. I'd like to see more of you Soren. Now you go back to whatever it was you were doing before I interrupted you."*

Soren's mouth dropped at the round—about blessing Nancy had just given her. Secretly she hoped that there would be a day that Merritt would bring her home to mom. "I'd like that very much. And Nancy? Thank you very much."

"You are quite welcome." Nancy said then wished Soren goodbye.

Soren hung up the phone and stared at the ceiling. The more she learned about Nina, the more she realized what an amazing person she was. It was no wonder Sam had fallen for her hook, line and sinker. Shaking her head, she picked up the Patricia Cornwell novel she'd abandoned earlier. She found her place and tried to get into it again, but something kept her mind from engaging. She finally shut the book again and set it on the table beside her. "Okay, okay, you win Sam."

Soren figured she could probably have tackled the entire diary by now, but she hadn't been able to emotionally. It had been hard to delve into Sam's feelings without feeling like she was spying on her. Plus, Soren's feelings for Merritt were starting to sound just like Sam's. No, reading a little at a time had been the only way she knew how to do it.

She refilled her wine glass, looking for some extra fortification then flipped the diary open and took a deep breath. She was relieved and disappointed when most of what she read was not much more than small entries about the summer. Sam and Nina had very little contact after that last meeting until late in 1896. The few times that Sam had run into Nina, she'd been with her father or Nina had been with her students. But an entry near Christmas 1896 turned out to be the most amazing one yet. By the time Soren finished reading, her hands were shaking and emotion gripped her heart in a vise. She closed her eyes, her mind sharing the tender ache that Sam had felt.

"Soren?" A voice whispered gently. "Soren honey, wake up."

Soren must have dosed off and when she finally stirred at the voice, she nearly jumped off the couch. "Jesus!"

Merritt backed away quickly, narrowly missing a hand to her stomach. She smiled at Soren apologetically. "I'm sorry I startled you."

Soren rubbed her eyes, still somewhat dazed. Finally she looked at Merritt questioningly. "How'd you get inside?"

"Key." She answered sheepishly, holding up the key Soren had given her when she started the renovations. "I knocked a couple of times, but you didn't answer." She anticipated Soren's next question and answered it before she could ask. "I saw the car and when you didn't answer, I was worried something might be wrong."

Soren shook her head. "No, I'm fine…aside from getting the shit scared out of me." She smiled and Merritt couldn't remember anyone that looked as sexy half asleep as Soren did. Even half awake, Soren recognized the look of desire in Merritt's eyes and it sent a shiver down her spine. She was finally awake enough to appreciate that Merritt looked as unbelievably sexy as she'd ever looked. Her long dark hair was loose from its normal braid and full waves of it framed her face in a way that made Soren's stomach jump. The long—sleeved white button down shirt she was wearing complimented her summer tan and made her green eyes sparkle. She'd traded in her normal cargo pants for loose fitting washed out jeans. Soren swallowed hard, knowing she'd never seen anyone as gorgeous as Merritt. Remembering the disastrous outcome the last time she'd allowed herself to succumb to Merritt's charms, she pulled her eyes away from Merritt and swung her feet to the floor, giving Merritt a place to sit.

Merritt sank into the couch, her leg brushing against Soren's and she jerked it away immediately, the electricity between them burning her to the core. She nodded at the empty wine glass. "Am I interrupting anything?"

Soren laughed nervously. "No, just reading and I needed to steel myself a little bit." Knowing what she did about Merritt's past, she wondered if her drinking bothered Merritt. It shouldn't, it was never more than a glass or two and not all the time. Of course if it did, Soren would gladly exchange all the alcohol in the world for a chance to be loved by Merritt. "I guess it made me a little sleepy."

Without thinking, Merritt reached up and brushed a lock of hair behind Soren's ear. Her knuckles grazed her jaw and she froze. If just touching Soren's face made her a quivering mess, how on earth was she going to spend an evening with her? Suddenly, she questioned whether coming here had been such a bright idea after all. When she'd first thought about it, it seemed like a great idea. She felt bad for leaving Soren last week under such bad circumstances and wanted to make it up to her, certain that now that she'd staked out their boundaries, she would be okay. She hadn't banked on her treacherous body putting up such a fight. She pulled her hand away quickly, but not before she saw the raw hunger in Soren's eyes. *God help me!* She pleaded not sure of her own ability to curb her ever strengthening feelings. She needed to rein her heart back in quickly. "Anything good?"

Soren grabbed the diary off the table and handed it to Merritt. "Read this." She said indicating the page with her finger.

"That good huh?" Merritt saw the date and realized it was close to Christmas. She focused on Sam's arching cursive and was pulled in after just a few seconds.

December 21, 1896.

Four days until Christmas and I'm certain I've already been given the most wonderful present any woman could ever hope for...love. Father's been beside himself for as many months as I can remember, appalled that I could turn down so many offers of marriage from eager suitors. Despite my Father's admonishment that one doesn't marry for love, one marries based on the sensibility of a good match, I cannot bring myself to accept that, much to my Father's dismay. You'll soon be past the age that any man will want you Samantha, and then where will that leave you? An old maid. An old maid, imagine my delight at the prospect. No man to take time away from my beloved Nina.

She came to see me today bearing gifts. A pipe and tobacco for Father, a beautiful broche for Mother and for me a reproduction of Foliage, a watercolor by Cezanne and her heart. The former I will admire, the latter I will cherish for the rest of my life.

When she arrived, she pulled me aside long enough to say that she'd missed me. My heart raced with the possibility that perhaps she too cared for me, but I dismissed it quickly as the foolish thinking of a silly mind. After spending an appropriate amount of time, we retired to my room to find a place for my new painting. My mind immediately went back to the last time Nina was in my room and the familiar

149

feelings began to stir again. I'm amazed that even being in the same room with her makes me feel things that I still cannot fathom. I had to hide my trembling hands behind me so as not to alarm her in the same fashion as before.

We hung the painting and as we were standing admiring it, my eyes found their way to Nina's face and I was powerless to look away. As if sensing my gaze, she turned and our eyes met and in one wonderful moment of clarity I knew that she felt as I did, and that what we felt was falling in love. The enormity of that struck us both and we both laughed nervously, unsure of what to do next.

My chest ached to touch her and I pulled her against me, our bosoms pressed tightly together. I could feel her heart beating against mine and it made me long to show her how I felt, express what I was feeling and words seemed to fail me. I did the first thing that I thought of...I kissed her. The feeling of her lips pressed against mine felt like fireworks on the Fourth of July. My body tingled and I felt Nina tremble against me, a moan escaping from her lips. My only thought was how right we felt together. And yet, I needed more. My hands found her chest and I pressed them against her core, earnestly trying to delve inside her. I felt her breasts full and soft against my palms, her body arched into mine. We stood there, our mouths exploring one another, my hands feeling the curves of her body and I was in heaven or as close to heaven as one humble person can be. I knew in that one moment that I would never feel for anyone the way I felt for Nina. My heart was hers! I could have spent the day with Nina, but she ended it too quickly. When we parted our eyes held the promise of a future for each other. I knew I had found my heart's mate and she hers.

"Wow!" Merritt said releasing a breath. "Wow!"

"I know. God, that first kiss is always the most amazing." Soren declared. "Is it wrong that I am turned on by that?"

Merritt smirked. "I don't think so." She shifted uncomfortably on the couch, her jeans rubbing on her already sensitive clit and threatening to push it into overdrive. The whole time she'd been reading, it wasn't Sam and Nina she pictured, it was Soren…kissing her. Which in and of itself was a very awkward predicament, given that she'd put a limit on how far the relationship would go and now her heart was asking for more. She tugged her jeans, trying to pull them away from her body. "It got to me too."

"God help me if Sam writes about their first time together." Soren winked. "It'll take more than a glass of wine to get me through that." She didn't need to say that anything more than what she'd just read would require a release, even if it meant putting that in her own hands…literally.

The vision of Soren stroking herself to an orgasm hit Merritt in the stomach and a surge of heat shot down her body and pooled in her already aroused center, wreaking havoc on her good intentions. She clenched her fists tightly, willing the image of Soren's naked, aroused body out of her mind. She rested her head against the back of the couch and stared at the ceiling, her breath coming in short, ragged bursts.

Soren noticed the flush of red in her face and knew her comment had hit home. She was willing to wait, but she'd be damned if she wasn't going to make it hard on Merritt. *Take that Merritt. That's how I feel every time I'm around you.* She had to smother a laugh. "So to what do I owe the pleasure of this visit?"

"I owe you for Saturday." Merritt answered quietly. "Given the turn to serious that our conversation took, I figured I owed you something fun and lighthearted to make up for it. And no talk about exes."

"You really don't," Soren answered coyly, "but far be it from me to turn down *something fun* with you. What'd you have in mind?"

"Dinner. But before that, I have a little surprise for you."

151

"Does it involve you and me naked?"

Merritt nearly choked. "Ahh, ahh, I mean…"

"Merritt." Soren rested her hand on Merritt's arm lightly. "I'm teasing. Dinner and a surprise is good. But…if naked were to happen, I'm totally open to that too."

Merritt caught her wink and laughed softly. "Duly noted. So you up for another adventure?"

Normally, the answer was no, but something about the way Merritt had asked made Soren realize she would say yes to just about anything. "Of course. Do I need to bring anything?"

"Just yourself. You may want to bring a jacket. It's supposed to actually cool down tonight…and we're walking."

Soren realized Merritt had worn tennis shoes and figured she'd grab hers and swap out her shorts for a pair of jeans. "Wait right here, I'm going to run upstairs and change…unless you want to change with me." Soren said suggestively then disappeared upstairs leaving Merritt to think about her offer.

For the second time in less than five minutes, Merritt pictured Soren naked in front of her and she knew if she didn't watch herself, her control was going to go right out the window. She stood up and raised her eyes to the ceiling. "This is your fault Sam." She was still trying to figure out whether or not she'd heard a mischievous chuckle at that when Soren came back downstairs. She'd switched her tee—shirt for a long—sleeve shirt that stopped just above the waistband of her jeans. The tight knit material hugged every curve of her body, adding to Merritt's already turned on state. She ached to rub her lips along the bare, tanned skin of Soren's flat stomach. She almost managed to pull her eyes away when they dropped to the spot between her legs. She felt her stomach turn inside out before she was finally able to wrench her eyes away, meeting Soren's very amused blue ones. Two more seconds inside with Soren and she was going to ignore every self—imposed line and ravish her with her lips. She smiled shyly. "Shall we?"

Soren followed Merritt to the front door, all the while admiring the seductive sway of her sexy backside. She smiled to herself. Merritt could tell her that she wasn't interested in a romantic relationship all she wanted, but her eyes didn't lie. No, they spoke volumes and left Soren silently praying that one day Merritt would follow her heart.

Chapter Fourteen

Soren read the sign twice before she spoke. "A ghost tour?"

"Yep." Merritt winked. "In honor of Sam and your newfound interest in spirits, I thought this would be right up your alley. Besides, it will give you a chance to see some really neat architecture."

"History I like, but if something jumps out and scares me, I can't promise I won't throw myself around you and hold on for dear life." Soren warned.

Merritt smiled mischievously. "I wouldn't expect anything less."

"You know if I didn't know you any better, I might think you chose this just so I would throw myself at you."

"Me?" Merritt asked innocently. "Now would I really do something like that?"

Soren narrowed her eyes. "Oh no, not sweet little innocent you."

Merritt winked mischievously. "Look at all the kids here. Do you honestly think their parents would bring them on a scary ghost tour?" She laughed when Soren rolled her eyes.

They stepped inside, registered and stepped back outside to wait. They had ten minutes to kill before the tour started. They fell back into the same easy conversation that they'd had started on their walk.

"So you messed around with the guitar as a kid…what got you into writing?" Merritt asked.

Soren smiled sheepishly. "Ex—girlfriend. Jordan, Brett and I had our own garage band in high school, but we didn't do much more than cover songs and after we all left for college, the band was a thing of the past...at least for them. I still played in college and my roommate's best friend, who was trying to make it big in the Nashville scene, was looking for a guitarist. I wasn't the best, but I had figured out along the way that I had a knack for writing. That and we started sleeping together, which sort of meant I was a shoe—in. We formed a country band our sophomore year with a couple of guys she knew. We never made it past some of the seedier dives downtown. After college, she and I broke up. Last I heard she had met a lawyer and was living the good life."

"So how was she responsible for getting you in this career?" Merritt nodded at another couple who had joined them outside for the tour. "Evening."

Soren greeted them then turned her attention back to Merritt. "Funny thing. Someone contacted her right out of school, liked our songs and wanted to know if she had written them…that they might be interested in buying some of them. She told them that aside from some *creative input*, she didn't have a whole lot to do with them other than singing. She gave them my contact info and the rest as they say is history."

"That's cool. So aside from a couple of years playing in bad bars, you made it into the business pretty easily…didn't go to the school of hard knocks huh?" Merritt teased.

"Well my dad didn't retire and leave me the business." Soren smirked wickedly. "If that's what you mean by school of hard knocks."

"Hey I bought the business from him fair and square." Merritt said with mock offense. "And I'll have you know, it wasn't without its share of knocks. That's a tough job."

155

"Aww poor baby. Did you have lots of ouchies?" Soren teased then smiled lasciviously. "You know what cures those don't you?"

"No...what?" Merritt's eyes were wide with feigned innocence. She pulled her sleeve up and showed a blackish—blue bruise to Soren. "Cause I've got one."

Soren stepped in front of Merritt, her back shielding them from the other couple. "I'm so glad you asked." She licked her lips and her gaze dropped to Merritt's mouth, the look sending shivers down Merritt's spine. She slid her hand around Merritt's arm, her thumb caressing the skin around the bruise gently. She took a small step closer, and she sensed Merritt's breathing quicken. She tilted her head slightly and narrowed the gap between them.

Merritt's breath caught in her chest. She could almost feel Soren's lips against hers and it ignited a fire deep in her body. She felt her knees tremble and she put her other hand on Soren's waist to steady herself. "No." She uttered a single whisper, but she wasn't sure if she meant no don't kiss me or no, don't make me wait any longer. Her head was swimming from the breath she had been holding. Everything around them disappeared until only the vision of Soren remained in front of her, her body aching to be touched.

Soren narrowed the distance between them, her eyes dark and hungry. She held them there, suspended in time, both so close to something that was better left unknown. She knew once they'd had a taste, they would be addicted. She held Merritt's gaze. "I'm sorry." She whispered and leaned closer. She registered the brief flash of fear before she lifted Merritt's arm to her lips and silently kissed away the pain.

Somehow new voices broke through the haze and Soren reluctantly broke the contact, gently dropping Merritt's arm at her side, both of them acknowledging the loneliness that filled them as they stepped away from each other.

When the tour started, they listened as the tour guides dressed in period garb began telling historical details about their starting point, John Reynolds Square. On the walk to the next stop of the tour, they fell in step at the back of the group. Despite the fact that they were on a ghost tour, the ambiance of Savannah at night was quite romantic. They walked along under the Spanish Moss hanging from the oak trees, listening to the sounds of summer all around them, half—listening to the guides in front of them. Their hands brushed together and neither one attempted to open the distance between them.

"So how's the writing coming along? I hope we haven't made it too hard with all the noise."

Soren smiled wryly. "You know it comes in waves. I've got three songs totally done and half as many more that are notes on a napkin, lines jotted here and there. I was in the park reading the other day, and my new Radclyffe book got some additional pages added to the story. I think the most difficult part is not being in my studio. Can't block out all the distractions and the acoustics in the house are, well not the greatest. So I guess that's the long answer to say it's quite slow right now."

"You want to bounce anything off me?" Merritt asked hopefully. "I have pretty good taste in music."

"No way!" Soren laughed nervously then apologized quickly at the look of hurt that flashed in Merritt's eyes. "I'm sorry, it's not that I don't appreciate the offer, it's just that…well I don't really let anyone hear it before I send it to my agent. That way I keep the criticism down to one source. Works better for my self esteem."

Merritt shrugged. "Well if you change your mind, I can flatter you shamelessly."

"I'll remember that. You know?"

"You know what?" Merritt asked suspiciously hearing the mischievous tone in Soren's voice.

"There is another way I would give in and let you listen." Soren said suggestively.

Merritt knew exactly what she was suggesting and it sent her body into overdrive. She swallowed hard, her stomach flip—flopping like crazy. She had to acknowledge the painful ache between her legs, her sensitive center was throbbing and she thought she might orgasm just thinking about the two of them together. For the first time, she thought maybe they could just have a physical relationship, no emotions involved. They were adults and both could definitely use a release. Just as quickly, she accepted that they were already beyond that point. No, falling for Soren hadn't been a problem, letting herself do something about it, that was an entirely different thing. She tried to steer her mind away from what Soren had offered and spoke lightheartedly. "Buy the CD?."

Soren laughed softly. "Nah, I'll give you a copy…just 'cause I like you so much." She winked as they caught up to the group who had stopped in front of the next house. They listened to the brief explanation of the Hampton Lillibridge House and Soren glared at Merritt. "An exorcism? I thought you said this tour wasn't scary."

Merritt held her palms up innocently. "Search me. It was supposed to be the non—scary type."

"You're gonna pay for this one." Soren warned with a smile. She followed everyone inside, grabbing Merritt's hand at the door. She felt Merritt's fingers curve around hers and warm comfort calmed her body.

"This house was built by an architect from Rhode Island in 1796 and one of the few to survive the great fire in 1820." The guide recited knowingly. "The house itself has a rather sordid history including a long—believed tradition that a sailor hung himself here when the home was still being used as a boarding house. There have been rumors of unexplained noises and even the sound of furniture being thrown around. Listen closely and you may even hear the sounds of laughter and a party from yesteryear." She said in a creepy whisper.

She stopped at a large fireplace in the living room. "In 1963, Jim Williams purchased the home and moved it from Reynolds Square to its current location. Strangely enough, one of the workers was killed when the home next door collapsed on top of him."

The male guide continued somberly. "Williams' crew reported feeling an unseen presence and one was so convinced that something was trying to throw him down this thirty foot fireplace shaft that he threw himself to the ground. When the rest of the crew finally found him, he'd been lying prone for hours, fighting the force." He walked away from the fireplace towards the stairs. "Jim Williams had to have a priest perform an exorcism in order to get the crew to stay on. Rumor however indicates that it wasn't successful." He started to walk up the dark stairway.

Soren's hand, that had gripped Merritt's so tightly her nails started to dig in, gripped even tighter. "I have to get out of here. I'm not sure if it's just me and the power of suggestion, but I'm a whole lot creeped out."

Merritt pulled her towards the front door as the guide led the rest of the group upstairs explaining the different ghosts that people had witnessed. They stopped on the sidewalk outside and Soren took a deep breath. "Sorry. That was all just a bit too much for me. That wasn't at all like the feeling I get with Sam. I, how do I explain it? It was different, darker. I didn't like that feeling at all." Soren confessed.

Merritt's thumb absentmindedly caressed Soren's palm, trying to calm her. "I'm sorry Soren. I didn't realize it would be so out there. I just thought with Sam and everything we could have some fun." She squeezed Soren's hand. "Maybe this was a bad idea. You wanna call it a night?"

"No, I'm just being a baby." Soren chastised herself, even going so far as to pull her hand away. "Besides I want to see the Low house. Especially since that was Nina's cousin."

"You sure?" Merritt searched Soren's face and saw her resolve. "It could be that you are more sensitive to this sort of thing. Your sixth sense is more highly developed."

Soren laughed wryly. "I'm going to go with no. I wouldn't say it was more intuitive at all. Before this, I don't think I had a sixth sense." She snorted. "If I did, there are quite a few things and people I would have avoided in the past."

"Don't I know it?" Merritt agreed. "Sometimes I think I was born on a Friday and it *was* yesterday."

"Yeah, Mr. Obvious, here's your sign." Soren laughed, obviously amused with herself. She leaned into Merritt and lowered her voice. "Kind of like you keep missing the fact that we should be together."

Merritt was saved from answering when the rest of the tour joined them outside and she let out a relieved sigh. She could have said she hadn't missed that fact but it would only lead to her having to explain again why she'd made the choice not to hook up with Soren. There were two reasons why she couldn't do that. First, she promised a light—hearted evening and second, her steadfast resolve was dangerously close to breaking. Talking about it only served to make it more difficult to remain in control. Instead, she caught up with Soren and attempted to pay attention.

The next stop was The Pirate's House. "Ahoy matey's! Welcome to the Pirate's House." One of the tour guides bellowed in a very convincing pirate's growl, bringing a round of laughter from the group. "Keep yur wits about ye, or be forced to walk the plank by the ghosts that frequent this haunt." He smiled when they all groaned at his pun.

"I should point out that the Pirate's House would be more aptly named the Privateers' House since when it was originally built in 1753, pirates had already been killed or scared off by the British Navy. The people that were actually sailing these waters were British and French sailors, or privateers as they were called, who had a commission from the British Government to pillage any ships they came across and give a portion to the King." He led them inside the house.

"Hey, did you hear the one about the sergeant who slept with a woman who had gonorrhea?" Soren whispered. "He figured he would be okay because it only affected the privates."

Merritt groaned loudly.

"Know what a buccaneer calls his package?" Soren asked quietly. "His privateers."

"Oh my god. They just keep getting worse." Merritt rolled her eyes. "Got anymore you need to get out?"

"Nah, I'm good." Soren smirked. "Oh wait, maybe one more. Did ya hear about the sergeant that was yelling at one of his privates?" She laughed when Merritt groaned again. "He told him to open up his privateers and listen? Get it? Privateers? Private ears?"

"Oh my God. I think I just threw up a little in my mouth." She tossed her head forward towards the tour guides. "I'm going to just go stand next to them for the rest of the tour."

Soren grabbed her elbow and hauled her back. "Uh-uh. Ghosts. Remember I may or may not be afraid of them and I need someone to throw myself around in case I am."

Merritt pointed discreetly at a man standing in front of Soren who was sweating profusely and every couple of seconds muttered something to himself. She leaned over and whispered in her ear. "He looks like a safe bet. Shit, he's probably already scared away the ghosts."

Soren smothered a snicker. "Yeah, and I'll get a bath while I'm at it. No way Tanner. You're mine." She gripped her arm and pulled her body flush against hers and smiled at the swift intake of breath. She knew the contact was affecting Merritt just as much as it was her. "You got me into this and you are getting me out. You aren't pawning me off on some guy."

They stopped in what was obviously the dining room of the current Pirate's House restaurant. "This house was originally used as a tavern and an inn, not only by the 'pirates' but by the less stellar citizens of Savannah. It had such a reputation for its unsavory characters that Robert Louis Stevenson based some of the events in *Treasure Island* on things that happened here."

"Think we'll get to see Long John Silver?" Soren asked referring to a character in the book.

"Probably not." Merritt shook her head. "Savannah's not real keen on chain restaurants."

"Oh real funny."

"Yeah, I know." Merritt smirked. "You're not the only one with bad jokes."

"Apparently not." Soren pulled on Merritt's arm. "Let's go."

They followed the group downstairs and listened as their guides explained that each one of the floors had their own apparitions. People reported seeing men dressed as sailors, hearing loud noises upstairs and even spotting a surly—looking man they referred to as Captain Flint.

They stopped in front of a large hole in the basement wall that had been bricked over. Soren leaned towards Merritt. "That thing is huge. What…did they sail into the restaurant?"

"This is actually a tunnel that leads to the water. When the privateers were here trying to recruit new members, they would come to the tavern and tout the benefits of sailing with them. If the men didn't join willingly, they would get them drunk, bop them on the head then drag them to their ships through the tunnel. For most men, that was the last time they saw their families."

"Holy cow!" Merritt exclaimed. "Kind of gives new meaning to getting hammered and not being able to find your way home."

"No kidding." Soren agreed. "And so far, none of these ghosts are nice like Sam.

"Just wait. I think you are in for a real treat at the Low House." Merritt winked. "Might even give Sam and Nina a run for their money."

Chapter Fifteen

"We'll have a large magical mystery tour." Merritt handed their menus back to the waitress and smiled at Soren. "Jalapenos okay? I thought that pizza would be fitting as an end to our night of adventure."

Soren nodded her head up and down. The pie made with pesto, mushrooms, spinach, feta and jalapenos at the Mellow Mushroom did indeed sound delicious. "Heck yeah. I like my pizza like I like my women. The hotter the better."

"And with a bite!" Merritt added thinking of the initial shock of heat the jalapenos provided.

"Well of course. If they bite, all the better." Soren winked mischievously. "Just not hard."

Soren did little to mask the look of raw hunger in her eyes when she said that and Merritt's body reacted immediately. She pictured them lying naked together, her teeth gently tugging Soren's nipple and she felt her clit tighten and wet tingling between her legs. She drained her coke in lieu of a cold shower, desperately trying to cool her racing hormones. She glanced at Soren over the top of her cup and swore she was smirking.

"Okay, so you like biting." Soren teased. "What else do you like? What's your type?"

Merritt crunched on a piece of ice half considering the question and half getting rid of some pent—up frustration. "Man, I don't know that I necessarily have a type. She has to be smart, good sense of humor, we have to be able to get along outside of the bedroom, family has to be important. It would be nice if we shared some of the same hobbies. I need someone that challenges me to be better and holds me accountable for it. She's not afraid to put me in my place if need be. I want someone that makes me feel insanely turned on one minute and totally safe and loved the next. I've never really had a preference as far as hair or eyes, that sort of thing. That about covers it. What about you?"

"Boy, you don't ask for much, do ya? You know we get along outside the bedroom…really well. I'm guessing in the bed or couch or wherever, we'd be great." Soren laughed when Merritt gave her the evil eye. "Fine. I *love* brunettes! Can't help it, I've just always been that way." She could tell that got Merritt's blood surging again and that drove Soren even more crazy. "Second thing I notice is the smile. I have this thing with a person's mouth."

"Oh I'm sure you do." Merritt smirked. "What lesbian doesn't?"

Soren rolled her eyes and took a drink of her coke. "I meant her smile. I usually wait till the third or fourth date before I start thinking about what her tongue can do. The next thing I notice is the eyes. A person can say all they want, but the eyes are where the truth comes out. Take yours for example. You tell me that you don't want to start anything, but when you look at me I know what you really want to do is rip my clothes off."

Merritt choked on her drink and nearly spit it out all over the table. When she finally regained her composure, she sent Soren an evil smile. "What are my eyes telling you right now?"

Soren looked her square in the eyes, holding them for several beats before smiling. "That you want to spank me."

Merritt was saved from replying by the waitress dropping off their pie. She thanked her then dished out healthy slices for the two of them. She took a huge bite and started waving her hand in front of her mouth. "Ow, shit! That's hot."

"What did you think she meant when she said it's hot?" Soren laughed.

Merritt rolled her eyes. "Well I figured hot, not burn the first three layers off the roof of my mouth. I seriously don't think I can feel my tongue. That's gonna hurt later."

"Well maybe I can come up with something to take your mind off the pain." Soren teased. "You know the body releases natural pain killing hormones during an orgasm."

For the second time in ten minutes, Merritt choked on her drink. Only this time she decided to fight back. She reached across the table and entwined her fingers with Soren's, her thumb lightly caressing her palm. She leaned forward, her eyes capturing Soren's and paralyzing her. "Maybe we should try that."

Soren inhaled, desire pooling in her stomach. She swallowed hard trying to breathe, the air between them was so charged it took her breath away. Merritt's eyes held her face and she swore she could feel Merritt's lips caressing hers. God help her, she had to look away before she did something insane and kissed her right there.

Merritt felt her pulse beating erratically, and she wanted to ignore the warnings that bounced loudly around her head. She saw Soren's eyes cloud over and look away for a beat and mercifully the spell was broken. But she wondered what would happen to break it the next time or the time after that? When she'd lost the will to fight against her destiny.

"So brunette with a great smile and tell all eyes? Anything else?" Merritt inquired with forced nonchalance.

Soren was still breathing raggedly and she took several deep breaths before she continued. "Mostly the same stuff as you. I want someone who inspires me. I want a moment with her that I can put in a song. When I'm with her, I want to hear the notes that would be our life. It's cheesy I know." Soren smiled wryly. "I want someone that I can spend the rest of my life with and that's into our relationship as much as me. She's someone that even though I may be having the worst day of my life, she can smile at me, or hug me, or I can just think about her and I know that everything will be okay. Someone who gets me despite all my quirky shit and loves me anyway. Definitely someone who is a good listener and knows what I want, even if I can't find the right words to tell her. And of course, I need someone that sends my hormones into overdrive even if I'm not in the mood to act on them."

"You forgot to say someone who can lasso the moon." Merritt teased.

Soren winked. "Maybe not actually lasso the moon, but at least be willing to try it if I asked her to." She eyed the pizza, trying to decide if she had the room to stuff down one more piece. She caught Merritt staring at her, eyes twinkling and she shrugged her shoulders as if to say can you blame me?

Before she could decide, Merritt read her mind and shoveled another piece on both their plates. "Eat. I walked our asses all over Savannah tonight. Besides you could use the calories."

"What?" Soren feigned offense. "You calling me skinny?"

"Nah. Just a little underfed maybe."

"Hey I resemble that remark." Soren said, bit off a huge bite and talked around it. "I'm trying to fatten back up. Give you a little more to hold on to."

Merritt couldn't make heads or tails out of what Soren was saying so she just laughed and attacked her own pizza.

"Tell me about your first crush." Soren said out of the blue when she finished her slice.

Merritt finished chewing then swiped a napkin over her face. "Wow...random. Let's see, my first crush." She leaned back in her chair and stared at the ceiling. "That would be Ms. Graham, my third grade teacher. She was the one that helped diagnose my dyslexia."

"You're dyslexic?" Soren asked puzzled. "I would never have guessed that."

"Yep." Merritt smiled. "Of course, she worked really hard with me even after I moved on past third grade to overcome it. Today you wouldn't know if I didn't tell you. I guess she was my hero after that and she was kind of hot. I liked her for a long time after that."

"So maybe if I dress up like Super Girl, you might get a crush on me?" Soren teased.

"Short skirt and red leather boots. I think that would work. What about you?"

"Mmm, Wendy Manning. French class my junior year. So hot and so straight." Soren said quickly and Merritt had to stifle a groan. "Actually you kind of remind me of her, except you're not straight." She jumped when she heard her phone ring.

She wiped her hands quickly and pulled the phone out of her pocket, catching it on the last ring. "'Ello." She said casually.

"Soren, hey it's Jordan." Her voice sounded hurried and Soren tensed.

"Jordan, what's up? Is everything okay? Is it Ali?" Soren was concerned and when she looked up, Merritt could see the concern in her eyes. She sat up quickly, suddenly alert, hoping everything was okay.

"Yeah, yeah, everything's fine. Ali's having some contractions and her doctor is a little concerned with them coming so early." Jordan paused and listened to someone talking in the background. *"Anyway, she's having us go see the on—call doctor just in case. I just wanted to give you a head's up."*

Soren's face broke into a slightly relieved smile, but her nerves were still on edge. "Okay, well call me back and let me know what's up. I can get a late flight out."

168

"No, don't do that." Jordan said quickly. *"You won't really be able to do much right now anyway. We'll need more help after she has the baby anyway."*

"True." Soren agreed. "But call me if this is for real. I want to be there as soon after as possible."

"I will." Jordan promised. *"I'm pretty sure this is just a false emergency, but keep your phone close just in case."*

Soren said she would then said goodbye. When she looked back at Merritt, her eyes were raised questioningly. "That was Jordan. Ali's having contractions."

"They're a bit early, aren't they?" Merritt asked. "She's not due for another couple of weeks."

"According to the doctor, but babies have a mind of their own." Soren laughed. "I guess her doctor must be a little concerned. She's having them see the on—call doctor just in case."

"Well then we need to get you home and packed…just in case." Merritt signaled for the waitress and paid their bill.

"Thanks for dinner." Soren said as they walked back to her house. "And for the adventure. I had a lot of fun tonight."

"You're welcome. Somehow I think we could both use some fun in our lives."

Soren was just about to respond when a loud clap of thunder rumbled across the night sky, followed by several flashes of lightning. "It's not supposed to rain tonight is it?"

"Small chance. I think they were saying there's a chance of pop—up thunderstorms developing this evening, but they are supposed to be scattered."

Another flash of lightning and thunder hit around them. "It sounds like it's just about ready to pop up right on top of us. How far to my house?" Soren asked not knowing the city well enough yet to judge their whereabouts and the darkness making it impossible to recognize any familiar landmarks.

Merritt checked the street sign as they crossed the road. "Three blocks."

Thunder rumbled loudly above them. "Well we are running the last three blocks then." She broke into a jog and yelled at Merritt. "Come on!"

They made it two blocks when the heavens opened up in a torrential downpour. Within seconds, they were both soaked. They sprinted the last block and dashed up the steps onto the porch, both of them gasping for air.

"God, what a fitting end to our night." Merritt said sarcastically.

"And you mean God literally." Soren laughed. "The timing couldn't have been any worse."

Merritt agreed. "We only needed two more minutes…that's all. Two." She shivered. "And now I'm freezing."

"You have to come inside and dry off. I'll give you some dry clothes." She unlocked the door. "They'll be a little short but at least they'll be dry."

"I think I'll be okay if I can just get a towel." She reached up and gathered her wet hair in her hands and twisted it behind her head.

Soren swallowed hard. Merritt's hands over her head pushed her breasts out and her nipples were hard against her white shirt. It was enough to bring all her desire for Merritt rushing back. Her knees almost crumbled at the intensity of her emotions. She ached to take Merritt's naked breast into her mouth and tease it till it was even harder.

Merritt made the mistake of looking at Soren right then. There was no mistaking what she wanted and the look of raw desire sent shudders through her body. It would be so easy to just let go and give in to what they both wanted. She stepped away, putting necessary space between them and crossed her arms over her chest. "Actually, I'm good. I'll just turn on the heater in the truck." She had to get out of there. The house, the two of them alone with no one there to keep them in line, it was all too intimate for her. She felt overwhelmed with desire.

170

"That's insane." Soren shook her head. "I don't want you to catch a cold."

Merritt tried to say no, but Soren grabbed her hand and pulled her towards the steps. In the brief millisecond before she followed her up the stairs, Merritt's mind flashed to the bedroom. The two of them standing a hair breadth apart, naked bodies longing to join, Soren's naked body writhing beneath her, her body poised waiting for Merritt to drive her over the edge. Merritt stopped in mid stride, gasping for air.

Soren turned around, her questioning eyes searching Merritt's. She saw lust mingled with apology and her heart ached for her.

Merritt shook her head. "I can't."

She didn't have to say what, Soren knew. She couldn't be alone with her and keep her promise. As much as she hated it, she had to respect her decision. The only way she would ever have Merritt is if she came to her willingly. She stepped down to the bottom step, at eye level with Merritt and held her hand, keeping her from backing away. "I know." She held Merritt's eyes and smiled softly.

"I'm sorry."

"Don't be. I understand." Soren consoled her. She ached to touch her, even briefly knowing that tonight might be the last time she saw her before she returned to Nashville. She needed to feel Merritt's skin against hers and for now she would settle for a small taste. She rubbed her knuckles lightly over Merritt's cheek, loving the feeling of her skin. "Please." She asked in an aching breath.

Merritt couldn't move, she could only nod, her skin on fire where Soren's knuckles rested, the chill from the rain gone completely. The look in her eyes matching the intensity in Soren's and the room vibrated around them. She felt Soren cup her cheek in her palm and she leaned into her, her skin on fire.

Soren caressed her thumb over Merritt's cheek then ran it lightly over her lips sending a new wave of desire through her body. She increased the pressure and Merritt put her hand over Soren's holding it against her face. Their eyes met again and Merritt felt the blood pool between her legs. Soren's thumb was wreaking havoc on her body as though it were her lips instead. Soren pulled Merritt towards her, brushing her cheek against hers, reveling in the feel of her soft skin. She closed her eyes and held her cheek there for a brief moment before grazing her cheek along Merritt's chin. She felt her heart catch and felt Merritt's ragged breathing on her skin. She only intended to touch her briefly, but the intensity stole her self—control. She caressed Merritt's cheek with her own and she felt her lips brush against Merritt's.

When she would have pulled away, Merritt started to move against her, amazed at how intimate the brief caresses had become. Her heartbeat pounded in her ears and she trembled against Soren. She'd never had an orgasm without her clit being stimulated, but Soren's cheek against hers was enough to almost make her come. God, just the briefest touch had her so turned on she could hardly see straight. She realized how easy it would be to capture Soren's mouth against hers and get lost in her. "Oh God. What are you doing to me?"

Soren heard the ache in Merritt's ragged voice and her mind reeled. She knew it would be so easy to pull Merritt against her and take what her body had craved since the moment she met her. She also knew it would hurt them both too much. She stilled her cheek against Merritt's and whispered in her ear. "I want you so bad...but I'll wait." She pulled away slowly, missing the warmth immediately.

Merritt opened her mouth but Soren silenced her with her finger. "No apologies. It's just the end of a chapter...not our story." She tried to keep her voice from shaking.

Merritt shook her head. "I need you to know that just because I'm afraid to show you, it doesn't mean that I don't feel it."

Soren squeezed her hand. "It's okay Merritt." She stepped off the stair and walked her to the door. "We're right where we need to be."

Merritt opened the door slowly, her eyes studying Soren. She didn't miss the look of hurt in her eyes and it broke her heart. She longed to pull her into her arms and kiss away the pain.

"We can talk about it when I get back from Nashville."

Merritt winced, already missing her. "I'm really am sorry." She said quietly then disappeared out the door.

Chapter Sixteen

Merritt slammed the truck door and ran her fingers through her hair, her body a tense ball of desire. Had she really just walked out of Soren's house after what happened between them? Her clit was throbbing painfully and she knew any efforts to assuage the ache would only leave her empty and wanting more. With shaking hands, she tried to insert the key into the ignition. "Fuck!" She exclaimed as she bent over to pick them up. Somehow she managed to get the truck started and drive away, her body still humming from the feelings she had for Soren. "Shit! Shit! Shit!"

Soren stripped her wet clothes off and pulled a robe tightly around her. She turned the water on in the shower, waiting for it to warm up. Parts of her needed a cold shower, but the chill from being soaked had returned and she opted on a hot one instead. She finally saw steam and was taking her robe off when she heard the doorbell. She thought about not answering and just slipping into the shower and letting the warm water envelope her and hopefully wash away the painful ache between her legs.

She was stepping into the shower when the bell rang again. "Damn it." She pulled her robe back on and tip--toed back downstairs, leaving the lights off. If it was someone she didn't know, she would just ignore them and go back to her shower.

She peaked out the small window and furrowed her brows. She opened the door slowly. "Merritt?"

Merritt pushed the door open, her hungry eyes meeting Soren's confused ones. She captured her face in her hands and pulled her close, their lips touching for the first time igniting a fiery passion that raced through their bodies.

Soren's lips parted and Merritt's tongue touched hers and a new wave of wetness flooded her. Her hands found Merritt's arms and she clung desperately to her, afraid that she would disappear as quickly as she had come. Merritt circled her arm around Soren's back and held her flush against her body, her thigh pressing against Soren's already sensitive clit and eliciting a moan from deep within her.

Merritt's hand left Soren's face and her thumb caressed the hollow spot at the base of her neck. She could feel Soren's pulse racing wildly, matching her own that was beating like a hammer. Her tongue plunged into Soren's inviting mouth and they tangled together wildly. Soren felt her knees tremble with desire and before she lost herself completely, she wrestled her mouth from Merritt's and searched her eyes, asking the question she couldn't voice.

Merritt met her gaze and barely nodded her head. She pulled Soren against her and answered, her voice a strangled whisper against Soren's ear. "I don't want to talk, I don't even want to think, I just want to touch you."

Soren laced her arms behind Merritt's back and raised up on her tip—toes. She felt a smile tugging at the corners of her mouth. She told her self to ignore the warning bells going off in her head. She would deal with the ramifications tomorrow…even if it meant finding out this wasn't going any further than tonight. She pulled Merritt's lower lip between hers and sucked gently, eliciting a growl of desire. She stopped when she felt Merritt's tongue seeking her own hungrily. Pulling away, she shut the door and turned toward the steps. "I want to shower with you."

Merritt felt electricity shoot down her spine and tie her stomach in knots. Wetness flooded her. If she had been weak before, the mere thought of their wet, naked bodies gliding

175

together in a hot shower was enough to almost knock her legs out from under her. She closed her eyes, mentally checking herself so that she could make it up the steps and not take Soren right here on the floor. She enveloped Soren's hand and she led them both upstairs, knowing that they'd reached the point where neither of them could turn around and she was damn sure neither one of them wanted to.

Soren followed her into the bathroom. Her stomach jumped when Merritt turned to face her, her green eyes almost obsidian with molten desire. Their lips met again and the heat they felt was not from the steam around them. Soren ran her palm over Merritt's abdomen and felt her muscles jump beneath her touch. She slid her palm higher along the small, perfect curve of Merritt's breast. The only thing between her and Merritt's soft skin was thin material. She moved her palm over Merritt's chest, delighting at the feel of her nipples hardened beneath her hand. She ran the pad of her thumb over Merritt's nipple and felt it grow even harder.

Merritt's body arched into her and her arm circled around Soren's waist, pulling her flush against her body. She was amazed at how well Soren's body molded into hers and wondered what her naked body would feel like pressed tightly against hers. Her other arm gently tugged the tie of her robe and she slipped her hand inside, feeling Soren's soft skin. Her hand ran along the soft skin at her side and her fingertips barely brushed the sensitive skin beneath her breast, sending shivers up and down Soren's spine.

When blind caresses would no longer sate their desire, Soren pulled away and her fingers found the buttons of Merritt's shirt. Her eyes met Merritt's and the look she saw there melted any restraint she had left. She undid each button, and slowly pulled the shirt open revealing small, perfect breasts. She smiled wickedly then leaned forward and caught Merritt's nipple between her lips. She tugged it gently feeling it grow inside her mouth. She swirled her tongue around it then nipped it between her teeth, pulling it towards her eliciting a groan of pleasure. She smiled around it, teasing her mercilessly.

Merritt gripped the towel bar for support. She was lost and felt a primal urge rising deep within her. She gently pushed Soren away from her, desperation evident in her features. "You'll make me come if you don't stop."

Soren smiled suggestively. "Then I'll stop. I want to make you come in my mouth the first time." She leaned her head against Merritt's shoulder. "God, I can't wait to taste you."

"Holy fuck!" Merritt exclaimed. She tugged her shirt off and undid her jeans, struggling to tug the wet material over her hips.

Soren felt desire sock her in the gut when she saw that Merritt was not wearing any panties. Her breath came in heavy, ragged gasps and her eyes were glued to the patch of dark hair that already glistened with desire. An overwhelming urge to touch her ignited a fire that tore through her body. She closed the gap between them and felt Merritt's hot skin against hers. She let the robe fall to the floor and her lips sought Merritt's mouth. She kissed her fiercely and her hand found Merritt's hip. She rubbed against Merritt's body and felt Merritt's juices wet her thigh.

She went wild after that, like an animal after its first taste of the hunt. Her hand skimmed along Merritt's thigh and her fingers grazed the glistening hairs. She ran her hand along Merritt's lips, spreading the slick moisture with her fingers. She felt Merritt jump when she touched her sensitive clit. Merritt arched against her hand, the gentle pressure sending desire slicing through her core. She tugged at Soren's lip, biting her gently, her body aching for release.

When she thought she could take the teasing no more, Soren broke the kiss and brought her fingers to Merritt's lips. Merritt opened her mouth and Soren slid her finger inside. Merritt could taste herself on Soren and it made her clit quiver uncontrollably. Soren pulled her finger away slowly, teasing Merritt then she lowered herself to the floor in front of her.

Soren put her hands on Merritt's thighs, her thumb brushing lightly against her swollen lips. She pushed her back against the wall. Soren kissed the sensitive skin between her thighs and felt Merritt's legs shudder against her. She inhaled the sweet scent of desire and knew she would forever want the woman in front of her. She kissed the dark triangle then stroked her tongue along her slick wet folds. Soren was lost the moment she tasted Merritt. She knew she'd never tasted anything sweeter than this.

Merritt trembled, her palms against the wall steadying her. She felt Soren's tongue stroke her expertly and when her tongue found her clit, she felt her body tighten in anticipation. God, she wanted this, no she needed this. Soren felt her juices on her chin and she hungrily swallowed them, her tongue plunging inside Merritt's body, bringing her closer and closer to orgasm. She felt Merritt's thighs tighten against her and her hands found Soren's shoulders. Soren pulled Merritt's clit into her mouth and she sucked it, her tongue swirling circles around it.

Soren knew she was close. This time she would not prolong her pleasure. She would give Merritt what they both needed, a release. She stroked her deftly and felt her body starting to convulse against her. Merritt's hips bucked wildly against her, arching to meet her mouth. Soren quickened her pace. Merritt felt the waves of her orgasm build to an apex, paralyzing her body then sent her crashing over the other side. She threw her head back and screamed a raw, primal scream as ripples of pleasure assaulted her body like the boundless waves of the ocean.

Soren waited till the shudders subsided then kissed Merritt's sensitive skin which elicited a new round of shudders. Merritt pulled her up and kissed her gently. "It's too much. Just let me hold you."

Merritt wrapped her arms around Soren and held her flush against her while their heartbeats returned to normal. She finally pulled her head up and faced Soren who smiled timidly. "Thank you. I've…I've wanted to do that since the moment I met you."

Merritt winked and smiled wickedly. "Looks like I've got to play catch up then. Shall we start with that shower you promised me?"

Soren pulled the shower door opened and stuck her hand inside testing the water then stepped in quickly. Her heartbeat had slowed and her body was starting to feel a slight chill. Merritt stepped in beside her and pulled the door shut. She watched Soren stand under the stream of water, her hands pushing her hair back as warm water cascaded around her. Merritt felt desire clench her stomach. Soren's body was beautiful. Despite being slender, her breasts were round and full and Merritt longed to feel the weight of them in her palm. Her waist was narrow and her hips curved seductively into well--muscled legs.

Soren finally opened her eyes and caught Merritt on the upswing of her full body perusal. She reached out and pulled her close, switching positions and putting Merritt under the hot water. "Here your turn to warm up."

"Oh I'm plenty hot now." Merritt said lasciviously. She pulled Soren against her and they stood together letting the water wash over them. It only took Merritt a couple of minutes of Soren's breasts pressed firmly against hers to get completely worked up all over again. She tilted Soren's chin up, shielding her from the spray and kissed her softly. Her lips were soft and wet and Merritt caressed her mouth gently. Soren's lips parted and Merritt's tongue found hers in short teasing strokes.

Soren felt wetness flood her body that had nothing to do with the shower. Her hands cupped Merritt's bottom and pulled her hips against hers sending waves of desire crashing through her. Merritt broke the kiss and gently spun her around towards the wall behind her. "Let me wash you." Soren's only response was a murmur.

Merritt poured some shampoo on her hands and swirled it around in her palms before applying it to Soren's hair. She lathered it through and then her strong fingers began to massage Soren's scalp. Soren moaned. "God that feels sooo good. I could get spoiled by you." Merritt kissed the back of her neck gently and continued massaging her fingers through Soren's hair. Before it could go from sensual to relaxing, Merritt guided her back into the spray and let the water rinse over Soren.

"Now for the rest of you." She poured body wash onto a sponge and started with Soren's back. She moved down her body stopping at her bottom and then down the outside of her leg. She started back up the inside of her leg. She let the sponge caress the inside of Soren's thigh and smirked when she was rewarded with a low moan. She repeated the process on the other side then wrapped her arm around Soren and let the sponge glide over her shoulders and down the front of her chest. She ran it gently around Soren's nipples and could feel her nipples harden instantaneously.

Merritt was wreaking havoc on Soren's body and she pressed her hands against the wall trying to steady herself. She felt the sponge glide over her abdomen and tease the triangle of light hair before dipping lower. She felt her stomach clench and she involuntarily arched towards Merritt's hand.

"Feel good?" Merritt teased as she ran her hand over her aching clit. "God, you're so wet." She let the sponge drop from her hand and she put both arms around Soren, pressing her body tightly against her. Her hands found Soren's breasts and she rolled the sensitive nipples between her fingers. Her breasts jumped at the contact and her nipples ached.

Soren rubbed against her seductively then stilled when she felt Merritt's fingers found her hardened clit. She arched her head, turning it so she could find Merritt's lips. Her tongue plunged into Merritt's mouth and danced in rhythm with hers. Merritt's fingers slid into her slick folds and she slipped the tip of her fingers inside before immediately pulling away only to tease her clit before starting anew. Merritt kept bringing her close and pulling back, driving Soren closer and closer to the edge. She finally broke the kiss, her eyes beseeching Merritt. "Please."

Merritt pulled her other hand away from Soren's breast and cupped her bottom, squeezing it gently. She ran her fingers along the inside of her thigh, brushing the slick folds of her very aroused center, her left hand still stroking and teasing her clit. She could hear Soren's labored breathing. She inserted her fingers then pulled it back quickly only to return again. Soren could feel Merritt's fingers fill her and start a slow, rhythmic dance. She moved with her, matching Merritt's even strokes.

Merritt could feel Soren's body tensing and knew she was close to climaxing. She squeezed her clit, rolling it between her fingers then started making fast circles steadily increasing the pressure. Her fingers delved deeper inside Soren's body and she could feel the muscles contracting around her. She stroked harder and faster, their bodies matched stroke for stroke. Soren knew she was going to come soon and she felt alive. Every cell in her body was on fire and she felt like she was close to exploding. "Harder. God Merritt, fuck me harder."

She felt the strokes deepen and her muscles coiled to spasm. She gripped the wall and closed her eyes, poised on the edge. Merritt grunted and it was lost as Soren's body shook violently, waves of pleasure spilling through her body. Merritt stroked harder, her other hand still rubbing violent circles around Soren's pulsating clit and Soren's body soared again. Her body shuddered with spasms as the second orgasm hit her right behind the first. She bit her lip, trying to contain her emotions and when the intensity of Merritt's touch was too much she threw back her head and screamed. Merritt pulled her close and held her, the warm water washing away more than just the remains of their lovemaking.

Several moments later she jumped, the warm water suddenly replaced by cooler water that threatened to chill them both. By the time Merritt had reached around and turned the water off, Soren was already handing her a towel. She wiped her face and was reaching up to dry her hair when she felt Soren cup her breast and rub her thumb over her taut nipple. Her arms froze above her head.

"Looks like I've got to get you warmed up again." She kissed her lightly then stepped out of the shower to finish toweling off. Merritt watched her through the glass and she felt the chill start to dissipate. Soren turned around and caught her looking. She smiled at Merritt's feigned embarrassment. "Come on. I'll build you a fire."

Merritt dried off and followed her into the bedroom. She glanced around and finally looked at Soren, confusion in her eyes. "Wood?" She asked.

"Don't need it. One of the few perks of the house...an existing gas fireplace." Soren picked up a remote and clicked a button. A whooshing sound caught Merritt's attention and when she looked an inviting fire was already going in the fireplace. "Ahh the benefits of gas...much faster to set the mood."

Merritt winked mischievously. "Sweetheart, you set the mood the first time I laid eyes on you."

Soren's heart melted. She had felt drawn to Merritt the first time she'd met her but had never known the exact moment the feelings were returned. "I wondered." She answered quietly. She watched Merritt stride confidantly toward her. She had never seen a more beautiful woman in her life. Her toned, well--sculpted body was curved in all the right places and watching her now made her stop breathing. "God, you really are gorgeous."

A smile spread over Merritt's face. She cupped her palm against Soren's cheek. "I was just thinking the same about you. I could get lost in your eyes."

Soren searched her face. "I'd let you."

"I know." Merritt said quietly. She pulled Soren towards her and captured her mouth in a slow, sensuous kiss. The impatient fury of their desire had been momentarily sated by their lovemaking. Now they were free to explore each other's bodies as long as they wanted and Merritt intended to take her time.

Their hands roamed freely over each other's bodies, memorizing every curve and hollow and burning it indelibly into their minds. Merritt wasn't sure how much time had passed but when her hand slid between Soren's legs and felt the slick warmth, she let out a deep guttural moan. She slid her hands around Soren's buttocks and lifted her body, pulling her flush against her. Soren's legs wrapped around Merritt's hips and she ground against her stomach, covering Merritt with her juices.

Merritt felt the wet warmth and she felt fires igniting everywhere that Soren's passion had anointed her. She strode quickly to the bed and with one arm still wrapped tightly around Soren, she broke their kiss long enough to position a pillow at the edge of Soren's bed. She found the edge of the bed with her knees and steadied herself, their passion making her body tremble fiercely.

Gently, Merritt lowered Soren to the bed with her backside resting against the pillow. She braced herself over Soren, her thigh between Soren's leg pressing into her sex incessantly and her lips began an impatient sampling of her body. She dipped her tongue in Soren's ear then ran it over the soft angles of her jaw line, finally caressing the hollow at the base of her neck. She kissed the erratic pulse and Soren's body arched exposing the seductive curve of her neck. Merritt ran her tongue along it and Soren shivered impulsively, her body pulsing everywhere.

183

Soren clinched her legs around Merritt's thigh and ground into her trying to ease the tight ache in her clit. She needed to come soon or she thought she might die. Merritt sensed this and trailed kisses down her throat, lowering still to her full breasts. She captured Soren's nipple in her mouth and raked her tongue over it, her other hand pinching its twin to a hardened peak. She caught her nipple between her teeth and gently bit, pulling it towards her. Soren's body came off the bed trying to feel more. "Oh God Merritt, please. I need you now."

Merritt let out a low, animal chuckle. God, this need was empowering. It threatened to undo every last bit of restraint she had. Her hand slid down the curve of Soren's waist and over her narrow hips. Everywhere she touched lit fires on Soren's skin. Her breathing came in short, desperate gulps and she bit her lip, an overwhelming feeling like she could crawl out of her skin. "Please Merritt. I need you now."

Merritt willingly obliged. The need to touch and taste Soren replacing all other conscience thought. She slid her fingers over Soren's hardened clit and spread her moist lips. She slid her finger in and gasped at the hot wetness. "God, you're so wet."

"You do that to me." Soren said breathily. "Please baby, I need you inside me."

Merritt knelt down and pulled Soren's aroused center towards her, inhaling her scent. She was heady with control, her only thought pleasing Soren. She slid two fingers inside her and she felt Soren's heat envelope her. She plunged in slowly and Soren's hips began to move with her. Using her other hand, she spread Soren's outer lips, exposing her pulsating sex. Her tongue found Soren's naked clit and she raked over it gently, not wanting to bring Soren to climax too soon. The moment her tongue tasted Soren's arousal, her own body tightened with desire. She'd never come just from tasting someone before but now her body ached and hinted at the raw power of her impending orgasm.

Soren pushed her hips against Merritt needing to increase the pressure but Merritt pulled away. Her eyes sought Soren's, and the naked desire there sent shock waves through her body. "Merritt, I need to come so bad...please baby." Soren said through gritted teeth, her need causing every muscle in her body to tighten with desire.

Merritt kissed the sensitive skin around the small triangle of hair and along the curve of her inner thigh before glancing up again and shooting her a devastating smile. "Soon, sweetheart. Soon, I promise." The tip of her tongue found Soren's clit again and she worked slow circles around it before pulling it into her mouth and sucking her gently. She felt a new flood of wetness surround her and she pulled her fingers out then slowly inserted three fingers, plunging gently as Soren's muscles relaxed.

Soren massaged her own breasts, her fingers rubbing and pinching her nipples, sending waves of pleasure rippling through her body. She moaned softly, her body climbing higher and higher towards a zenith of pleasure. She felt Merritt pull her fingers away and she instinctively arched her hips, needing Merritt to fill her again. "Soren?"

Soren opened her eyes and met Merritt's intense gaze. "Can you take more?"

It took Soren a second to register what she meant and when she did, it took her no time at all to say yes. She had seen the unmasked desire smoldering in Merritt's eyes, but also she had seen love and trust to such depths that it seared her to her very core. "Please."

Merritt slowly eased four fingers inside her, waiting patiently as Soren's body opened to receive them. She sucked Soren's clit into her mouth and raking her tongue across it. New waves of wetness surrounded her fingers and she plunged them in deeper until she felt like she was at the center of Soren's soul. And when Soren's hips moved against her, she withdrew them only to plunge them in deeper.

Soren felt her muscles clench around Merritt. She had never taken that much before but the brief tingling of pain disappeared, replaced by a new longing, almost animal in its intensity. She moved against Merritt's mouth, her body arching and taking her fingers in deeper and deeper. She could feel the beginning waves of her orgasm as they started to build, stoked like the low, burning embers of a small fire. Each stroke of Merritt's tongue over her aching clit fueled the flames, threatening to fan them into a raging fire.

Merritt's fingers moved slowly not wanting to hurt Soren. She could feel Soren's muscles contracting around her and she knew she was close. She plunged in deeper, finding a sweet spot buried deep inside Soren and stroked it deftly, matching the expert strokes of her tongue on Soren's hardened clit, threatening to send her tumbling over the edge. Her own orgasm was so very close.

Soren needed more, wanted more. "Harder Merritt, fuck me harder."

It was all the encouragement Merritt needed. She felt her own wetness overflow its gates and pour down her body. She plunged her fingers in harder and deeper, meeting Soren's quick thrusts. She felt Soren's muscles clench around her fingers and her hips jerked off the bed against her mouth.

The orgasm ripped through Soren's body like a viscous tidal wave decimating all her control. She tried to scream, but every ounce of energy was pulsating in the roaring epicenter of her climax. Ripples of pleasure crashed over her once, twice, a third time before the orgasms let go of her and finished their merciless onslaught. She trembled in the aftermath of the storm, her body a quivering mass of sensitive nerves. She pulled Merritt towards her with her legs, needing to feel their bodies together.

Merritt rubbed her wet center along Soren's body as she came up to join her on the bed. Everywhere her arousal touched left warm hints of the delicious secrets that longed to be found. Soren trembled at every intimate touch, her once

186

sated appetite pulsing anxiously. She needed to taste Merritt again, the brief encounter earlier serving only to awaken the animal need inside her and she knew she must feed her hunger or be in desperate want forever. She pulled Merritt's face to hers and captured her lips in a fierce kiss, tasting herself there. Her clit clenched expectantly.

She slid her fingers between Merritt's legs and inhaled a breath. She was soaked with her arousal. "I think I need to take care of you." She withdrew her fingers, capturing Merritt's juices and ran them along her lips, her eyes dark with an almost carnal glint of need. "I need my mouth on you now." She grabbed Merritt around the waist and moved her forward until her hot arousal rested above her face.

Merritt hovered above her. She pulled away laughing, but the sound caught in her throat when Soren slid her tongue deep inside her. All thoughts of teasing replaced by a need so primal it threatened to rip her open and lay her bare for all to see. She shuddered with caged desire, shock waves of electricity reverberating to her core and leaving her shaking with want. She clamped her hands on the bed in an attempt to gain some semblance of control over her body and keep her anchored. Soren's tongue stroked expertly in and out as she deftly teased her engorged clit.

Soren took all that was offered and then some. Each time her tongue plunged into Merritt, she unleashed a surge of electricity that raced straight through Merritt's body, threatening to undo the tenuous vestiges of her fight to keep her heart locked away. She'd long ago felt the fortress she hid behind weakening under the fiery onslaught of Soren's affections. Fear mingled with desire in a fierce battle for domination over her trembling body.

"Oh God Soren, what are you doing to me?" She cried out feebly as the beginning tendrils of her orgasm sent waves rippling through her body. "Yes, yes baby. I'm coming." She screamed as wave after wave of pleasure assaulted her and ripped her from her moorings. She barely felt Soren's arms snake around her and anchor her as she rode the crest of pleasure and surrendered to her soul shattering climax. She lowered herself on top of Soren, her body quivering in the aftermath.

When she finally trusted her muscles to function, she pushed herself up on her elbows and smiled drowsily. "Thank you."

Soren kissed her lightly on the lips, a small smirk playing on the corner of her mouth. "No, thank you. If you only knew how long I've wanted to do that."

Merritt kissed her chin and chuckled. "I think I have a pretty good idea." She slid onto her side and Soren snuggled into her, her firm bottom pressing into the sensitive area between Merritt's legs. Soren heard Merritt growl quietly and she wriggled provocatively. Merritt put her hand on her hip and stilled her. "Please, I don't think I can take anymore. I'm completely unraveled as it is."

Soren grabbed her hand and pulled it to her breast, feeling the warmth of her palm cupping her gently and she sighed contentedly. "I'll stop for now. But I make no promises about later."

Merritt growled again and kissed the nape of her neck. "Damn it woman. You'll be my undoing."

Soren snuggled in closer, loving the feel of Merritt's body pressed against hers. "I certainly hope so darlin'".

Sometime later, Soren awoke with a start, the warmth of Merritt's body no longer wrapped around her. She reached across the bed and it felt empty and cold and as the doubts and fears of earlier replaced the dreams of their lovemaking, she felt cold with ache. She lay there, staring at small fragments of moonlight filtered through the glass droplets of her chandelier, wondering if tonight with Merritt was all she would be given and if so, what had she done to so royally piss off the fates.

Knowing sleep would not come again, she wandered into the library and picked up the one thing she'd finally realized could tame the restless musings of her mind. She slid her fingers along the cold strings and told them everything she hadn't been able to say out loud.

Chapter Seventeen

Soren rubbed her eyes wearily. She had made the decision to drive home instead of flying so she would have her car and now still 180 miles outside of Nashville, she was feeling every bit of the overnight drive and several nights with no sleep. She'd resorted to taking Tylenol PM, but it hadn't helped get Merritt off her mind. She was still smarting from Merritt's hasty retreat from her bed Saturday and her repeated attempts to talk to her going unanswered.

After talking to Jordan again, she'd decided to postpone her trip till Thursday. Ali's contractions had been a false alarm, but given the fact that she'd already started to efface, the doctor was almost positive the baby would come within the week. Soren figured if she got there by Thursday, it was a safe bet she'd be there in time for the birth.

The first rays of dawn were streaking low across the sky and she saw signs for the Chattanooga exit and let out a relieved breath. She needed a Venti triple shot something or other from Starbucks. She hadn't originally intended to leave in the middle of the night but when it was obvious to her that she wasn't sleeping anytime soon, she headed out early. She figured she might as well beat the traffic anyway.

Being alone on the road had given her plenty of time to reflect on the past week and Saturday especially. She could still taste Merritt and it made her stomach flip—flop wildly. She touched herself through her shorts and felt the beginning tremors of desire shoot through her body. She'd never had an orgasm before like the one that Merritt had given her and never, ever had she come three times in a row. She pulled her hand away quickly knowing how embarrassing it would be to have an accident and have to explain why.

She had called Merritt once and gotten her voicemail, which didn't come as a surprise. The message she'd left had been simple and to the point. They had passed a point with each other Saturday and Soren saw no reason to hold anything back. She told Merritt she hoped that being together meant as much to her as it had to Soren, and that she didn't have any regrets. She understood that Merritt needed time to sort through her feelings and she would give her as much time and space as she needed. She planned on spending at least a month in Nashville and they could talk when she got home. Even when she'd outlined her plan to be gone a month with no contact, Soren wondered how on earth she was going to last a month without hearing Merritt's voice. It would be a definite test of her resolve.

Her last three words were *I love you.* Not exactly the most ideal way to break it to Merritt that she was in love with her, but Soren knew she needed to say it and it had seemed like her only opportunity for the time being. When Merritt finally realized that she couldn't fight her heart any longer, Soren knew that she would tell her and show her everyday that she was completely and totally in love with her. She had long ago accepted the fact that she and Merritt's hearts were destined to be entwined together forever. That was the one constant thought that kept her going the last four days. Otherwise she was tempted to allow herself one giant meltdown.

Soren checked back from the past long enough to order a breakfast sandwich, Venti coffee and get a full tank of gas before hitting the road again. She dove into the food and coffee, eager to get the caffeine coursing through her veins and wake her up enough to drive the last 150 miles. A quick glance at her watch told her she would get into the city in the middle of rush hour and she hoped Thursday morning traffic wouldn't be too bad. She'd made the drive almost completely distracted and knew that facing heavy traffic with her mind anywhere but the road could prove to be dangerous.

Ten miles outside of Nashville, her phone rang. She blindly reached for it wondering who would be calling her that early in the morning. She checked the display and didn't immediately recognize the number, but did know it was a Savannah exchange.

"Hello?" Soren wasn't sure whose voice she expected to hear, but Gay's was not the one that had come to mind.

"Good morning darlin'. Sorry to call you so early but I needed to ask you something." She said jovially, her always friendly voice putting an immediate smile on Soren's face.

"No, it's cool. I've been up awhile. What's up?" Soren kept her eyes on the busy road.

"You gonna be around awhile this morning? I've got a couple gardenia topiaries I want to run by. Darlin', I'm fixin' to make your house not only the best looking, but the best smelling."

Soren groaned. "Actually no. I'm in Nashville. My best friend and her wife are expecting their first baby."

"Oh." Gay sounded surprised. *"Merritt didn't mention that...but then I haven't seen her much lately. She's kind of been the invisible roommate the past few days. Figured she'd been hanging out with you."* Gay teased.

A pang of loneliness gripped Soren's chest. "Umm, you know what? I haven't really seen much of Merritt this week. I'm sure things have just been really busy for her lately."

Gay laughed softly. *"Maybe so. Well I won't keep ya any longer. I reckon I'll just run these by while you're gone. I'll make sure Merritt or myself keeps 'em watered while you're away."* She paused a moment. *"By the by, how long you figuring on being gone?"*

"Probably a month at least." Soren said quietly. "I figure they will need a couple of extra hands for awhile."

Gay let out a breath. She wondered if that was why Merritt was in her own world these days. *"Does Merritt know?"*

Soren told her she did not. "I told her it would be about a month. She just doesn't know that I've left…since we haven't really talked lately. I didn't have a chance to say goodbye."

"She doesn't?" Gay asked surprised. *"Wow! Not sure how she's gonna feel about that."*

Secretly, Soren hoped she felt as lonely as she did. The more she thought about the time frame, the more she felt her determination to give Merritt space weakening. "Speaking of that, can you do me a favor?"

"A sexual favor?" Gay said suggestively. *"Darlin', I can do you…a favor anytime."*

Soren laughed out loud. She could see Gay winking. "Any chance you want to come up to Nashville? I'm gonna need your sense of humor…I think."

"I could…" Gay replied hesitantly. *"…but who would take care of the gardenias?"*

"Good point." Soren agreed. "I guess I can make do with memories of our rock hunting adventure together."

Gay cackled loudly. *"Darlin', that was priceless! I will never forget the queen of the magic touch flying straight onto her ass. How's that concrete burn healing up?"*

"Healing just fine, no thanks to you." Soren said sarcastically. "Guess that pretty much means you have to do me a favor now."

"Fine." Gay said in a resigned voice. *"But if it has anything to do with hugging or kissing my cousin goodbye, forget it. I may be from the South, but it ain't Kentucky, if you know what I mean."*

Soren groaned loudly. Living just below she was all too familiar with the term kissing cousins and Kentucky being one of the states that had either rightly or not earned the term. "No worries. There'll be no touching required." Soren smiled when she heard Gay's relieved sigh. "I just need you to make sure Merritt gets something I left her. It's in the library. She'll know what it is when she sees it."

Gay was immediately intrigued. *"Mmm, naked pictures of you?"* She laughed wickedly. *"I may just have to sneak over there and take a gander myself."*

"Why darlin'?" Soren purred. "Wait a month, and I'll show you the real thing." She knew that Gay could dish it out but backed down immediately if Soren called her bluff. She could picture Gay's cheeks red with embarrassment and she had to stifle a laugh. She took the loud gulping as her queue to continue and save Gay from anymore discomfort. "If you'll just tell her to make sure she gets it, I'd really appreciate it."

"Sure thing honey." Gay said finally. She heard shuffling and saw Merritt making her way into the kitchen, her hand covering a big yawn. Her eyes were red and puffy and she looked like she hadn't slept in days. *"I guess I better let you go. I'll get those plants over there and take care of you know what. Call me if you need anything done while you're away."*

Soren smiled. Whatever idiosyncrasies Gay had, she had learned quickly that underneath it all beat a heart of gold…no matter how hard she tried to hide it. "Thanks Gay. I appreciate it…I *really* do."

Gay hung up the phone and turned her attention to Merritt, who was sitting at the breakfast bar watching her curiously. "Soren." Gay said as if that was enough explanation. "You want coffee?" She pulled a cup from the cabinet, poured Merritt a cup and set it down in front of her.

"Oh yeah, what'd she want?" She inhaled the scent and took a cautious sip.

"She's gone to Nashville." She watched a look of pain flash across her cousin's face. "Guess she's gonna be gone for a bit."

"She might have mentioned that in passing." Merritt tried to act nonchalant, but Gay saw right through her. Merritt had never been able to keep her feelings from showing up in her eyes.

In passing my ass Gay thought to herself. "I have a couple of plants I have to run by the house, you wanna join me? I think they are heavier than I can lug up the porch steps myself."

Merritt froze. The last time she'd been at Soren's house was Saturday night, or rather Sunday morning early. The morning she'd snuck away like a frightened child. She hadn't been able to face waking up next to Soren and accepting what she'd done. And she certainly hadn't worked up the nerve to reply to her voicemail. What would she say? Last night was a mistake. I think we should take it all back. Except it was the most wonderful mistake she'd ever made and admitting that to herself meant moving forward and she wasn't sure she was ready. She couldn't make promises when she wasn't sure she wouldn't hurt Soren. "Can't you have one of the guys help you out?"

"I don't understand why you can't do it." Gay retorted. "You're gonna be there anyway."

"Maybe. Maybe not." Merritt's reply was evasive.

"Why not?" Gay countered quickly.

"No need to. The guys are doing great." Merritt crossed her arms defensively. "It's not like they need me looking over their shoulders all the time."

"Well you need to get over there sometime. Soren left something for you in the study. So while you are there helping me, you can get that too." Gay saw the surprise in her eyes at that revelation. She continued knowing she was pushing buttons that were better left alone, but she loved her cousin too much to let ker keep pushing away the woman that Gay was pretty sure could make her happier than she'd ever been. "You can follow me over there."

195

"I can't today. I'll make it over there sometime." Merritt muttered then snapped back when she saw Gay open her mouth. "Let it go, will ya? I'll get there when I get there."

Gay didn't get offended. She knew Merritt didn't mean anything by snapping at her. "You wanna talk about what's buggin' you?"

Merritt glared at her. She was in no mood to talk about her feelings about Soren. "There's nothing to talk about."

"You don't think? How about the fact that the woman you love is going to be gone for a month and it's got you in a pissy mood?"

"We're just friends."

"Are you darlin'?" Gay asked quietly. "'Cause I've never been that upset about one of my *friends* leaving?"

Merritt growled and stood up. "Drop it Gay. You don't know what you're talking about." She pushed the stool in and started to walk out of the kitchen.

"Listen cuz." Gay said quickly. "I love you, but good grief, you are so stubborn, you could argue with the wall and win. It doesn't take a genius to see y'all fancy each other. That's plum easy to figure out." She put her hand up to silence Merritt. "I'm talking and I reckon it's about time you listen. Right now, you ain't got the sense God gave an ant. I know you're scared you'll mess up like ya did with Kate. I understand that. But let me tell you a little secret missy, you're fixin' to lose the best thing that's ever happened to you by being a chicken shit. I see you standin' back waitin' till you think you're all good and fixed and you think you're in some magical place that you won't mess up and hurt Soren. Well darlin', that place don't exist. There are no guarantees. You don't know that you won't ever hurt each other. I know you won't mean to, but it happens. But instead of givin' this a chance, you're so hell bent on saving Soren from you, that you don't realize you're hurtin' her even more. You better wake up, darlin'."

196

"Thanks for the sound relationship advice." Merritt said sarcastically. "That's like me telling you how to cook."

Gay laughed, completely unoffended at the reference to her lack of a stable relationship at any point in her life. "Darlin', I'm single 'cause I choose to be. You're just being stupid."

Merritt winced but she knew Gay's assessment was spot on. "If I go and help you with the plants, will you get the fuck off my back?"

"Yes."

Merritt ignored the smirk on her face and walked out of the room. She yelled from the stairway. "You can wipe that smartass grin off your face or I'll do it for you." She heard Gay's laughter echo all the way into her room.

Chapter Eighteen

Merritt set her lemonade on the coffee table and leaned back into the couch with Sam's journal in her hand. She took a deep breath. She wasn't sure what awaited her, but if it were anything like the entries they'd read together, she was in for trouble. Her emotions were already raw and frayed. It had been almost a week since she'd seen Soren and she missed her desperately. That part scared Merritt because it meant having to accept that she was beyond the point of being able to run away. No, she needed to feel like her control wasn't spiraling away from her.

She hadn't been able to listen to the song Soren had written for her either. She glanced at the CD again. She knew she needed to but every time she got close to playing it, she started to shake. She was on edge and figured it would certainly send her tumbling over the brink. Soon, she told herself, soon.

Finally, she put her finger where the bookmark was and opened the journal up to the page Soren had marked. She noticed the date was well after the last entry she'd seen. It was the summer of 1899, almost two—and—a—half years after the Christmas when Sam and Nina had kissed the first time and four years since they'd met the first time. Looking back, the time must have crept along slowly for the two of them, but in Merritt's mind it was the blink of an eye.

June 12th, 1899

My soul died today. It is with a grief—stricken heart that I pen the words of my soul's ultimate demise. A few short years with my Nina and now she is torn away from me with such fierceness that I wonder if we shall ever recover. Breaking her heart is like a sharp dagger buried deep within me, twisting violently and shredding the very fiber of my soul. Oh Nina, I cannot fathom my life without you, especially when fate is so wicked as to rent you from me and yet leave you in my presence so my eyes can look upon you and remember my treachery.

My father threatened to send me away to relatives in Maryland if I do not accept James's proposal of marriage. He feels it is not right for a young woman of my age and class to remain single and keep the company of other single young ladies. It makes other tongues waggle and think us too modern and he does not agree with the Feminist movement that is endangering American families. If only they knew what Nina and I share, oh how their tongues would waggle then.

I know my father to be a very stubborn and sometimes extreme in his love and knew that if he promised to send me away, he would certainly do so and I would die if I were never to see my beloved again. So with only the thought of keeping her in my life even if it weren't as I wished, I told Nina the news that I knew would devastate us both. I can only say that the pain that comes from breaking a lover's heart is more than any one person should have to bear in this short lifetime. I would just as soon rip my heart out and set it aflame. God help me, for I have looked upon hell and felt the pain it inflicts.

There is no one to share my grief other than the pages of my journal which from today forward shall only be a faint, painful memory of my brief taste of heaven on earth. I cannot begin to describe the aching emptiness that has eclipsed my soul. My father could not possibly know the immense sadness he has forced upon his only daughter.

Merritt swiped adsentmindedly at a tear. *That's one way to get my attention* she thought. She knew from the beginning that Sam and Nina had not ended up together, but to actually hear the painful details about their breakup brought it a little too close to home. She didn't have an overbearing father pushing her to be something she wasn't, but she was at a crossroads. It reminded her of the *Choose Your Own Adventure* books she'd been hooked on as a kid. *If you choose Soren, go to page 4. If you are a dumbass and choose to remain single, go to hell.*

The only problem was she couldn't see the last page of the story. She couldn't be sure if she followed her heart and chose Soren that everything was going to be fine, that she wouldn't hurt her somewhere down the line. She hated the fact that she had become the type of person that needed a guarantee. Hadn't Soren *and* Gay both told her life didn't come with a guarantee, you just jumped and hoped the parachute opened. Something deep in her gut told her she didn't want to end up like Sam, heartbroken and alone. She just needed to figure out a way to convince her brain what her heart already knew.

She glanced at the CD again. She picked it up. "Shit, I'm already crying. Might as well keep the party going." She put the CD in, hit play and closed her eyes. Soren's voice filled the room. "Merr, you're the first woman I've ever wanted to write a song for." Merritt's heart jumped as Soren's words hit her. She almost fainted when Soren started to sing. The first lines she sang a capella and Merritt could hear the anguish in her beautiful voice.

> *God, I need something to fix this condition,*
> *Fix this pain that's tearing me apart,*
> *Can you hear my heart screaming?*
> *You know how much it hurts to be alive*
> *When every breath utters your name*
> *And I wonder if you feel the same?*

Merritt felt her chest gripped in a vice. *God yes! I feel the same* she thought. The subtle beat of Soren's guitar blended in with her voice on the next stanza. Merritt had to smile. Soren was incredibly talented and she found herself drawn in, imagining Soren in front of her singing to her. She didn't think she could stand to see the tears she knew she heard.

Felt you come inside, a devil on a quest
Stirring feelings better laid to rest.
See you fighting my reasons
Afraid of letting yourself fall too far.
Can't you see that I'm going crazy
For you? Won't you save me from myself?

Merritt tightened her fist into a ball and let out a strangled cry that sounded like a wounded animal. She wondered if she could save herself much less save Soren. Soren's sultry voice hit the chorus and Merritt could feel all of it resonating through her body, she felt Soren's fingers move from the guitar to stroke her gently.

Can't stop myself, I'm falling for you.
Can't change what I'm feeling,
Got you wrapped around me, stuck in my head
Givin' you my heart, hoping it won't break
Long past reason, can't take it all back
I look at you and I'm completely undone, completely undone.

Merritt thought completely undone was a perfect way to describe how Soren made her feel. Anytime she was with her, she lost all self control. Her heart went wild and all her common sense went out the door. She wondered how she actually made it as long as she had before taking what they both longed for. *'Cause I'm an idiot!*

Wonder if you can feel me calling to you,
Silent tears sent across space and time?
An angel cloaked in darkness
Won't you save me from the night, come to me

Wipe away the fears of the past
Mend the fraying edges of my heart.

Was she an angel or really was Merritt the devil? Could she mend Soren's heart or would she end up breaking it even more in the long run? No wonder Soren had given her so long to figure things out. She was a freaking basket case, stuck in a self imposed prison. Merritt held the key in her hand trying to decide if she should use it.

Won't face love without you, feelings left unsaid,
Wrap this shelter of love around you
Steal this ache that doesn't end.
You can't deny what's written in my eyes.
Took my chance with naked honesty,
Give you my heart till the end of time.

She knew the ache all too well and she knew that love was what Soren was offering—plain and simple. No strings, no hidden agenda, just love. The head over heels, knock you on your ass, outta the ballpark, once in a lifetime kind of love. "God Merritt, you really are an idiot." She muttered acerbically.

She listened as the chorus repeated then faded out before hitting replay. She wasn't sure how many times she'd hit replay or how long she'd been sitting in the dark when a shadow appeared in the doorway.

"Good song?"

"Gay." Merritt said and rubbed her eyes. "Sorry I didn't hear you come in."

Gay walked over and held out a glass of amber liquid. "You look like you need this more than me."

Merritt watched her for a second before taking the glass and throwing back its contents. The initial sting of the alcohol almost took her breath away since she hadn't had a drink in months. She gestured at the couch and Gay sat down beside her.

"What's all this?"

Merritt shrugged. "It's the stuff Soren left at the house for me."

Gay crinkled her forehead. "The song too?"

"Yeah. She wrote it for me." Merritt answered quietly. "She's in love with me."

"Kinda sounded that way…the few times I heard it." Gay teased. "Reckon it's gonna be a long month for you." Merritt turned away and Gay knew that she was hurting pretty badly. "She's real good, ya know."

Merritt's mind flashed to Saturday night and it felt like someone had turned on an oven around her head. Her face and ears were on fire.

"Well I'll be hornswaggled." Gay exclaimed.

"What?"

"You slept with her." Gay punched her in the arm.

Merritt couldn't meet her gaze. Keeping secrets from Gay had never been her long suit. Not that sleeping with Soren was a secret per se, but also probably not something she would voluntarily offer either.

Gay slapped her leg. "Darlin' that's just about the best news I've heard all day. How's it feel to rejoin the living?"

"Incredibly amazing and scary at the same time." Merritt admitted.

"Perfect! That's how it should feel. I'd be worried if you weren't scared shitless."

Merritt ran a hand over her face. "I've never been so confused before, you know? God, I'm thirty—nine years old and I am more unsure of myself and my decisions than I was as a kid. Isn't it supposed to get easier the older you get?"

Gay laughed. "No darlin', it's supposed to get harder the older you get. You aren't deciding between a grape or cherry freeze pop anymore. You know if this was an easy decision it wouldn't be worth making. The harder it is means that it's worth it. It means Soren is worth it. Hell even I'm half—way in love with Soren."

Merritt gave her a sideways glance.

Gay winked. "Simmer down, I'm kidding. Here's the thing…Soren's laid her cards out on the table. She loves you and my guess is she's in it for the long haul, which means she's willing to wait for you. Course, you're not much of a catch so I'm not sure if that makes her a really good person or just plain dumb."

Merritt glared at her.

"Hey I like you…" Gay said quickly. "…but you're my cuz so I kinda have to."

"Yeah, well if my mom hadn't told me to like you, I wouldn't." Merritt replied sarcastically.

Gay burst out laughing. "Speaking of that, what does Nancy think of Soren?"

A smile played on the corner of Merritt's mouth. "Actually, she really likes her…unlike any of my past girlfriends."

"Shit, that should be reason enough…especially after Kate. There was no love lost there." Gay said cautiously. "And before you say it, what happened with Kate is not your fault. I've watched you hold on to guilt for too long. I reckon we all deal with situations differently. You can't keep holding yourself back out of fear that this will happen all over again."

"God, I know. But I love her too much to go into anything knowing I might mess up." Merritt sounded anguished and Gay knew she was struggling with powerful demons.

Gay threw up her hands in frustration. "Well fuck it then. I forgot you were God."

"Huh?"

"Well I reckon you must think you are with the harebrained crap that's coming out of your mouth. Guess I forgot you can control everything and guarantee no one will get hurt. Pretty powerful credit you're giving yourself. While you're at it, would ya mind ending war and reversing the greenhouse effect?" She put her finger on Merritt's heart. "If you still need something to tell you the right decision, it's right here."

Merritt opened her mouth to reply then stopped. It finally hit her how ridiculous she was being. She understood what Gay had tried repeatedly to tell her. She was human and in life there were no guarantees no matter how badly she wanted to have them and all the time she spent sitting back waiting till she felt perfect for Soren had gotten her nowhere fast. She was in love with Soren, that much she was sure of. The rest, well the rest would work itself out. She grinned sheepishly. "I'm an idiot."

"Yeah you kinda are." Gay agreed wryly. "Course trying to convince you of that's like trying to boil corn in ice water."

"It's the German in me." Merritt teased.

"Ha! Reckon it's more the dumbass in you." Gay said with a smirk. "So…is she good in bed?"

Merritt smiled cryptically. "That, my dear cousin, is something you will never know." She waited till Gay left then pulled her phone out of her pocket. She scrolled through the numbers till she found Soren's and stopped with her hand over the send button, a flash of panic. She knew she couldn't talk to Soren until she was absolutely sure she was ready to give herself completely. She couldn't constantly fear that she would mess things up, she had to trust herself and until she could do that, she had to wait. And she knew that was going to make for a long month.

#

Brett sank into the chair between Soren and Jordan who were laughing hysterically. He eyed them suspiciously. "Am I interrupting something?"

Soren shook her head from side—to—side. It took her several seconds to get her laughter under control enough to even attempt to speak. "We were just remembering the time we played spin the bottle at your thirteenth birthday party."

Brett groaned loudly and tried to stand up when Jordan reached over, grabbed his arm and pulled him back into the chair. "Uh—uh, that was your idea." She winked at Soren. "Although I'm glad you suggested it."

"I know Ren's glad I did." Brett smiled cockily. "I'm the only guy she's ever wanted to kiss."

Soren rolled her eyes and poked her finger in her mouth pretending to gag. "I sure did, *Mr. I peed my pants every time Lauren walked by.* God, what lesbian wouldn't want to go straight for you?"

Jordan burst out laughing. "You know we just tease you 'cause we love you." It was an attempt at an apology, albeit a small one. "We do have you to thank though for helping us discover our true superhero identities."

"Yeah the Gay Wonder Twins." Soren joked. She leaned back, took a swig of her beer and chuckled. "Man that was quite a day though."

Jordan readily agreed. "Found out I liked kissing girls…a lot. Just not you."

"Hey!" Soren objected. "Well I didn't like kissing you either."

Brett cleared his throat. "Well that's probably more than I needed to know."

"Guess I shouldn't tell you what I do now that I'm all grown up." Jordan quipped.

"Yeah, he probably still thinks the stork dropped his kids off." Soren added.

"Three words ladies. Rain…tonight…paybacks." Brett said punctuating his words.

Soren and Jordan stopped laughing. At the same time they remembered when they were eleven and Brett had locked them outside in the rain for making fun of him. "Okay, okay, no more teasing." They agreed.

The three of them sat in silence enjoying the Tennessee summer night. "Just like old times." Brett said reminiscently. "We've missed you around here."

"How could I miss you guys? You call me almost everyday." Soren teased. "I'm kidding. I've missed you too."

"Brett said you've been keeping yourself rather busy lately with some hobbies. You've taken up sub—contracting I hear." Jordan teased.

Soren raised her eyebrow. "Oh he did, did he?"

Brett hit his sister on the arm. "You weren't supposed to tell her I told you."

"What!" Jordan yelled. "You didn't say it was a secret."

Soren laughed. Brett and Jordan still acted like they were ten sometimes. They fought but she knew they loved each other fiercely. "It's fine. I have been busy…not like that." She said quickly when Jordan wriggled her eyebrows suggestively.

"Oh so you're saying you haven't slept with her?" Jordan queried.

A blush crept over Soren's face and she hid behind her beer bottle.

"So how's that working out for you? Working *underneath* another woman?"

"Oh I'm not always underneath her. Sometimes I'm on top."

Brett jumped out of his chair and walked to the back door. "That would be really hot, if you weren't my best friend. Now, it's just gross."

Jordan watched him walk inside then moved into his chair. "Okay dish. What's really going on with the tall, dark and obviously gorgeous contractor you hired? Brett said she had a girlfriend."

"Had is the operative word. Merritt, that's her name, broke it off."

"Mmm, Merritt." Jordan said her name slowly. "Sounds sexy."

"Undeniably sexy." Soren acknowledged with a smile.

"She must be for you to even give her a second thought."

"She made it impossible not too. She's..." Soren paused contemplating her next words. "God Jordan, she's beautiful inside and out. She's warm and funny and sensitive. We can talk for hours and never stop. I think I fell for her the second I met her."

"Jeez Ren, who cares about her personality?" Jordan rolled her eyes and raised her voice impertinently, making fun of Soren. "Umm, she likes to knit, she loves to do crossword puzzles, her favorite flower is the lily and she takes in stray animals. Tell me about the important stuff. What does she look like and is she good in bed?"

"Phhbbtt." Soren snorted loudly. "I seem to remember a certain someone who didn't like Ali at first because she thought she was a snob."

Jordan smiled sheepishly. "Snobby, shy. Anyone could confuse that."

"Right." Soren replied sarcastically. "'Cause they are so similar. Almost didn't marry your baby momma cause you were so stuck on her personality."

Jordan laughed at her chiding. "Good thing I had someone as wise as you to set me straight about her." She caught Soren's smirk. "Okay so not straight, but you know what I mean."

Soren laughed. "Yeah, I do."

"Seriously though, Ren. Tell me about her." Jordan pressed impatiently.

Soren leaned her head back and stared at the sky, picturing Merritt. She let out an appreciative moan. "God, where do I start? Beautiful doesn't even begin to describe her. She is so fucking gorgeous. She's taller than I am with the most incredible body I've ever seen. She's got these green eyes that when she looks at me I just want to get her naked and have my way with her. The sexiest lips that do things to me I never imagined. Hmm, what else? Oh, she has

208

long, dark brown hair that I find myself wanting to, uhm, pull on…hard."

"Wow, she must be perfect." Jordan licked her lips. "The look in your eyes is enough to get me hot and bothered."

Soren chuckled softly. "She's just like Mary Poppins…*practically* perfect in every way."

"Practically?" Jordan said skeptically. "So what's her problem? She smells funny?"

"Not so much really." Soren sighed. "I'm not sure she is ready for a big time commitment."

"And you are."

Soren shook her head. "With her yes. I'll admit I was definitely not looking for one, in fact it was about the furthest thing from my mind, but somehow she got inside of me and now I don't want to let go. I'll be honest though…I'm scared I won't have a choice. What if she decides she can't give herself to me?"

"So keep it strictly physical and see what happens. Maybe she'll come around."

"I wish it were that easy." Soren smiled wryly. "When I tell you I want the whole nine yards, I mean I want it all. House, white picket fence, dog, 2.4 kids, the works. I'm not sure how long I would last with it just being sex."

Jordan whistled quietly. "Wow, kids huh? You are hooked."

"Yeah, kids, I know. I wasn't sure if I'd ever want that again after losing Olivia, but something in my gut just tells me if Merritt makes the leap, it's going to be for good and I would want to share that with her. We talked about it and we both feel like given the right person we would definitely be up for having children together."

"Do you have any idea…aside from the use of her obviously superhuman bedroom skills on you that she is in the same place?"

"Honestly, I think her heart is there, just not sure if her head is." Soren drained the last of her beer and started picking at the label. "Without going into too much detail, she's afraid that she'll mess up like she did in her last relationship and things will end badly and she'll end up hurting me. Long and short, she is taking the blame for everything that went wrong with her ex."

"I can't say that I don't know how that feels. I hope she knows that you can't predict how a relationship will go based on past history." Jordan reached into a cooler, pulled out two bottles and handed Soren one. "So where did you leave things with her?"

"Thanks." She took the proffered bottle and opened it, chucking the lid into a small trash can beside her. "I figured she could use the month I was away to sort things out. I told her how I feel and that she owes it to herself to give us a chance. I hope she feels the same but I'll understand if she's not ready. I won't like it, but I'll understand it." She pulled out her phone half expecting it to ring and when it didn't, she shoved it back into her pocket, disappointment evident on her face.

Jordan saw the look and cocked her head. "Why don't you call her?"

"I can't." Soren said shaking her head. "The balls in her court. I'm not going to push. I've just got to sit back and wait…as patiently as possible. And hope I don't go crazy in the process."

"Well we'll try our hardest to keep your mind occupied." Jordan teased sarcastically. "Can't have you…"

"Hey guys."

Both women jumped at the sound of Lauren's voice.

"It's time." Lauren watched matching looks of disbelief cross their faces. "For real. Ali's water just broke."

210

Chapter Nineteen

Soren stared at the small bundle that Ali held against her chest. A tuft of soft blond hair was peaking out and she could just make out her tiny forehead before the rest of her face got lost in a blur of blanket and Ali's breast.

Emily Grace Kendrix hyphen Carothers had finally decided to grace the world with her presence at 3:54 in the morning on an otherwise nondescript July day. Surprisingly enough, after a pregnancy that hadn't been the easiest, Ali had only had to survive eight hours of labor which surprised them all. Still a day later, Soren could tell by looking at her that she was exhausted, as could be expected.

The birth had brought back a flood of memories sending Soren on a rollercoaster ride, remembering with vivid detail the night of Olivia's birth. Her excitement at Emily's arrival had been somewhat tempered by the pain she would always feel since she'd been forced out of her own daughter's life. Rather than put a damper on Jordan and Ali's day, she'd chosen to wait outside the delivery room and only went to see them when she'd gotten her emotions reigned in.

"Ren?" Ali's quiet voice broke through her reverie and Soren looked up expectantly. "I think Emily wants her aunt to burp her."

Soren scooped Emily into her arms and propped her up on her shoulder, before settling back into the rocking chair in the corner of the room. For several moments, the only sound in the sterile room was the rhythmic tapping on Emily's back and an occasional creak from the chair.

She craned her head to look at Emily, inhaling her scent. She smelled exactly like she remembered Olivia, a hint of Baby Magic and powder. Her stomach tightened at the scent and her heart jumped into her throat. She blinked back tears, but instead of sad ones, they were tears of hope. Emily's birth was a sign that life does indeed move on and so had she. Obviously, she would give anything to get Olivia back, but Soren could finally admit that she wouldn't change where she had ended up today. Nor would she stress about tomorrow.

"So are you ready to have another one yet?" Ali asked after several moments.

Soren felt Emily's warm body wriggle against hers and she smiled. "I think so. I just have to find someone special to do it with."

"What about your new girl? Jordan says you're in love already." Ali teased.

Soren rolled her eyes. "Jeez, what is it with brother and sister big mouth? I swear neither one of them can keep anything quiet."

"Neither one of who can keep quiet?" Jordan asked as she joined them in the room. She set two bags of fast food on a small table and bent over to give Ali a kiss. "Hello Mother."

"Seriously, do not call me that. It makes me feel like I'm sixty years old and living on a farm." Ali glared at Jordan. "And you can't keep your big mouth shut."

"What?" Jordan asked innocently. "I haven't even been here, what did I do now?"

Soren shot her a glare that matched Ali's earlier one. "Does everyone need to know about my love life?"

Jordan colored slightly and started to stammer. "Uhm, no, well I…" She shot Ali a desperate look and Ali merely laughed as if to say you're on your own with this one. "It's not a big deal Ren. Besides I only told Ali and a couple of the nurses and maybe the doctor."

"That's great Jordan. Why don't you just put out an announcement?" She narrowed her eyes thoughtfully. "Wait a minute. Why on earth would you tell the doctor or the nurses? And you better have a better reason than you were just making conversation."

"It just so happens, missy, that one of them was interested in playing some naughty nurse games with you." Jordan teased. "I figured I would let her know that your heart was already spoken for...but that you may want to borrow a set of scrubs, just in case."

Soren rolled her eyes at Jordan's suggestion, but her thighs clenched at the idea of role playing with Merritt. She felt her ears getting warm and tried to hide the blush creeping up her cheeks.

"I knew it!" Jordan smiled cockily. "You do want to borrow some scrubs. Naughty girl."

"Maybe...whatever. But you still have a big mouth." Soren stuck her tongue out at Jordan then turned back to Ali and raised her eyebrows. Ali nodded her head and Soren laid Emily back in the small bassinet beside the hospital bed. "Anyway, as you may have already heard, I did meet someone. And God help me, I am head over heels in love with her."

Ali waited while Jordan pulled hamburgers and fries out of the bag and passed them around. She took a large bite of the burger and moaned appreciatively. "Man, that's a good burger. So you're in love. How's she feel?"

Soren dipped a handful of fries in ketchup and shoved them in her mouth before answering. "She hasn't said as much, but I get the feeling her heart's already mine. I just know, ya know?"

"Have you told her how you feel?" Ali mumbled around another bite of her burger.

Soren shook her head. "Yeah, kinda. I told her voicemail."

"Wow, romantic." Jordan teased. "I can't believe she hasn't fallen all over herself to be with you."

Ali punched Jordan in the arm. "Quit it! Like you have any room to talk."

"I'm romantic." Jordan countered feigning offense.

"Ahh yeah, sure you are honey." Ali teased. "Asking me to marry you over a text message is the epitome of romance."

"Well you were married." Jordan sputtered quickly. "How else was I supposed to ask you when your ex— husband was always around?"

Ali ran her finger lightly along Jordan's cheek and smiled. "I'm sure we could have arranged some alone time sweetheart. He was just a minor roadblock at times. But it all worked out in the end…and I'm sure it will for you too, Ren." She said fixing her eyes on Soren.

Soren shrugged. "At the time, voicemail was all I could get. After we sl…after we spent a significant amount of time together, I think it scared her and she ran. I would rather have told her in person but what are you going to do? At least this way she knows."

"Has she tried calling you since then?"

"No." Soren shook her head. "I didn't exactly tell her not to call while I was here, but I did sort of tell her to take the time that we were apart to figure out where she was and where she wanted to be."

"It's going to be a long month." Ali said quietly. "Are you sure you can go that long without talking to her?"

"I don't know. One week without talking to her and I'm going out of my mind." Soren chucked her trash into a waste container with an expert flick of her wrist. "I just hope she's missing me at least as much and it helps her realize she doesn't want to lose what we have."

#

Merritt set her phone down with a loud sigh. She missed Soren terribly, the aching in her chest similar to what she thought it may feel like to suffocate. She felt like her life support had been ripped away from her and the feeling of happiness was a cold, distant memory that had left her needing Soren like she needed air. Again, she had to wonder at her own stubborn foolishness. She knew Soren believed that Sam was stuck here because she hadn't been strong enough to choose love and she figured she'd be damned if she made the same mistake. She just hoped when the time came Soren's heart would still be hers.

"Looking at it ain't gonna make it ring." Gay teased. "Same as the last hundred times you checked. If you want to talk to her, call her."

Merritt growled. "I can't, not yet anyway. There are…there are things that I need to say that I won't say on the phone."

Gay raised an eyebrow and regarded Merritt quizzically. "Reckon you're finally going to admit you're in love with her?"

"I don't think that was ever in question." Merritt said quickly and turned the key letting them into Soren's house. "Whether or not I would act on those feelings was the issue."

"You'd be a fool if you didn't." Gay pushed the door shut behind them. "So why are we here again?"

"I want to do something for Soren and I need your input." She opened the door to the study.

"Sure, shoot." Gay slumped into an arm chair and stared at Merritt. "What's your big idea?"

Merritt recounted their conversation about the less than ideal setting that Soren had to use to record her music. She outlined her plan for the study adding that they would have to hustle since she should be home in just over three weeks. "And big mouth, you have to keep it a secret."

Gay laughed out loud. "What makes you think I'm talking to her while she's away?"

"Oh please." Merritt snorted. "I know someone's been taking her mail in and watering. Plus, you're guys are so incredibly tight, I assume that includes regular chats."

Gay just smiled cryptically. "Guess you'll never know will ya cuz?"

Merritt rolled her eyes and shook her head. "Dude seriously, if you weren't my cousin."

"You'd what, tough guy?" Gay quipped. "Don't take your pent up frustration out on me. I told you to go after her, remember?"

Merritt opened her mouth then shut it quickly. "I'm sorry. I know it's not your fault, you just happen to be an easy target right now."

"Darlin', you need to figure out how to deal with whatever's going on inside or you and I are gonna have a rough month. And don't worry, I won't tell her *our little secret.*"

Chapter Twenty

Soren tucked the blanket around Emily. "I can't believe she's almost a month old." She whispered. "Time has flown by."

Jordan nodded in agreement. "I know. It seems like just yesterday we were at the hospital having her." She turned the monitor on and set it on the diaper changing station close to the crib. She raised her hand to her mouth and tipped it back pretending to drink.

Soren nodded and followed her out of Emily's room and into the kitchen. She sat on a barstool and watched Jordan pour them each a glass of lemonade, hand her one and take a seat on the stool next to her. "She really is beautiful. You and Ali did a great job."

Jordan's smile widened exponentially. "Yeah, the little booger is pretty cute. She looks a lot like Ali already. I hope she loses the cross—eyed thing soon. That's a little creepy."

Soren nudged Jordan with her elbow. "Stop it. She's just a baby. It will go away." She took a drink of her lemonade and her mind flashed to the first day she'd met Merritt. *Tea or lemonade okay?* She was pretty sure it was the very moment Merritt had said that she'd have what Soren was having that she started to fall in love. She took another sip and her mind replayed their last night together, her thighs tightened reflexively as the tendrils of remembered pleasure tingled through her body. She felt her face flush and she put the glass against her forehead to cool the surge of heat that pulsed from deep inside her.

"I imagine you're ready to get home." Jordan said speculatively. "Ready to see Merritt?"

"I'm ready to see the house finished." Soren sighed loudly. "I'm not sure how it will go seeing Merritt for the first time on a month. I'm nervous. I think the hardest part is not really knowing where we stand. She's had a month. What if she decided this isn't something she's ready for?"

"Then she's a damn fool." Jordan set her glass down loudly for emphasis splashing liquid all over the bar. "Shit." She grabbed a towel off the bar and made several swipes over her mess. "She'd be crazy if she didn't give it a chance."

"Thanks." Soren smiled appreciatively. "I think so, but my fate rests pretty much on her shoulders. I've kind of prepared myself for anything at this point."

"Does she know you'll be home Saturday?"

"Probably. I told Gay I was leaving early Saturday morning. I'm sure Merritt knows by now."

"Will you call her when you get back in town?" Jordan tilted her head towards the baby monitor and listened as Emily cooed several times then quieted down. "Guess she's still asleep." She turned back to Soren.

"I don't know. I think I need to let her initiate any conversation we have." Soren picked at her shorts distractedly. "I've put everything on the table. I think she respects me enough to be completely honest with me. Just cross your fingers that she decides to follow her heart."

"How about I break her fingers if she doesn't?" Jordan quipped. "I know it's totally cliché and you probably already know this, but if it's meant to be it will happen. That was what I finally had to tell myself when Ali was going back and forth between staying in her marriage or running away with me. I waited, maybe impatiently and I ended up with the girl."

"No, you're right, I do know that." Soren smiled sheepishly. "I guess you know patience has never been my long suit, but I'm learning quickly." A look of sadness flicked across her face and disappeared just as quickly.

Jordan saw the look and didn't comment immediately. Instead she went to the freezer, grabbed a carton of Ben & Jerry's and two spoons. She plopped back on the stool and handed Soren a spoon. "Maybe this will help. Ali's asleep and that is the only time I can eat out of the carton." She pulled off the lid and took a quick bite. "It'll be just like old times."

"With lemonade?" Soren crinkled her nose. She caught Jordan's eye roll and shrugged. "You're right. Ice cream is good with anything and it does help." She stuck her spoon in and swiped a large deposit of caramel much to Jordan's chagrin.

#

Merritt wiped the sweat off her forehead and glanced at the clock wearily. She was stunned to discover it was almost midnight. She'd been hard at work since seven that morning and a quick inventory of the room made her realize she was still a few hours away from being done. And it needed to be done before Soren returned the next day.

Her eyes made a broad sweep of what had once been just a study and she smiled at the modifications. She knew in her heart that Soren would love this room like she did. Merritt had poured her blood, sweat and most importantly her soul into the project and she smiled broadly, knowing the ache she felt inside was worth the result. More than just her body ached, her soul ached, longed for Soren.

The month they'd been apart had given her time to do the soul searching she knew was necessary and in her self reflection, she'd discovered the woman she lost so long ago and remembered that she actually liked herself. She found

219

her self respect and confidence again. Those were the things she'd had to rediscover to be able to finally realize what she wanted in her life. And what she wanted was to be with Soren…forever. She could finally accept that their hearts and souls were entwined.

She recalled the exact moment that she'd finally accepted that realization and the overwhelming emotional and physical response her body had to it. She laughed when she thought about yelling to anyone that would hear that she was in love and the only person or being around to witness her declaration had been Sam, assuming Sam was more than just a fleeting feeling at the back of her neck. But she'd felt alive in that moment, more alive than she'd ever been. The only thing that would eclipse the warm effusion of life that she'd experienced was when she got to take Soren into her arms and proclaim her love to her. For that moment, she'd waited as impatiently as a man in the desert begging for water.

Her thirst for Soren raged through her body like hot flames scorching away the parts of her that held onto yesterday leaving only hope for tomorrow. Her spirit rose and flew like the phoenix on a quest for completion and her body ached for the heart that would make her whole again. Soren's love had freed her from her self—imposed prison of uncertainty and doubt. She knew she would give the woman who'd filled her dreams everyday since they'd met the one thing she'd never fully given before…her heart. Merritt knew the thing she was doing in return for her freedom was small, but the gift she gave with it was all Soren had ever asked for.

Merritt glanced at the clock again. It was well past midnight and she knew she should be exhausted, except she didn't feel it. She felt excitement tempered with nervousness extending to every part of her body and energizing her. It was what had kept her going this long, every day for the past month she'd functioned under the influence of some other worldly power and she knew if she thought about it, she would collapse.

Instead, she surged forward and when she finished, she took one final look around and felt her heart jump. She saw herself but more importantly, she saw Soren. She knew without a doubt that her gift represented all that she had and all that she wanted to share with Soren. What she was offering was so much more than the small confines of this physical manifestation, it was Merritt's heart and soul and that in its entirety was the greatest thing she could bestow.

Chapter Twenty—One

Soren shut the door behind her, dropped her bags on the kitchen floor and slumped wearily into the nearest chair. She didn't need to look at a clock to know how late it was. Her early morning start had gotten later and later when leaving proved more difficult than she expected. It was hard to say goodbye but even harder knowing she was coming home completely in the dark as to her immediate and long term future.

Her insecurities had heightened making her a jumbled ball of nerves the entire way home. An accident in Atlanta that closed all southbound lanes for several hours did little to calm her wary anxiety and by the time she hit her driveway, she thought she might cry. "Enough Ren. You're stronger than that." She admonished herself all the while wondering if she really was that strong.

After a few minutes, she used her hands to push herself up from the table, her body threatening to give in and sleep at the table out of sheer exhaustion. She looked around the kitchen and was startled to realize how different it looked. Only a complete lapse in alertness had made her miss it when she'd first walked in. She walked along the new row of cabinets, her hand gliding across the cool granite countertops. She ran her hand along the inlaid wood detail in the cabinets and smiled. God, the renovation was even more amazing then she'd imagined.

Again sleep threatened to overtake her and she decided she would finish the tour tomorrow. She bent to pick up her bags when she caught sight of something sitting on the island tucked next to a large wooden bowl. Letting go of the handles, her legs followed the path her eyes had charted and an overwhelming surge of energy swept through her body. She picked up the small, tidily wrapped box and she ran her fingers over the small bow with the impatient reverence of a small child eager to open presents on Christmas morning.

She gently tugged the knot and watched it fall away, as the twisted ropes in her stomach simultaneously disappeared replaced by the flutterings of excitement. Nervous fingers shook as she pried the lid open, her breath caught somewhere in her throat, breathing long forgotten in her haste to reveal a secret treasure. She peered inside the small box and pushed tissue paper aside with the barest of rustling, her heart threatening to hammer out of her chest. Her fingers brushed over cool metal and she forced herself to breathe, all vestiges of her previous exhaustion disappearing.

Her eyes fixed on the shape of a small key and she felt warmth building deep within her. Soren pulled it out and ran her fingers over the smooth metal, her eyes narrowed thoughtfully as she tried to assimilate what she was seeing. Her key had still worked in the back door so she knew it wasn't to that lock and that meant that the front door was probably still the same as well. She looked back into the box and noticed a small sheaf of paper tucked into the bottom. She pulled it out, unfolded it and inhaled a sharp breath when she read the words written there. *For you.*

She recognized Merritt's narrow, sweeping strokes and her heart skipped a beat. She looked around anxiously, wholly unsure of what her key unlocked. She felt an invisible pull and she let herself be led, her body on a seemingly preordained journey. She found herself at the door to the study and a shudder went through her. Trying the handle, she found it open. She turned it and opened the door, unsettled excitement humming in her ears. Her eyes widened in surprise when she realized the spacious room had been transformed into a cozy sitting area.

The row of shelves still flanked the far wall, but they had been meticulously redone and the stain now matched the dark walnut of the hardwood floors. Two oversized wingback chairs kept a stately watch over the comings and goings. Pictures of Olivia covered the remaining wall space. The biggest change came in the form of a new wall that had been erected, narrowing the space and dividing it neatly. She narrowed her eyes as her mind took in the changes. She stopped at a door that was in the middle of the newly built wall with a small envelope taped to it.

Whatever was behind the door was something new and she knew Merritt was responsible for the change. Soren grabbed the envelope and she could almost feel her presence surround her and it calmed her and aroused her all at once. Her chest danced in a breathtaking amalgam of white hot desire and unsettled fear. Somehow she knew that inside the envelope and behind the door was her future, and she was suddenly unsure of what awaited her. She inhaled a deep breath and slid the envelope open. She bit her lower lip nervously as she pulled out a single sheet of paper bearing Merritt's strong handwriting.

The key you are holding is my gift to you. It unlocks the thing I have kept safeguarded my whole life. I hope you use it.

Soren's heart leapt wildly. She tried to insert the key and failed twice, her hands trembling uncontrollably. She wasn't sure what she would find on the other side of the door, but her desire to find out left her edgy and raw, more than she'd ever been. She had to put her hands on the door and brace herself, her stomach an out of control pendulum of nerves. Finally, she managed to still her body. She slid the key in and undid the bolt, the clicks of the lock thundering in her ears like a loud cacophony of drums.

She hesitated briefly, not wanting to open the door and find nothing. She felt the lightest press against her back, propelling her towards her destiny. She opened the door and her eyes met Merritt's anxious ones and in that brief second she knew that her heart was safe. She felt her lower lip start to quiver. A rush of emotions hit her in the gut and she had only a moment to acknowledge the feeling of peace that she finally had before tears streamed down her face.

Merritt strode from across the room where she'd been pacing nervously and gathered Soren against her. "It's alright baby, it's alright, I'm here."

Soren melded her body against Merritt's and felt waves of love wash over her. Her mind took in all the things about Merritt that she'd longed for since she had left--her scent, her feel, her strength, everything about her stirring feelings that Soren had tried to keep at bay and although no words of reassurance had been spoken, Soren knew that she could love her without abandon. Here in Merritt's arms was where she belonged, where she'd longed to be since they had met.

Merritt finally eased their bodies apart keeping Soren's hands captured in hers, her gaze searched Soren's face and what she saw there overwhelmed her. She knew she had made the right decision. "Soren, I love you, I'm in love with you. You gave me your love wanting nothing in return. You gave me my life back and ever since then only one thought has existed inside me. To share it with you. I love you."

Merritt's thumb caressed the top of Soren's hand, a silent declaration of the words she'd spoken. Soren held her gaze and saw love mingled with unspoken questions. She knew she needed to put Merritt's mind at ease, but words were not enough. She pulled her hand away and curved it around Merritt's neck, her fingers lightly caressed her delicate skin and sparks of electricity danced along Merritt's body. She pulled Merritt towards her and their lips melded together in a sweet mingling of passion and promise.

When desire threatened to overtake them, Soren summoned all her strength and wrenched her lips away, a faint smile playing at the corners of her mouth. "Merritt, my love, I am and always will be yours."

There were no words for the rush of emotion that coursed through Merritt's body at Soren's sweet, earnest declaration. Anything that she would have said would have paled in comparison to the heat that surged through her body. Instead, she hugged Soren against her, a fierce promise of her undying love.

Neither woman knew how long they stayed pressed together. Since their first vision of each other, the normal passage of minutes and hours ceased and time stood still around them. When reality finally pulled them apart, Soren looked around. She cocked her head and stared at Merritt. "What's all this?"

Merritt smiled sheepishly. "This is the other part of your present." She flipped another light switch and as lights flickered behind a large pane of glass, she heard Soren's sharp intake of breath.

"Is that what I think it is?" Soren asked breathlessly.

"Mmm—hmmm." Merritt rocked back on her heels, a small smile on her face. She opened another door and Soren saw a small control room complete with soundboards and mixing equipment. "It's small, but it should have everything you need. I know how much you miss your recording studio back home."

"Merritt, it's wonderful!" Soren gasped. "It's more than wonderful. It's amazing. I don't know what to say."

Merritt shrugged her shoulders. "I know it's kind of small…"

Soren threw her arms around Merritt and kissed her soundly. "It's perfect!" She put her hand over Merritt's heart. "It's the second best present I ever received."

Epilogue

Two Years Later

Merritt leaned against the door frame and watched the love of her life and the mother of her beautiful daughter Samantha. Sam lay snuggled against her mother's chest and Soren's cheek rested lightly on her head. Her eyes were closed and the only sound coming from the room was the quiet squeak of her rocking chair.

Merritt's smile widened. God, she was so in love with Soren, more now than she had been two years ago. Sam was an extension of that amazing love and Merritt couldn't think of a more wonderful thing than two people in love sharing such an awe—inspiring responsibility.

As if sensing she was being watched, Soren's eyes flickered open and she smiled drowsily. Merritt's heart melted as she realized that even in repose, Soren was the most beautiful woman she'd ever met. Merritt flicked her eyes towards the ceiling and whispered quietly. "Is she still here?"

Soren kissed Sam's head gently and something caught her eye. A shimmering visage, the face of a beautiful woman, her hand raised in a silent farewell, a contented smile played at the corners of her mouth. Soren blinked, believing that the vision had been the sun teasing her playfully, but in her heart she knew she'd finally seen Sam. She smiled at Merritt and shook her head from side to side. "No, she finished what she needed to do. She brought love back to this house."

Syd Parker is an aspiring author and avid reader. She resides in Indiana, where she and her partner enjoy golfing, running and cycling. Growing up in the Midwest gave her a strong sense of family and she loves spending time with her ten nieces and nephews.

Check her out on Facebook.

Made in the USA
Lexington, KY
24 February 2012